"Popular romance writer Debbie Macomber has a gift for evoking the emotions that are at the heart of the genre's popularity." —*Publishers Weekly*

"It's clear that Debbie Macomber cares deeply about her fully realized characters and their families, friends and loves, along with their hopes and dreams. She also makes her readers care about them." —*Bookreporter.com*

"Debbie Macomber is one of the most reliable, versatile romance writers around." —*Milwaukee Journal Sentinel*

"Readers won't be able to get enough of Macomber's gentle storytelling." —*RT Book Reviews*

"Bestselling Macomber...sure has a way of pleasing readers." —*Booklist*

"It's impossible not to cheer for Macomber's characters.... When it comes to creating a special place and memorable, honorable characters, nobody does it better than Macomber." —*BookPage*

"Macomber is a master storyteller." —*Times Record News*

DEBBIE MACOMBER

Fresh Starts

The Cowboy's Lady and *My Funny Valentine*

 MIRA

/||MIRA™

Recycling programs
for this product may
not exist in your area.

ISBN-13: 978-0-7783-6846-5

Fresh Starts

Copyright © 2025 by Harlequin Enterprises ULC

The Cowboy's Lady
First published in 1990. This edition published in 2025 with revised text.
Copyright © 1990 by Debbie Macomber
Copyright © 2025 by Debbie Macomber, revised text edition.

My Funny Valentine
First published in 1991. This edition published in 2025.
Copyright © 1991 by Debbie Macomber

TM is a trademark of Harlequin Enterprises ULC.

Mira
22 Adelaide St. West, 41st Floor
Toronto, Ontario M5H 4E3, Canada
MIRABooks.com

Printed in U.S.A.

CONTENTS

THE COWBOY'S LADY

To Merrily Boone
Friend
Title Finder
Speller of Impossible Words
Discoverer of Great Restaurants

One

Everyone in Cougar Point, Montana, knew the bowling alley had the best breakfast in town. For a buck ninety-five they served up eggs, sausage, hash browns and toast, plus all the coffee a body could drink. Russ Palmer was hungrier than a bear in springtime, but food wasn't the only thing on his mind.

He wanted company—of the female variety.

"Mornin', Russ," Mary Andrews, the lone waitress, called out when he walked into the restaurant. Her greeting was followed by a chorus from several other ranchers.

Russ removed his black Stetson and hooked it on the peg by the door. Although it was only a few days into September, the air was decidedly cool and he'd worn his blanket-lined denim jacket.

Sliding into the booth with a couple of friends, Russ picked up the tail end of what Bill Shepherd was saying.

"Pretty as a picture."

Russ's interest was instantly piqued. "Who?"

"The new schoolteacher, Taylor Manning," Harry Donovan answered eagerly. At twenty-three Harry still had the peach-faced immaturity of youth and fine, blond hair he couldn't seem to control.

A schoolteacher. Russ's curiosity level fell several notches. "Taylor's a funny name for a woman," he muttered, reaching for the menu, which was tucked between the sugar container and the salt and pepper shakers.

"The missus and I met her yesterday," Bill went on to say. "She rented old man Halloran's place on the edge of town."

Russ nodded as he scanned the menu. He ordered the "special" every Saturday morning, but he liked to see what was offered in case something else struck his fancy.

"She moved here from Seattle," Harry informed Russ enthusiastically.

"Then she's a city girl," Russ said, and a hint of sarcasm slipped into his voice. The kid had it bad. Personally Russ didn't hold out much hope of the new teacher sticking it out past Christmas. Seattle was known for its mild climate. At best Taylor Manning could deal with four or five days of drizzle, but he'd bet his ranch and five hundred head of cattle that she had no idea what a Montana winter could be like.

"Whether she's a city slicker or not, I couldn't rightly say," Harry said with no lack of fervor, "but I can tell you one thing. She's real pretty. I swear she's got the bluest eyes I've ever seen and dark, silky hair that falls to about here." He gestured with his hand to a point well below his shoulder blades. "A man could see himself running his fingers through hair that soft," he said dreamily. Pink tinged Harry's cheeks as he stopped abruptly and cast a self-conscious look at his two friends.

Russ laughed outright. "Hell, Harry, she hasn't even been in town a week and already you're sweet on her."

"I can't help myself." Harry grabbed his mug so fast he nearly spilled his coffee. "Wait until you meet her yourself, then you'll know what I mean."

"I'm not going to be mooning over any schoolmarm," Russ told the two men. He hadn't gotten to the age of thirty-four safely unmarried only to be taken in by the charms of a citified schoolteacher. Especially one Harry Donovan would fantasize about.

Bill and Harry exchanged glances, then Harry snickered loudly, apparently amused by Russ's attitude. "You just wait till you see her yourself," he said again.

"What do you mean I can't use my American Express card here?" Taylor Manning demanded of the clerk at the small store. "I could use this card in Kodiak, Alaska!"

"I'm really sorry," the older woman said, "but as far as I know, no one in town takes American Express."

Shaking her head, Taylor pulled her Visa card from her wallet and set it on the counter. "I'll use this one instead." She pushed her chocolate-brown hair over her shoulder and looked around. This situation was becoming embarrassing. Taylor had used her meager savings to rent the house. She'd gone shopping for some kitchen things she was going to need, thinking she could use her credit card and pay for them when it was more convenient.

She was grateful there were only two other people in the store. A cowboy and his daughter. No, Taylor decided on second thought. The teenage girl was too old to be his daughter, but too young to be his girlfriend.

"I'm very sorry, but we don't take Visa, either."

"You don't take Visa," Taylor echoed in shocked disbelief. "*Everyone* takes Visa."

"No one in Cougar Point," the woman said apologetically.

Taylor smiled blandly. "Then what *do* you take?"

"Cash would work."

Taylor rummaged through her purse, drawing out a checkbook. She studied the meager balance and sighed inwardly. "I don't suppose you take out-of-state checks, do you? Don't answer that," she said quickly. "Anyone who doesn't honor American Express or Visa isn't going to take a check from a Seattle bank." She stared down at the few items longingly and made her decision. "I'll simply put everything back and wait until the checks come through from my new account." She'd also have to wait until she'd deposited her first pay two weeks from now, but she didn't feel announcing that was necessary.

"I'm really sorry, miss."

Taylor nodded. "No problem," she murmured, and even managed a respectable smile. She turned, nearly colliding with the cowboy she'd noticed earlier.

"Oh, sorry," she said, slipping past him.

"Just a minute. Did I hear you mention Seattle?" His voice was deep and masculine. Without giving her a chance to respond, he added, "You wouldn't happen to be Taylor Manning, would you?"

"Yes. How'd you know?" Not that she should be surprised. Folks had been introducing themselves all week, telling her how pleased they were that she'd accepted the teaching assignment in their town.

Setting his black Stetson farther back on his head,

the rancher explained. "The kid mentioned something about you this morning over breakfast."

"The kid?"

"Harry Donovan."

Taylor didn't recall meeting any youngster by that name, but there'd been so many names and so many faces that she'd long since lost track.

The cowboy smiled, and their eyes held for a moment. His reaction hinted at curiosity, but for her part, Taylor had no feelings one way or the other. Oh, he was good-looking enough. His head was covered with a crisp black Stetson; all the men in town seemed to wear them. His dark hair curled along the nape of his sun-bronzed neck as if he'd delayed getting a haircut a couple of weeks too long. He was tall, easily six-three, and he wore tight-fitting blue jeans and a plaid shirt beneath a thick denim jacket.

"Mabel," the rancher said, looking past Taylor. "This is the new schoolteacher."

"Well, for goodness' sake, miss, why didn't you come right out and say so?" Without a second's delay the clerk reached beneath the counter and brought out a tablet and started listing the items Taylor had wanted to purchase.

"Does this mean you'll accept my American Express? My Visa? My check?"

"No, I feel bad about that, but most of the commercial people in these parts don't do credit card business with those big banks. I'll just write down these items here and send you a bill at the end of the month the way I do with most folks."

"But…you don't know me." The woman hadn't so much as requested identification.

Mabel waved her hand, dismissing Taylor's concern. "I feel terrible about this."

Taylor turned her gaze to the cowboy once more. "Thank you."

He touched the brim of his hat in a quick salute and started down the aisle toward the younger girl.

While Mabel was writing up the sale, Taylor watched the exchange at the rear of the store. The teenager was standing beside a cosmetic display, gesturing wildly.

"If you could just sign here," Mabel instructed, turning the tablet around for Taylor. "I can't tell you how pleased we are that you've come to Cougar Point. There won't be much of a social life for you, but we have our moments."

"Yes, I know," Taylor murmured. She hadn't accepted this teaching assignment because of the potential nightlife. She'd specifically chosen the backwoods of Montana in an effort to give herself the necessary time to heal after her disastrous affair with Mark Brooks. She'd moved to Cougar Point so she could immerse herself in her chosen profession—and deal with the bitterness of losing Mark. Next year she'd leave Cougar Point again, rejuvenated and whole. Her family, especially her father, had assumed she'd taken this job on impulse, and although her actions were often spontaneous, for once her father was wrong. The decision to spend a year in Montana had been well thought out, the pros and cons carefully weighed. She was taking this time to mend a badly broken heart, hoping twelve months in the country would do what six months in the city hadn't.

"I want a second opinion," the teenager cried as she rushed toward the front of the store. "Excuse me," she said brightly, holding out her hand. "I'm Mandy Palmer

and this is my brother, Russ, who happens to be obstinate and stubborn and completely unreasonable and—"

"Mandy," Russ threatened in a voice few would challenge, "I said no."

"That's just too bad," the girl returned. Tears glis-
tened in her green eyes. She was petite and very pretty,
and wore her thick blond hair in a long French braid. It
swayed when she jerked her head toward her brother.

"Mandy," Russ threatened again.

The girl ignored him with a defiant tilt of her chin
and looked at Taylor. "When a girl's fourteen years old
and going into her first year of high school, she's old
enough to wear a little makeup, isn't she?"

"Uh…" Taylor hesitated. Mandy was staring at her
with imploring eyes while her brother glared heatedly,
silently demanding that Taylor mind her own business.
"What does your mother say?"

"Our parents are dead," Russ said gruffly. "I'm Mandy's
legal guardian and I say she's too young to be painting her
face with all that garbage. She's only fourteen!"

"Were you wearing makeup when *you* were my age?"
Mandy asked Taylor, the appeal in her eyes desperate.

"A little," Taylor admitted reluctantly. She clutched
her purchases tightly, not wanting to get caught in the
middle of this family fight.

"Mascara?"

"Yes," Taylor confessed.

"Blush?"

Taylor nodded, ignoring the fierce scowl being directed at her by the girl's brother.

"How about lip gloss?"

"I was wearing that in junior high," Taylor said,
gaining a bit more confidence. In Taylor's opinion—

although it clearly wasn't wanted or appreciated by the male faction here—Mandy should be allowed to experiment with a little makeup.

"See," the girl said enthusiastically. "And you turned out to be a fine, upstanding citizen, didn't you? I mean a little lip gloss at fourteen didn't automatically turn you into a…a lady of the night, did it?"

Taylor couldn't help laughing; that was the most ridiculous thing she'd ever heard. "No. But it was close. It all started with too much mascara, followed by blue eye shadow. Before I realized what I was doing, I was into perfumes." She hesitated and lowered her voice to a whisper. "The French kind."

Mandy gasped for effect.

Taylor didn't hide a smug smile as she continued. "From there it was a natural descent. I found myself standing on street corners…"

"It's time to go," Russ ordered. He gave Taylor a look that could have curdled milk. "We've heard more than enough."

Still amused, Taylor left the store. She sure hadn't made a friend of the rancher, but Russ was being too strict with his younger sister. It wasn't like her to take sides in something that didn't involve her, but his attitude had struck a familiar chord. Taylor's own father was often hard-nosed and outdated in his views. More than once the two of them had fought over the most ridiculous issues. If her mother hadn't been there to run interference, Taylor didn't know what would have happened. The crazy part was, she thought the world of her father. They could argue until the cows came home, but that never dampened the deep affection they shared.

Till the cows came home! Taylor paused midstep.

Good grief, she was already beginning to think like a cowgirl. If this was the way she sounded after ten days, heaven only knew what she'd be like in a year's time.

Taylor was walking to her car when she ran into Mary Beth Morgan, another teacher. They'd met earlier in the week during a staff meeting. Mary Beth was in her mid-fifties, friendly and a country girl through and through. She was the type of woman who personified everything good about small towns.

"You're looking pleased about something."

Taylor nodded. "I just met Russ and Mandy Palmer. They were debating whether Mandy's old enough to wear makeup and somehow I got stuck in the middle. That man is certainly opinionated."

"Mandy can give as good as she gets. I once heard Russ say that even Napoleon couldn't stand up to Mandy when she truly wanted something."

That seemed like a comment the cowboy would make and, despite herself, Taylor discovered she was smiling.

"Russ has a good heart, so don't judge him too harshly," Mary Beth said as they strolled down the sidewalk together. "He's raising Mandy on his own and genuinely cares about her. His views may be kind of outdated, but he tries hard to be fair."

"What happened to their parents?"

"Actually Mandy's his half sister. Russ's mother ran off when he was a toddler. I doubt Russ even remembers her. Fred Palmer took his wife's leaving really hard. I'm sure there are two sides to that story, though. Fred could be ornery and was as pigheaded as they come."

"Russ must take after his father then."

"He does," Mary Beth said, missing Taylor's joke. "Most folks around here would rather tangle with a grizzly bear than mess with Russ when he's in one of his moods. I suppose that has a lot to do with his living all these years without a woman's influence. Once Betty died…"

"Betty must be Mandy's mother?"

"Right. To everyone's surprise, Fred up and married again. Betty was the sweetest thing, and just the right kind of woman for someone like Fred. She was sweet and kindhearted and as good as the day is long. Mandy arrived a year later.

"Fred and Betty were happy. I don't think there was a dry eye in town when she died. Not long afterward Fred died, too. The doctors may have a complicated name for what killed him, but I'll tell you right now, Fred Palmer died of a broken heart."

"How sad." The humor drained from Taylor. No one could be unaffected by that story.

"Russ reminds me of his father when Fred was around that age. What Russ needs is a wife—someone like Betty who'll cater to his whims and pamper him and let him have his way."

That left her out. The thought startled her. She would no more consider marrying a rancher than she'd entertain the idea of riding a horse. As far as she was concerned, cows smelled, hay made her sneeze and the sight of a horse sent her scurrying in the opposite direction.

"I'm sure if Russ said anything offensive…"

"He didn't," Taylor was quick to assure the other woman. But not because he didn't want to, judging by the look in his eyes. If ever there was a man who longed to put her in her place, it was this formidable rancher.

Unfortunately, or fortunately as the case might be, it would take a lot more than one cowpoke to do it.

Mary Beth and Taylor said goodbye at the corner, and Taylor went to the grocery store. With a limited budget and a distinct lack of imagination when it came to cooking, she headed for the frozen food section.

Without much enthusiasm she tossed a frozen entrée into her grocery cart. The local supermarket didn't carry a large selection, and it was either the salisbury steak or the country fried chicken.

"Was that really necessary?" a gruff male voice asked from behind her.

"The country fried chicken?" she asked, turning to face the very man she and Mary Beth had been discussing.

"I'm not talking about your pathetic choice for dinner. I'm referring to my sister. She's going through a rebellious stage, and I don't appreciate your taking her side on an issue. We can settle our differences without any help from you."

Taylor was about to argue when she noticed the teenager coming down the aisle.

"Oh, hi," Mandy greeted her, brightening. She hurried to Taylor and her brother. "You're not eating that for dinner, are you?" the girl asked, eyeing the frozen meal in Taylor's cart. A horrified look spread across her face.

"It seemed the least amount of trouble," Taylor admitted. She'd spent a full day unpacking and cleaning, and even a frozen dinner was more appealing than being forced to cook for herself. As far as she could see, there wasn't a single fast-food place in town. The nearest McDonald's was a hundred miles from Cougar Point.

"I've got a big pot of stew simmering at home," Mandy said eagerly. "Why don't you come over and have dinner with Russ and me? We'd love to have you, wouldn't we, Russ?"

Her brother's hesitation was just long enough to convey his message.

"It's the neighborly thing to do," Mandy prompted.

"You're welcome to come, if you want," Russ said finally, and Taylor had the impression it took a great deal of resolve to echo his sister's invitation.

There wasn't any question that Taylor should refuse. But something perverse in her, something obstinate and a bit foolish, wouldn't allow her to do so. Perhaps it was because she recognized the same mulish streak in him that she knew so well in her father. Whatever the reason, Taylor decided she was going to enjoy this dinner. "Why, thank you. I'd be honored."

"Great." Mandy beamed. "We live about ten miles east of town."

"East?" Taylor repeated, turning in a full circle in an effort to orient herself. She wasn't sure which way was east, at least not from where she was standing in the grocery store.

"Take the main road and go left at the stand of sycamore trees," Mandy continued. "That's just past Cole Creek, only don't look for any water because it's dried out at this time of year."

Further directions only served to confuse Taylor. She wasn't even all that confident she could tell a sycamore from an oak. And how was she supposed to identify a dried-out creek bed? Usually Taylor was given directions that said she should go to the third stoplight and take a left at the Wal-Mart.

"Why don't you ride along with us?" Mandy suggested next, apparently sensing Taylor's confusion. "Russ can drive you back into town later."

"It'll probably work better if I follow you," Taylor said. "My car's at the house, but it would only take a minute for me to swing by and get it."

"It wouldn't be any trouble. Russ has to come back, anyway. Besides, I wouldn't want you to get lost once it turns dark."

Taylor noted that Russ didn't echo his sister's suggestion. The temptation was too great to ignore, and once more Taylor found herself agreeing to Mandy's plan.

"My truck's parked outside," Russ grumbled. He didn't seem very pleased by this turn of events. But then he hadn't looked all that thrilled about anything from the moment they'd met.

Russ's truck was a twenty-year-old dented Ford that most folks would have hauled to the scrap heap a year earlier. The bed was filled with supplies. Grain sacks were stacked in one corner, fertilizer in another.

The front fender was badly bent and had begun to rust. The license plate was missing, and Russ had to completely remove the passenger door for the two women to climb inside. Once they were seated he replaced the door and latched it shut.

Taylor squirmed around in the bench seat, searching for the seat belt.

"There aren't any," Russ explained as he slipped in next to her and started the engine.

The seat was cramped, and Taylor had to dig her elbows into her ribs. Her shoulders were touching his on the left side, his younger sister's on the right. It had been a long time since Taylor had sat this close to a man. At first she tried to keep her thigh from grazing his, but it was nearly impossible. So their thighs touched. Big deal.

Only it soon got to be.

There must've been something in all that fresh country air that was adversely affecting her brain cells. Without much difficulty, Taylor could actually imagine herself smitten with this man. *Smitten?* Oh dear, her mind was doing it again, tormenting her with this old-fashioned country jargon....

Suddenly they turned off the main road and headed down a lengthy rut-filled section that tossed her up and then down. Every time they hit a dip, Taylor would bounce off the seat as if it were greased. It was all she could do not to land on top of Russ or Mandy. They were obviously accustomed to this thrashing about, and each managed to stay neatly in place. Taylor, on the other hand, was all over the inside of the cab.

Whenever the truck hit an uneven patch, some part of Taylor's anatomy came into intimate contact with Russ's. Their thighs stroked each other. Their shoulders collided and their waists jostled together. Again and again their bodies were slammed against each other.

Taylor couldn't help noticing how firm and muscular Russ felt. She didn't want to acknowledge it. Nor did she want to experience the heat of his body and the warm muskiness of his skin. He felt solid. Strong. Virile. A host of sensations, long dormant, sprang to life inside her.

Not once had Russ Palmer purposely touched her, and yet Taylor felt as though his hands had caressed her everywhere.

"Would you mind slowing down?" she cried. She hated having to ask.

"Why?" Russ asked, his voice filled with amusement.

"Russ," Mandy snapped, "Taylor's not used to this."

Amused or not, Russ slowed the vehicle, and Taylor went weak with relief. She could feel a headache coming on, but she wasn't sure it had anything to do with the skipping, hopping and jumping she'd been subjected to for the past ten minutes.

They arrived at the ranch house a couple of minutes later, at just about dusk. The first thing Taylor noticed was the huge red barn. It was the largest she'd ever seen, but that wasn't saying much. She knew next to nothing about barns, although this one seemed enormous. The house was sizable, as well. Four gables stood out against the roof of the huge white structure, and the windows were framed by bright red shutters.

Taylor climbed out of the truck on the driver's side after Russ, not wanting to be trapped inside while he walked around to remove the passenger door. It took her a minute to steady her legs.

Mandy bolted ahead of them. She raced up the back steps that led into the kitchen, holding open the door for Taylor. "The stew's in the Crock-Pot."

Taylor saw that Russ had gone in the opposite direction, toward the barn, probably to see about unloading the contents of the truck bed. Her gaze followed him, and she wondered briefly if the close confines of the truck had affected him the same way they had her.

Probably not. He looked a lot more in control of himself than Taylor felt.

A thin sheen of perspiration moistened her upper lip. What the hell was the matter with her? Groaning silently, Taylor closed her eyes. She knew precisely what was wrong, and she didn't like it one bit.

Two

Russ remained silent for most of the meal. He didn't like this schoolteacher. But he didn't exactly dislike her, either. She was as pretty as Harry had claimed, and her hair was thick and rich. A couple of times he'd been tempted to lift a strand and let it slip through his fingers, but that would've been impossible. And what she did to a pair of jeans ought to be illegal. On the ride to the ranch he'd purposely driven over every pothole he could just because he liked the way her body had moved against his.

"You're from Seattle?" Russ asked. He'd been trying to ignore her for most of the meal, not because he wasn't interested in learning what he could about her, but because—dammit—he was as taken with her as Harry had been.

Taylor nodded, smiling. "I was born and raised in the shadow of the Space Needle."

"Ever had snow there?"

"Some."

The thought of her smooth pale skin exposed to the elements knotted his stomach.

"I understand winters are harsher here than in western Washington," she said stiffly. "I came prepared."

"I doubt that you have a clue how severe winters can get in these parts." Russ had seen too many cases of frostbite to have any illusions.

It was clear that Taylor resented the way he was talking to her. He didn't mean to imply that she was stupid, only unaware, and he didn't want her learning harsh lessons because no one had warned her.

One quick look told him he'd raised Taylor's hackles. She seemed to need several minutes to compose her response, then she set her fork next to her plate, placed her elbows on the table and joined her hands. Staring directly at him, she smiled with deceptive warmth and said, "You needn't worry, Mr. Palmer. I'm perfectly capable of taking care of myself. I've been doing so for many years. I may be a city girl, but let me assure you, I'm both intelligent and resourceful."

"Do you know what happens to skin when it's exposed to temperatures below thirty degrees? How about the symptoms for hypothermia? Would you be able to recognize them in yourself or others?"

"Mr. Palmer, please."

"Russ." Mandy's outraged eyes shot from him to Taylor and then back again. "You're being rude to our guest."

Russ mumbled under his breath and resumed eating. Maybe he was overreacting. Perhaps his motives weren't so lily-white. Perhaps he was more angry with her than concerned about her welfare. She'd certainly done enough to upset him in the past few hours. Taking Mandy's side on that makeup issue had bothered him, but that hardly mattered after the way she'd pressed herself against him during the ride from town. He couldn't get the feel of her out of his mind. Her skin was soft and she smelled like wildflowers. That thought led to another. If she smelled so good, he couldn't help wondering how she'd taste. Like honey, he decided, fresh from the comb, thick and sweet. The knot in his stomach tightened. If he didn't curb his mind soon, he'd end up kissing her before the night was through.

"You're an excellent cook," Taylor said to Mandy in a blatant effort to lighten the strained atmosphere.

Mandy beamed at the compliment. "I try. Rosa and her husband retired last year, and I talked Russ into letting me do the cooking, and it's worked out pretty well, hasn't it, Russ?"

He nodded. "There've been a few nights best forgotten, but for the most part you've done an excellent job."

"She took over all the cooking at age thirteen?" Taylor asked, obviously astonished, although Russ had trouble figuring out why. He'd long suspected that city kids didn't carry anywhere near the responsibility country kids did.

Mandy eyed Russ. He knew that look well by now, and it meant trouble. He bit his tongue as she opened her mouth to speak.

"It seems to me that any girl who can rustle up a decent meal every night is old enough to buy her own clothes without her older brother tagging along, don't you think?"

The way things were going, Mandy was angling to be sent to her room without finishing dinner. "That's none of Taylor's concern," he said tightly, daring their guest to challenge his authority with his younger sister.

"You agree with me, don't you, Taylor?" Mandy pressed.

"Uh…" Taylor hedged, looking uncomfortable. "I have a limit of answering only one leading question per day," she explained, reaching for another piece of bread. "I don't think it's a good idea to get on Russ's bad side twice in only a few hours. I might end up walking back to town."

"Russ would never do that."

Want to bet? Russ mused. Okay, so he wouldn't make her walk, but he'd sure as hell hit every pothole he could. The problem there was that he'd be the one likely to suffer most.

"What do you honestly think?" Mandy repeated.

"*I* think you should eat your dinner and leave Taylor out of this," Russ ordered harshly. The girl had turned willfulness into an art form.

"I… Your brother's right, Mandy," Taylor said, lowering her gaze to the steaming bowl of rich stew. "This is something the two of you should settle between yourselves."

"Russ and I'll settle it all right," Mandy responded defiantly, "but he won't like the outcome."

Russ didn't take the bait. "More stew, Taylor?"

"Ah…no, thanks. My bowl's nearly full."

"When did you start buying your own clothes?" Mandy asked, clearly unwilling to drop the issue.

Russ stared at Taylor, daring her to question his authority a second time. She glanced nervously away. "As I recall, I had the same problem with my father at this age. I got around him by taking a sewing class and making my clothes."

"When was this?"

"Oh, about the eighth grade or so. To this day I enjoy sewing most of my own things. It's economical, too."

"The eighth grade?" Mandy cast Russ a triumphant look. "You were basically choosing and sewing your own clothes when you were only thirteen, then."

"It's not a good idea for me to get involved in a matter that's between you and your brother, Mandy. I did earlier and I don't think it was the right thing to do."

Russ felt a little better knowing that.

Mandy's shoulders sagged, and Russ was pleased to note that she was gracious enough to accept Taylor's word. Finally.

"I didn't mean to cause such a scene in the variety store," Mandy murmured apologetically. "All I wanted was Russ's okay to buy some lip gloss."

Russ set his napkin on the table. "I wouldn't mind letting you wear some lip gloss, but you insist on overdoing it. I walked past your bedroom the other night and I swear your lips were glowing in the dark."

Mandy glared at him, her eyes filled with indignation. What had he said *now*? Before he could ask her what was so all-fired insulting, she threw her fork and napkin onto the table and promptly rushed out of the room.

"Amanda Palmer, get back here this minute," he shouted in the same steely tone that sent his men scurrying to obey. When Mandy didn't immediately comply, he stormed to his feet, ready to follow her.

"Russ," Taylor said softly, stopping him. He turned toward her, wanting to blame her for this latest display of pique.

Taylor sighed and pushed aside her bowl. "Give her

a few minutes. She'll be back once she's composed herself."

"What did I say?" he demanded, sitting back down, genuinely perplexed.

Taylor hesitated, then said, "It might've had something to do with the joke about her lips glowing in the dark."

"It's true. I told her she couldn't wear any of that war paint you women are so fond of, so she defied me and started putting it on before she went to bed."

"She's exercising her rights as a person."

"By spurning my rules? I swear that girl drives me to the edge of insanity. What's gotten into her the past couple of years? She used to be an all-right kid. Now it seems I can't say a word without setting her off."

"She's a teenager."

"What's that supposed to mean?" he barked.

"Don't you remember what you felt like at fourteen? How important it was to dress and act like everyone around you?"

"No," Russ stated flatly. His features tensed. He didn't want to discuss his sister with Taylor. She didn't know any more about raising kids than he did. The problem with Mandy was that she was getting too big for her britches.

Standing, Taylor reached for her bowl and glass. "I'll clear the table."

"Leave it for Mandy," Russ insisted.

Taylor ignored him, which was getting to be a habit with her. Russ had yet to understand what it was about women that made them constantly want to challenge him—especially in his own home.

"Why?" Taylor demanded, startling him out of his

reverie. Even more astonishing was the fact that she looked angry.

"Why what?"

"Why would you want to leave the dishes for Mandy?"

"Because that's woman's work," he explained.

"You're possibly the worst male chauvinist I've ever encountered," she said, carrying what remained of the plates to the sink. "In my opinion, those who cook shouldn't have to wash dishes."

"It'll be a cold day in hell before you'll ever see me washing dishes, lady." He found the thought comical. He hadn't taken kindly to being called a chauvinist, but he refused to argue with her. They were having enough trouble being civil to each other without further provocation from him.

Taylor hurried to the sink, filling it with hot water and squirting in soap. "Since the task apparently belongs to a woman, I'll do the dishes."

"No guest of mine is washing dirty dishes."

"Fine then," she said, motioning toward the sink. "Everything's ready for you."

Although he was struggling against it, Russ was thoroughly irritated. He was standing directly in front of her. Not more than two inches separated them.

Taylor stared up at him and must have recognized his mood, because she swallowed hard. It wasn't consternation he saw in her eyes, but something that stabbed him as sharply as a pitchfork. Longing and need. The same emotions he'd been battling from the moment he'd laid eyes on her.

He saw something else. She didn't want to experience it any more than Russ wanted to feel the things he'd been feeling for her. When they'd sat next to each other in the truck, he'd never been more profoundly aware of a woman in his life. The air had been alive with tension—a tension that seemed to throb between them all evening long.

Russ felt it.

Taylor felt it.

Both seemed determined to ignore it.

Bracing her hands on the edge of the sink, she anxiously moistened her lips. Russ's eyes fell to her mouth. Her eyes reluctantly met his, and the look they exchanged was as powerful as a caress.

"I...I should be going," she whispered.

"You called me a chauvinist."

"I...apologize." Her pride was obviously crumbling at her feet. The fight had gone out of her.

He pulled his gaze back to her mouth, experiencing a small sense of triumph at the power of his will. "Where'd you ever get a name like Taylor?"

"It was my mother's...maiden name."

Once more her voice came out sounding whispery and soft. Too soft. Too whispery for comfort.

"My mother's from Atlanta, and it was an old Southern tradition to give the first daughter her mother's maiden name." By the time she finished, her voice was a mere thread of sound.

Neither of them spoke for the longest moment of Russ's life. Taking a deep, shaky breath, he was about to suggest he drive her home. Instead, Russ found himself leaning toward her.

"I'm sorry I ran out of the kitchen like that," Mandy announced, coming back into the room.

Russ frowned at his younger sister, irritated. The girl

couldn't have chosen a worse time to make her entrance. For her part, Taylor appeared ready to leap across the room and hug Mandy for interrupting them.

"I was about to take Taylor back to town," Russ announced gruffly.

"Do you have to leave so soon?" Mandy asked. "It's barely even dark."

"It'll get dark anytime, and I still have a lot to do before school starts. Thank you so much for having me—both of you. You're a wonderful cook… I really appreciate this."

"You'll come again, won't you?" Mandy asked.

"If you'd like."

"Oh, we would, wouldn't we, Russ?"

He made a response that could have been taken either way.

Mandy walked to the door and down the porch steps with them. Her arms hugged her waist against the evening chill. "You're driving the Lincoln, aren't you?"

Russ gave another noncommittal reply. His truck was in the shop, having the transmission worked on, and he'd been forced to take the older one into town that morning. Mandy's implication that he'd bring Taylor home in that dilapidated thing was an insult. The look he gave her suggested as much.

"I was just asking," she said with an innocent smile.

Taylor and Mandy chatted while Russ went around to the garage and pulled out the luxury sedan. The two women hugged goodbye, and Taylor got inside the car and ran her fingertips over the leather upholstery before snapping the seat belt into place.

"You ready?" he asked more brusquely than he intended.

"Yes."

They drove a few minutes in uncomfortable silence. "How large a spread do you have here?" she eventually asked.

"A thousand acres and about that many head of cattle."

"A thousand acres," Taylor echoed.

The awe and surprise in her voice filled him with pride. He could have gone on to tell her that the Lazy P was anything but lazy. His ranch was among the largest in the southern half of the state. He could also mention that he operated one of the most progressive ranches in the entire country, but he didn't want to sound as if he was bragging.

They chatted amicably about nothing important until they got to town. Russ turned off the side street to old man Halloran's house without even having to ask where Taylor was living. If she was surprised he knew, she didn't say.

When he pulled in to her driveway, he cut the engine and rested his arm over the back of her seat. Part of him wanted her to invite him inside for coffee, but it wasn't coffee that interested him. Another part of him demanded he stay away from this schoolteacher.

"Thank you again," she said softly, staring down at her purse, which she held tightly in her lap.

"No problem."

She raised her eyes to his, and despite all his good intentions, Russ's hungry gaze fixed on her lips. He became aware that he was going to kiss her about the same time he realized he'd die if he didn't. He reached for her, half expecting her to protest. Instead she whimpered and wrapped her arms around him, offering him her mouth. The sense of triumph and jubilation that Russ experienced was stronger than any aphrodisiac. He wrapped her in his arms and dragged her against him, savoring the pure womanly feel of her.

His kiss was wild. His callused hands framed the smooth skin of her face as he slanted his mouth over hers. He kissed her again and again and again.

Her throaty plea reluctantly brought him back to reason. For an instant Russ worried that he'd frightened her, until he heard his name fall from her lips in a low, frantic whisper. It was then that he knew she'd enjoyed their kisses as much as he had.

"Do you want me to stop?" he asked, his voice a husky murmur. He spread damp kisses down her neck and up her chin until he reached her mouth. Drawing her lower lip between his teeth, he sucked gently.

"Please...stop," she pleaded, yet her hands grasped his hair, holding him against her.

But then Taylor lowered her hands to his shoulders and pulled herself away, leaving only an inch or so between them. Her shoulders heaved.

"I can't believe that happened," she whispered.

"Do you want an apology?"

"No," she answered starkly. Then, after a moment, she added, "I wanted it as much as you did. I can't imagine why. We're about as opposite as any two people can get."

"Maybe so, but I think we just discovered one way we're compatible, and it beats the heck out of everything else."

"Oh, please, don't even say that," she moaned, and pushed him away. She leaned against the back of the seat and ran a hand down her face as if to wipe away all evidence of their kissing. "This was a fluke. I think it might be best to pretend it never happened."

Russ went still, his thoughts muddled and unclear. What she'd said was true. He had no business being attracted to her. No business kissing her. She was from the city and didn't understand the complexities of his life. Not only that, she was the new schoolteacher, and not a woman the community would approve of him dallying with.

That they *were* attracted to each other was a given. Why seemed to be a question neither of them could answer. One thing Russ knew: Taylor was right. It was best to forget this ever happened.

For the next week Taylor did an admirable job of pushing Russ Palmer from her mind. It helped somewhat that she didn't have any contact with either member of the Palmer family.

Taylor didn't question what had come over her or why she'd allowed Russ to kiss her like that. Instead she'd resolutely ignored the memory of their kiss, attributing it to a bad case of repressed hormones. That was the only thing it could've been, and analyzing it would accomplish nothing.

Now that school had started, Taylor threw herself into her work with gusto, more convinced than ever that she was born to be a teacher. She was an immediate hit with her third- and fourth-grade students.

On Wednesday afternoon at about four, an hour after her class had been dismissed, Taylor was sitting at her desk, cutting out letters for her bulletin board, when there was a polite knock at her door. Suspecting it was one of her students, she glanced up to discover Mandy standing there, her books pressed against her.

"Mandy, hello," Taylor said, genuinely pleased to see the girl. "Take a seat." She waved the scissors at the chair next to her desk.

"I'm not bothering you, am I? Russ said I wasn't to visit you after school if you were busy. He thinks I'll be a pest."

"You can come and visit me anytime you want," Taylor said, as she continued to cut out blunt letters from the bright sheets of colored paper.

Plopping down on the chair, Mandy crossed her legs and smiled cheerfully. "Notice anything different about me?"

Taylor nodded. "Isn't that war paint you're wearing? And that sweater looks new. Very nice—that light green suits you."

Russ's sister giggled shyly. "I came to thank you. I don't know what you said to my brother, but it worked. The next morning he said he'd thought about it overnight and decided that if I was old enough to cook dinner and wear a little makeup, then I was mature enough to choose my own clothes without him tagging along."

Taylor wasn't convinced that Russ's change of heart had anything to do with her, but nevertheless, she was pleased. "That's great."

"I heard from Cassie Jackson that you're a really good teacher."

Cassie was a fourth-grader in Taylor's class. She smiled at the compliment.

"I hear half the boys in your class are in love with you already," Mandy told her. "I told Russ that, and I think he's a little jealous because he frowned and grabbed the paper and read it for ten minutes before he noticed it was one from last week."

The last person Taylor wanted to discuss was Russ Palmer. "I don't suppose you'd like to help me cut out letters, would you?" she asked, more to change the subject than because she needed any assistance.

"Sure, I'd love to." Within a half hour she and Mandy had assembled a bright brown, yellow and orange autumn leaf bulletin board festooned with the names of every child in the class.

Once they'd finished, Taylor stepped back, threw her arm around her young friend's shoulders and nodded happily. "We do good work."

Mandy grinned. "We do, don't we?"

Noting the time, Taylor felt guilty for having taken up so much of the girl's afternoon. "It's almost five. Do you need me to give you a ride home?"

"That's all right. Russ said he'd pick me up. He's coming into town for grain and I'm supposed to meet him at Burn's Feed Store. It's only a block from here."

Mandy left soon afterward. Taylor gathered up the assignments she needed to grade and her purse and headed toward the school parking lot. Her blue Cabriolet was there all by itself. She was halfway to the car when a loud pickup barreled into the lot behind her. From the sick sounds the truck was making, Taylor knew it had to belong to Russ.

He rolled to a stop, his elbow draped over the side window. "Have you seen Mandy?"

She nodded, her eyes avoiding his. "You just missed her. She's walking over to the feed store."

"Thanks." His gears ground as he switched them,

and he looked over his shoulder, about to back out, when he paused. "Is that your car?"

"Yes." Normally Taylor walked to and from school. It was less than a mile and she liked the exercise, but it had been raining that morning, so she'd brought her car.

"Did you know your back tire's flat?"

Taylor's eyes flew to her Cabriolet, and sure enough the rear tire on the driver's side was completely flat. "Oh, great," she moaned. She was tired and hungry and in no mood to deal with this problem.

"I'll change it for you," Russ volunteered, immediately vaulting from his truck.

It was kind of him, and Taylor was about to tell him so when he ruined it.

"You independent women," he said with a chuckle. "You claim you can take care of yourselves and you're too damn proud to think you need a man. But every now and then we have our uses. Now admit it, Taylor. You couldn't possibly handle this without me." He was walking toward her trunk, as haughty as could be.

"Hold it!" Taylor raised one hand. "I don't need you to change my tire. I can take care of this myself."

Russ gave her a patronizing look and then chose to antagonize her even more. This time he laughed. "Now that's something I'd like to see." He leaned against her fender and crossed his arms over his broad chest. "Feel free," he said, gesturing toward the flat.

"Don't look so smug, Palmer. I said I could take care of it myself and I meant it."

"You wouldn't know one end of the jack from the other."

Taylor wasn't going to argue with him about that.

"Would you like to make a small wager on my ability to deal with this?"

Russ snickered, looking more pompous every minute. "It would be like taking candy from a baby. The problem with you is that you're too stubborn to admit when a man's right."

"I say I can deal with a flat tire any day of the week."

"And I say you can't. You haven't got enough strength to turn the tire iron. Fact is, lady, you couldn't get to first base without a man here to help you."

"Oh, come off it. It's about time you men understood that women aren't the weaker sex."

"Sure," Russ said, without disguising his amusement.

"All right," Taylor said slowly. She deliberately walked past him, then turned to give him a sultry smile. She narrowed her eyes. "Perhaps you don't care to place a small wager on my ability. Having to admit you're wrong would probably be more than a guy like you could take."

His dark eyes flared briefly. "I didn't want to do this, but unfortunately you've asked for it. What shall we bet?"

Now that he'd agreed, Taylor wasn't sure. "If I win…"

"I'd be willing to do something I consider women's work?" he suggested.

"Such as?"

Russ took a moment to think it over. "I'll cook dinner for you next Saturday night."

"Who'll do the dishes?"

Russ hesitated. "I will. You thought I'd have trouble going along with that, didn't you? But I don't have a thing to worry about."

"Dream on, Palmer. If I were you, I'd be sweating."

He snickered, seeming to derive a good deal of plea-sure from their conversation. "Now let's figure out what you'll owe me when you realize how sadly mistaken you are."

"All right," she said, "I'd be willing to do something you consider completely masculine."

"I'd rather have you grill me a steak."

"No way. That wouldn't be a fair exchange. How about if I…do whatever you do around the ranch for a day?" Taylor felt perfectly safe making the proposal, just as safe as he'd felt offering to make her dinner.

"That wouldn't work."

"I'd be willing to try."

Russ shrugged. "If you insist."

"I do," Taylor said.

Still leaning smugly against the side of her car, Russ pointed at the trunk. "All right, Ms. Goodwrench, go to it."

Taylor opened her front door, placed her papers and purse inside and got out the key to her trunk.

"You might want to roll up your sleeves," Russ sug-gested. "It'd be a shame to ruin that pretty blouse with a grease stain. It's silk, isn't it?"

Taylor glared at him defiantly.

Russ chuckled and raised both arms. "Sorry. I won't say any more."

Opening the trunk, Taylor systematically searched through it until she found what she was looking for.

"A tire iron is about this size," he said, holding his hands a couple of feet apart, mocking her.

Carrying the spray can, Taylor walked around to the flat tire and squatted down in front of it. "I like my steak medium rare and barbecued over a hot charcoal grill. My baked potato should have sour cream and chives and the broccoli should be fresh with a touch of hollandaise sauce drizzled over the top." Having given him those instructions, she proceeded to fill her deflated tire with the spray can.

"What's that?" Russ asked, his hands set challengingly on his hips.

"You did say this Saturday, didn't you?" she taunted.

He scowled when she handed over the spray can for him to examine. "Fix-it Flat Tire?" he said, reading the label.

"That's exactly what it is," Taylor informed him primly. "Whatever this marvelous invention is, it fills up the tire enough so I can drive it to a service station and have the attendant deal with it."

"Now wait a minute," Russ muttered. "That's cheating."

"I never said I'd *change* the tire," Taylor reminded him. "I told you I could deal with the situation myself. And I have."

"But it's a man who'll be changing the tire."

"Could be a woman. In Seattle some women work for service stations."

"In Seattle, maybe, but not in Cougar Point."

"Come on, Russ, admit it. I outsmarted you."

He glared at her, and despite his irritation, or perhaps because of it, Taylor laughed. She got inside her car, started the engine and drove out of the parking lot. Then she circled back, returning to Russ who was standing beside his pickup.

"What do you want now?" he demanded.

"I just came to tell you I like blue cheese dressing on

my salad." With that she zipped out of the lot. She was still smiling when she happened to glance in her rear-view mirror in time to see Russ slam his black Stetson onto the asphalt.

Three

No doubt psychologists had a term for the attraction Taylor felt for this rancher, she decided early Saturday evening. Why else would a woman, who was determined to avoid a certain man, go out of her way to goad him into a wager she was sure to win? Taylor couldn't fathom it herself. Maybe it was some perverse method of inflicting self-punishment. Perhaps her disastrous relationship with Mark had lowered her to this level. Taylor didn't know anymore.

She'd prefer to place all the blame on Russ. If he hadn't made her so furious with his nonsense about a woman needing a man, she probably would've been able to stand aside and smile sweetly while he changed her tire. But he'd had to ruin everything.

During dinner at least, Mandy would be there to act as a buffer.

"What do you mean you're going over to Chris's?" Russ asked his sister.

"I told you about it Thursday, remember?"

Russ frowned. Hell, no, he didn't remember. He

needed Mandy to help him with this stupid dinner wager he'd made with Taylor. The woman had tricked him. In his view, she should be cooking, not the other way around. He would've been happy to take her to dinner in town and be done with it, but he knew better than to even suggest that. She'd insisted he make dinner himself.

"What's so important at Chris's that you have to do it now?"

"We're practicing. Drill team tryouts are next week, and I've got to make it. I've just got to."

She made it sound like a matter of life or death. "Couldn't the two of you practice some other time?"

"No," Mandy said. "I want to see Taylor, but I can't. Not tonight."

Grumbling under his breath, Russ opened the refrigerator and stared inside, wondering where the hell he should start. Make the salad first? Cook the broccoli? Earlier in the day he'd bought everything he was going to need, including a packet of hollandaise sauce mix.

"I'm sorry, Russ," Mandy said. "I'd offer to help..."

His spirits lifted. "You will? Great. Just don't let Taylor know. If she found out, she'd have me strung from the highest tree for allowing another woman to slice lettuce for me."

"I *can't* help you, Russ. That would be cheating."

"All I want you to do is give me a few pointers."

"It wouldn't be right." She lowered her voice to a whisper. "Don't slice the lettuce, and I shouldn't even be telling you that."

"What do you do with salad if you don't chop it?" Russ asked wearily. He followed Mandy into the living room where she collected her homemade pom-poms. "What am I supposed to do with the lettuce?"

"I can't answer that," she said, looking apologetic.

"You can't tell me how to make a salad?" he roared. His temper was wearing precariously thin. "Why not?"

"It'd be unfair. You're supposed to prepare this meal entirely on your own. If I gave you any help, you'd be breaking your agreement with Taylor." A car horn blared from the backyard, and Mandy grabbed her jacket. "That's Chris's mom now. I've got to go. See you later, and good luck with dinner."

She was out the door before Russ could protest.

Russ wandered around the kitchen for the next five minutes, debating what to do first. Grilling the steaks wouldn't be a problem. Anyone with half a brain knew how to cook a decent T-bone. The baked potato wasn't a concern, either. It was everything else. He took the head of lettuce and a bunch of other vegetables from the refrigerator and set them on the counter. Without giving it much thought, he reached for an apron and tied it around his waist. God help him if any of the ranch hands walked in now.

Taylor was impressed with the effort Russ had made when she arrived at the Lazy P. He opened the door for her and jerked the apron from his waist.

"I hope you're happy," he muttered, looking anything but.

"I am. Thanks for asking," she said, but inwardly she was struggling not to laugh. This entire scene was almost too good to be true. Next to her own father, Russ was the biggest chauvinist she'd ever met. The sight of him working in a kitchen, wearing an apron, was priceless.

"Something smells delicious," she said.

"I'll tell you it isn't the hollandaise sauce. That stuff tastes like sh—" He stopped himself just in time. "You can figure it out."

"I can," she said. Smiling, she strolled across the kitchen and set a bottle of wine on the counter. "A small token of my appreciation."

She couldn't hear his reply as he furiously whipped the sauce simmering on the front burner. "Maybe it'll taste better once it's boiled," Russ said, concentrating on the task at hand.

The table was set. Well, sort of. The silverware was piled in the center between the two place settings. The water glasses were filled.

"The broccoli's done." Russ turned off the burner. "It looks all right from what I can tell." He drained the water and sprinkled a dash of salt and pepper over the contents of the pan.

"I'll open the wine, if you like."

"Sure," Russ said absently. He opened the oven door, and Taylor felt the blast of heat clear from the other side of the room.

"What's in there?"

"The baked potatoes," he said, slamming the door. "How long does it take to cook these things, anyway? They've been in there fifteen minutes and they're still hard as rocks."

"Normally they bake in about an hour."

"An hour?" he echoed. "Dammit, the sauce!" he cried. Grabbing a dish towel, he yanked the saucepan from the burner. He stirred frantically. "I hope it didn't burn."

"I'm sure it'll be just fine. Where's Mandy?"

"Gone," he grumbled. He stuck his finger in the sauce and licked it, then nodded, apparently surprised. "She's over at Chris's practicing for drill team. And before you ask, she didn't help me any."

"Mandy's not here?" Taylor said. A sense of uneasiness gripped her hard. After what had happened the first time she was alone with Russ, she had reason to be apprehensive.

She was overreacting, she told herself. It wasn't as if she was going to fall spontaneously into Russ's arms simply because his sister wasn't there to act as chaperone. They were both mature adults, and furthermore, they'd agreed to forget the night they'd kissed. The whole thing was as much of an embarrassment to Russ as it was to her. *She* certainly wasn't going to bring it up.

"Don't think I had anything to do with Mandy being gone, either."

"I didn't," she said with a shrug of indifference, implying that it hadn't even crossed her mind—which was true, at least before Russ mentioned it.

He was scowling as if he expected her to argue with him.

"Can I do anything to help?" she asked in an effort to subdue her nervousness.

"No, thanks. This meal is completely under control," he boasted. "I'm a man of my word, and when I said I was going to cook you the best steak you've ever eaten, I meant it."

"I'm looking forward to it." Wordlessly she opened a series of drawers until she located the corkscrew and proceeded to agilely remove the cork from the wine.

"I know it's traditional to serve red wine with beef, but I prefer white. This is an excellent chardonnay."

"Whatever you brought is fine," he mumbled as he swung open the refrigerator and took out a huge green salad.

It looked as if there was enough lettuce to feed the entire town, but Taylor refused to antagonize him by commenting on the fact.

"I want you to know I didn't slice the lettuce," he said proudly as he set the wooden bowl in the center of the table, shoving aside the silverware.

"Oh, good," Taylor responded, hoping she sounded appropriately impressed. The second cupboard she inspected contained crystal wineglasses. Standing on tiptoe, she brought down two. They were both thick with dust, so she washed and rinsed them before pouring the wine.

"I wanted to bring dessert, but there isn't a deli in Cougar Point," she said conversationally as she handed Russ his wineglass.

He stepped away from the stove to accept the wine. Scowling, he asked, "You were going to buy dessert at a deli?"

"It's the best place I know to get New York cheesecake."

Russ muttered something she didn't quite catch before returning to the stove. He turned down the burners and took a sip of his wine. "Since it's going to take the potatoes a little longer than I realized, we might as well sit down."

"Okay," Taylor agreed readily, following him into the living room. The furniture consisted of large, bulky

pieces that looked as if they'd been lifted from the set
of an old western series on television. *Bonanza,* maybe.

A row of silver-framed photographs lined the fireplace and, interested, Taylor walked over to examine
them. A picture of Russ, probably from his high school
graduation, caught her attention immediately. He'd been
a handsome young man. Boyishly good-looking, but
she could easily tell that his appeal was potent enough
to cause many a young woman more than one sleep-
less night.

"That's my dad and Betty," he said, pointing out the
second large portrait. "It was taken shortly after they
were married." The resemblance between father and son
was striking. They possessed the same brooding, dark
eyes, and their full mouths were identical. She looked at
Russ's high school picture again and found herself zero-
ing in on his youthful features. Even back then, there'd
been a wildness about him that challenged a woman.
No man had provoked, defied or taunted her the way
Russ had, and she barely knew him. By all rights she
should stay as far away from him as possible, yet here
she was in his home, studying his picture and theoriz-
ing about his secrets.

She turned away from the fireplace and sat in an
overstuffed chair. "You were telling me before that
you've got a thousand cattle," Taylor said, making conversation while her fingers moved nervously against the
padded arm of the chair.

"I've sold half the herd. I'm wintering five hundred
head, but by summer the numbers will be much higher."

"I see." She didn't really understand what he meant
but didn't know enough to ask intelligent questions.

Thankfully Russ seemed to grasp her dilemma and explained of his own accord.

"The men are rounding up the cattle now. We keep them in a feed ground."

"A feed ground?"

"It's a fenced pasture with no irrigation ditches."

"Why? I mean, don't they need water?"

"Of course, but the heavy snows start in December, sometimes earlier. When the ground's covered, the cattle can't see the ditches, and if a steer falls into one, he often can't get out, and I've lost a valuable animal."

"If the snow's that high, how do you get the feed to them?"

"Sometimes by sleigh."

Taylor smiled at the thought of riding through a snow-covered field. She could almost hear the bells jingling and Christmas music playing while she snuggled under a warm blanket, holding tight to Russ.

Shaking her head to dispel the romantic fantasy, Taylor swallowed, furious with the path her daydreams had taken. She drank some of her wine, hoping to set her thoughts in order before they became so confused that she lost all reason. "That sounds like fun."

"It's demanding physical labor," Russ told her gruffly.

His tone surprised her, and she raised her eyes to meet his.

He might be saying one thing, but Taylor would bet her first paycheck that he was battling the same fiery attraction she'd struggled with from the moment he'd first kissed her. He continued to stare at her in that restless, penetrating way that unnerved her.

He seemed impatient to escape from her, and unexpectedly vaulted to his feet. "I'd better check on dinner."

Once he was out of the room, Taylor closed her eyes and sagged against the back of the cushion. This evening had seemed safe enough until she'd learned Mandy was gone. The air seemed to crackle with electricity despite even the blandest conversation.

Taylor heard Russ move back into the room, and assuming dinner was ready, she leaped to her feet. "Let me help," she said.

Russ caught her by the shoulders.

"The potatoes aren't done."

As she tilted her head, her hair fell over her shoulder and down her back. Mark had liked it styled and short, and in an act of defiance, she'd allowed it to grow longer than at any other time in her life.

"You have beautiful hair," Russ murmured, apparently unable to take his eyes from it. He slid his hand from her shoulder to the dark curly mass, and ran his fingers through its length. The action, so slow and deliberate, was highly exciting. Against every dictate of her will, Taylor's heart quickened.

Soon his other hand joined the first and he continued to let his fingers glide through her hair, as if acquainting himself with its softness. Taylor seemed to be falling into a trance. His hands, buried deep in her hair, were more sensual than anything she'd ever experienced. Her eyes drifted shut, and when she felt herself being tugged toward him, she offered no resistance. His mouth met hers in a gentle brushing of lips. Their breaths merged as they each released a broken sigh.

"Tell me to stop," Russ said. "Tell me to take my hands away from you."

Taylor knew she should, but emotions that had been hiding just below the surface overwhelmed her. She meant to push him away, extract them both from this temptation—and yet the instant her hands made contact with his hard, muscular chest, they lost their purpose.

"Russ…"

His answer was to kiss her, a kiss that felt anything but gentle. His hands were tangled in the wavy bulk of dark hair as he bent her head to one side and slanted his demanding mouth over hers.

Their kisses were tempestuous, intense, exciting, and soon they were both panting and breathless.

Suddenly Russ tore his mouth from hers. His eyes remained closed. "I haven't stopped thinking of you all week," he confessed, not sounding very pleased about it. "I didn't want to, but you're there every night when I close my eyes. I can't get rid of the taste of you. Why *you?*" he asked harshly. "Why do I have to feel these things for a city girl? You don't belong here and you never will."

Taylor's head fell forward for a moment while she thought about his words. He was right. She was as out of place in this cattle town as…as a trout in a swimming pool. She raised her head while she had the courage to confront him. Anger was her friend; it took away the guilt she felt for being so willing to fall into his arms.

"You think I'm happy about this?" she cried. "Trust me, a cowpoke is the last person in the world I want to get involved with. A woman in your life is there for your convenience, to cook your meals and pleasure you in bed. I knew exactly what you were the minute we met and I could never align my thinking with yours."

"Fine then, don't," he barked.

"I don't have any intention of getting involved with you."

"Listen, lady, I'm not all that thrilled with you, either. Go back to the big city where you belong, because in these parts men are men and women are women. We don't much take to all that feminist talk."

Taylor was becoming more outraged by the minute. Russ clearly had no conception that they weren't living in the nineteenth century anymore.

"Let's eat," he snarled.

Taylor had half a mind to gather her things and leave. She would have if she'd thought she could get away with it. But Russ had made this dinner on a wager, and Taylor strongly suspected he'd see to it that she ate every bite. Knowing what she did about Russ, Taylor wouldn't put it past him to feed her himself if she backed out now.

Taylor wasn't sure how she managed to force down a single bite. Yet the salad was undeniably good. The broccoli was excellent, the sauce marginal, the baked potato raw, but the steak was succulent and exactly the way she liked it—medium rare.

Silence stretched between them like a tightrope, and neither seemed inclined to cross it. At least ten minutes passed before Russ spoke.

"I shouldn't have said that about you not belonging here," he murmured, stabbing the lettuce with his fork.

"Why not?" she asked. "It's true and we both know it. I *am* a city girl."

"From everything I hear, you're a fine teacher," he admitted grudgingly. "The kids are crazy about you and I don't blame them."

She lifted her eyes to his, uncertain if she should believe him, feeling both surprise and pleasure.

"Word has it you're enthusiastic and energetic, and everyone who's met you says nothing but good. I don't want you thinking folks don't appreciate what you're doing. That was just me running off at the mouth."

Her voice dropped to a raspy whisper. "I didn't mean what I said either, about not wanting anything to do with you because you're a cowpoke."

Their eyes met, and they each fought a smile. Knowing she was about to lose, Taylor lowered her gaze. "I will confess to being a little shocked at how well you managed dinner."

Russ chuckled softly. "It wasn't that difficult."

"Does that mean you'd be willing to tackle it again?"

"No way. Once in a man's lifetime is more than enough. I may have lost the wager, but I still consider cooking a woman's job."

"I thought for a moment that our wager would change your mind. But at this point, why do anything to spoil your reputation as a world-class chauvinist?"

Russ chuckled again, and the sound wasn't extraordinary, but it gladdened Taylor's heart. Something about this cowboy intrigued her. He wasn't like any other man she'd ever dated. His opinions were diametrically opposed to her own on just about every subject she could mention. Yet whenever he touched her, she all but melted in his arms. There wasn't any logic to this attraction they shared. No reason for it.

Russ helped himself to more salad and replenished their wineglasses. "Now that you know what Cougar Point thinks about you, how are you adjusting to us?"

"It's been more of a change than I expected," she said, holding the wineglass with both hands. She rotated the stem between her palms. "It's the lack of conveniences I notice the most."

He arched his brows in question. "Give me an example."

"Well, I came home from work the other night, exhausted. All I wanted to do was sit down, put my feet up and hibernate until morning. The problem was, I was starving. My first impulse was to order a pepperoni pizza, and when I realized I couldn't, I felt like crying with frustration."

"The bowling alley serves a decent pizza."

"But they don't deliver."

"No," Russ agreed, "they don't."

Feeling a twinge of homesickness, Taylor finished her wine and stood. "I'll help you with the dishes," she said, feeling sad and weary as she glanced at Russ. Even in the friendliest conversation their differences were impossible to ignore.

"I'll do them," he responded, standing himself.

"Nope, you made dinner," she said firmly. "You're exempt from washing dishes—this time." She turned on the tap and squirted a dash of liquid soap into the rushing water. Monster bubbles quickly formed, and she lowered the water pressure.

She was clearing off the table when Russ suggested, "How about a cup of coffee?"

"Please," she said, smiling over at him.

He busied himself with that while Taylor loaded the dishwasher with plates and serving dishes, leaving the pots and pans to wash by hand.

"Here," he said from behind her, "you might want this."

She turned around to discover Russ holding the very apron he'd been so quick to remove when she'd arrived.

Her hands were covered with soapsuds. She glanced at them and then at Russ.

"I'll put it on for you," he said.

She smiled her appreciation and lifted her arms so he could loop the ties around her waist and knot them behind her back.

Russ moved to within two steps of her and hesitated. Slowly he raised his eyes to her face. Hungry eyes. They delved into hers and then lowered just as slowly until they centered on her lips.

Unable to resist, Taylor swayed toward him. Once more she found herself a willing victim to his spell.

Their eyes held for a long moment before Russ roughly pushed the apron at her. "You do it."

With trembling hands, Taylor shook the suds into the sink and deftly tied the apron behind her. "I wish Mandy was here," she murmured, shocked by how close they'd come to walking into each other's arms again. Obviously they both enjoyed the lure of the forbidden. Whatever the attraction, it was explosive, and she felt as though they'd been stumbling around a keg of lit gunpowder all evening.

"I think I'll call her and tell her to come home," Russ said, but he didn't reach for the phone.

Once the dishwasher was loaded, Taylor vigorously scrubbed the first pan, venting her frustration on it.

"Are you going to the dance?" Russ asked her next, grabbing a dish towel and slapping it over his shoulder.

"I...don't think so."

"Why not? It'll give you a chance to meet all the young guys in town and you can flirt to your heart's content."

"I'm far beyond the flirting stage," she returned coolly.

He shrugged. "Could've fooled me. Fact is, you've been doing an admirable job of trifling with *me* from the moment we met."

Taylor's hand stilled. "I beg your pardon?"

"Take those jeans your wearing."

"What's wrong with these jeans?"

"They're too tight. Stretched across your fanny like that, they give a man ideas."

Closing her eyes, Taylor counted to ten. The effort to control her temper was in vain, however, and she whirled around to face him.

"How *dare* you suggest anything so ridiculous? You nearly kissed me a minute ago and now you're blaming *me* because *you* can't control yourself. Obviously it's all my fault."

He grunted and looked away.

"My jeans are too tight!" she echoed, her voice still outraged. "What about my sweater? Is that too revealing?" She bunched her breasts together and cast a meaningful look in their direction. "Did you notice how far the V-neck goes down? Why, a mere glimpse of cleavage is enough to drive a man to drink. Maybe I should have you censor my perfume, as well. It's a wonder the good people of Cougar Point would allow such a brazen hussy near their children. And one with a big-city attitude, no less."

"Taylor—"

"Don't you say another word to me," she cried, and jerked off the apron. Tears sprang to her eyes as she hurriedly located her purse. "Good night, Mr. Palmer. I won't say it's been a pleasure."

"Taylor, dammit, listen to me."

She raced down the stairs to her car, barely able to see through the tears in her eyes. The whole world looked blurred and watery, but Taylor was in too much of a hurry to care. This man said the most ridiculous things she'd ever heard. Only a fool would have anything more to do with him. Taylor had been a fool once.

Never, never again.

Russ sat in the living room, calling himself every foul name he could think of, and the list was a long one. When the back door opened, he knew it would be Mandy and reached for a newspaper, pretending to read.

"Hi!" She waltzed into the room. "How'd dinner go?"

"Great," he mumbled, not taking his eyes off the front page.

"Has Taylor already left?"

"Yeah."

"Oh, shucks, I wanted to talk to her. Do you want to see the routine Chris and I made up?"

Russ's interest in his sister's drill team efforts was less than nil. Nevertheless, he grinned and nodded. "Sure."

"Okay, but remember it's not the same without the music." She held the pom-poms to her waist, arms akimbo, then let loose with a high kick and shot her arms toward the ceiling. She danced left, she leaped right, her arms and legs moving with an instinctive grace that astonished Russ. This was Mandy? Fourteen-year-old Mandy? She was really quite good at this.

She finished down on one knee, her pom-poms raised above her head. Her smiling eyes met his, seeking his approval. "So?"

"There isn't a single doubt in my mind that my sister's going to make the high school drill team."

"Oh, Russ," she shouted, "thank you!" She vaulted to her feet and threw her arms around his neck. "Just for that I'll finish the dishes."

"Thanks," Russ said absently. He didn't want to think about dinner or anything else connected with this disastrous evening. That would only bring Taylor to mind, and she was the one person he was determined to forget. He'd suffered enough. All week she'd been nagging at his conscience. He'd even dreamed of her. He hadn't felt this way about a woman since he was sixteen years old.

Then he had to go and say those stupid things. The reason was even worse. He'd been jealous. The thought of her attending the Grange event and dancing with all the men in town was more than he could bear. Other men putting their arms around her. Someone else laughing with her.

If anyone was going to dance with Taylor Manning, it would be him. Not Harry Donovan. Not Les Benjamin. Not Cody Franklin.

Him.

"Russ?"

He turned and found his sister staring at him. "What?"

"You've been pacing for the past five minutes. Is something wrong?"

"Hell, no," he growled, then quickly changed his mind. "Hell, yes." He marched across the kitchen and grabbed his hat, bluntly setting it on his head.

"Where are you going?" Mandy demanded, following him.

"To town," he muttered. "I owe Taylor an apology."

Mandy giggled, seeming to find that amusing. "You going to ask her to the dance?"

"I might," he said, his strides long and purposeful.

"All right!" his sister cheered from behind him.

Four

"Taylor!" Russ pounded on the front door with his fist. This woman sure was stubborn. "I know you're in there. Answer the door, will you?"

"I can't," a soft, feminine voice purred from the other side. "I'm wearing something much too revealing." The purr quickly became an angry shout. "Army boots and fatigues!"

"I need to talk to you," Russ insisted.

"Go away."

Exhaling loudly, Russ pressed his palms against the door. "Please," he added persuasively, knowing few women could resist him when he used that imploring tone.

"If you don't leave, I'm calling the police."

"The deputy's name is Cody Franklin, and we went to school together."

"That doesn't mean he won't arrest you."

"On what charge? Wanting to apologize to my lady?"

The door flew open with such force that Russ was surprised it stayed on its hinges. Taylor's index finger poked him in the chest and he stumbled back a step.

"I am not your lady! Understand?" Deep blue eyes sliced straight through him.

Russ's grin was so big, his face ached. "I figured that comment would get a reaction out of you. I just didn't think it would be quite this zealous. Did anyone ever tell you you've got one hell of a temper?"

"No." She obviously resented being tricked. She crossed her arms protectively around her waist and glared at him. "There's only one other man in this world who can make me as angry as you do and I'm related to him."

"Which means you can't avoid him, but you *can* avoid me."

Taylor rolled her eyes skyward. "The cowboy's a genius."

Russ removed his hat and rotated the rim between his fingers. "I'm here to apologize for what I said earlier. I don't know what came over me," he hesitated, realizing that wasn't entirely true. "All right, I have a good guess. I was jealous."

"Jealous," she exploded. "Of what?"

This wasn't easy. Confronting her was one thing, but admitting how he'd been feeling... An uncomfortable sensation tightened his chest. "I was thinking about other men dancing with you and it bothered the hell out of me," he said in a low murmur, none too proud of it.

"That makes as much sense as my jeans being too tight. I already told you I wasn't going to the dance."

"Yes, you are," he countered swiftly. "You're going with me."

To his consternation, Taylor threw back her head and laughed. "In your dreams, Palmer."

There were any number of women in town who'd

leap at an invitation to attend the Grange dance with him; he could name four off the top of his head. So it didn't sit right that the one woman he really wanted to take had mocked his invitation. He could feel the red burning his ears, but he swallowed his protest. Still, he supposed he and Taylor were even now.

"Some women might appreciate those caveman tactics of yours," she informed him, smiling much too broadly to suit his already wounded pride. "But I'm not one of them."

"What do you want me to do? Get down on one knee and beg? Because if that's the case, you've got a hell of a long wait!" He slammed his hat back on his head.

Some of the amusement and indignation left her eyes.

Russ tried once more, softening his voice. "There isn't anyone in Cougar Point I'd rather attend the dance with," he said. Their eyes held for a few seconds longer before Russ added, "Will you go with me, Taylor? Please?" That wasn't a word he said often; he hoped she realized that.

It was clear she was wavering. Maybe she needed some inducement, Russ decided. He settled his hands on her shoulders and brought her against him. She remained as stiff as a branding iron, refusing to relax. He could kiss her; that might help with her decision. Every time his mouth settled over hers it was like drinking rainwater, sweet and fresh from the heavens. He rested his chin on the crown of her head and felt some of the fight go out of her. A smile twitched at the edges of his mouth. He knew she'd come around once she'd had a chance to think about it.

"Taylor?" he whispered, lifting her chin so he could look into her eyes. What he saw puzzled him. Russ expected to find submission, perhaps even a hint of desire. Instead he discovered bewilderment and distress.

When she spoke, her voice was a little shaky. "I... It'd be best if you asked someone else, Russ."

"You're going to the Grange dance, aren't you?" Mary Beth Morgan asked, popping into Taylor's room after class on Wednesday afternoon.

Taylor shook her head and riffled through a stack of papers on her desk. "I don't think so."

"But, Taylor," the other teacher said, "everyone in town will be there."

"So I heard." Taylor stood and placed the papers inside her folder to take home and grade that evening.

"Why wouldn't you want to go?"

Taylor hedged, wondering how she could explain. "First, I don't have anything appropriate to wear, and second—" she hesitated and lifted one shoulder in a half shrug "—I don't know how to square dance."

Mary Beth smiled and shook her head. "You don't have a thing to worry about. You could show up at the Grange in a burlap bag and you'd have more offers to dance than you'd know what to do with. As for the square dancing part, put that out of your head. This isn't a square dance."

"I'll think about it," Taylor promised.

"You'd better do more than that," Mary Beth said. "I personally know of three young men who'll be mighty disappointed if you aren't at that dance."

"I suppose I could sew a dress," Taylor said, her spirits lifting. She knew the minute she arrived that Russ would believe she was there because of him, but the thought of staying home while everyone else was having fun was fast losing its appeal.

"Listen, Taylor, there aren't that many social functions in Cougar Point. Take my advice and enjoy yourself while you can because there probably won't be another one until Christmas."

"Christmas?"

"Right," Mary Beth said with a solid nod. "Now I'll tell you what I'll do. My husband and I will pick you up at seven."

"I know where the Grange Hall is," Taylor said, brightening. "You don't need to give me a ride."

Mary Beth laughed. "I just want to see if it's Russ Palmer, Cody Franklin or Harry Donovan who takes you home."

True to her word, Mary Beth and Charles Morgan came by to pick up Taylor promptly at seven on Saturday night.

"Oh, my, we're in for a fun evening," Mary Beth said as she walked a full circle around Taylor. Slowly she shook her head. "That dress is absolutely gorgeous."

Taylor had been up until midnight two evenings straight, sewing. There was an old-fashioned dry goods store in town, where she'd found a respectable—and surprisingly inexpensive—assortment of fabrics and notions. She'd chosen a pattern for a western-style dress with a tight-fitting lace-up bodice and snug waist. The skirt flared out gently at her hips and fell to midcalf. An eyelet-ruffled petticoat of white dropped three inches below the lavender dress. Brown boots complemented the outfit.

"Yup, we're in for a really good time tonight." Mary

Beth chuckled as she slipped her arm through Taylor's and led her out the door.

The music coming from the Grange Hall could be heard even before they parked the car. Bright lights poured out from the large brick structure on the highway outside town. The parking lot was filled with trucks and four-wheel-drive vehicles. Without meaning to, Taylor started looking for Russ's truck, then quickly chastised herself.

She was hardly in the door when Mandy flew to her side. The girl's face was glowing with a warm smile.

"I knew you'd come! Russ said you wouldn't be here, but I was sure you would. Oh, Taylor," she whispered wide-eyed when Taylor removed her coat. "Where did you ever find a dress that pretty?"

Taylor whirled around once to give her the full effect. "You like it? Well, I told you before there are advantages in knowing how to use a sewing machine."

"You *made* your dress?"

"Don't look so shocked."

"Could I ever sew anything that complicated?"

"With practice."

"If I took all the money I've been saving for a new saddle and bought a sewing machine, would you teach me to sew? I'm not taking home economics until next term, and I don't want to wait that long to learn. Not when I can make clothes as pretty as yours."

"I'd be happy to teach you."

"Howdy, Taylor." A young man with soft ash-blond hair stepped in front of her, hands tucked into the small front pockets of his jeans.

"Hello," she said, not recognizing him, although he apparently knew her.

"I was wondering if I could have the next dance?"

"Ah…" Taylor hadn't even hung up her coat yet, and she would've liked to find her way around and talk to a few people before heading for the dance floor.

"For crying out loud," Mandy muttered. "Give Taylor a minute, will you, Harry? She just got here."

Harry's cheeks flushed with instant color. "If I don't ask her now," he said, "someone else will and I won't get a chance the rest of the evening." He blushed some more. "So can I have this dance?"

"Ah…sure," Taylor said, not knowing what else to do. Mandy took her coat and Harry led her to the dance floor, smiling broadly as if he'd pulled off a major coup.

Once they reached the dance floor, Harry slipped his arm around her waist and guided her through a simple two-step. They hadn't been on the floor more than a few minutes when the music ended. Reluctantly Harry let his arm drop.

"I don't suppose you'd consider dancing the next one with me?" he asked hopefully.

Taylor hesitated. The room was growing more crowded, and she still hadn't talked to anyone.

"I believe the next dance is mine," a deep masculine voice said from behind her. Taylor didn't need a detective to know it was Russ. She stiffened instinctively before turning to face him.

Russ stood directly in front of her in a gray western-tailored suit with a suede yoke, his gaze challenging hers. His look alone was enough to silence the denial on her tongue. His eyes moved over her like a warm caress, tiny glints of mischief sparking in their depths.

The music started again, and as Harry stepped away, Russ placed his arms around her. There wasn't an ounce of protest left in Taylor as he caressed the small of her back. She closed her eyes and pretended to be engrossed in the music when it was Russ who held her senses captive.

Several minutes passed before he spoke. His mouth was close to her ear. "I knew you'd come."

Taylor's eyes shot open, and she jerked away from him, putting several inches between them. "Let me tell you right now that my being here has absolutely nothing to do with you, and—"

He pressed a finger over her lips, stopping her in midsentence.

Slowly Taylor lifted her gaze to his. Deeply etched lines from long hours in the sun crinkled around his eyes.

"Thank you for coming," he whispered, and his warm breath tinged her cheek. Then he removed his finger.

"It wasn't for you," she felt obliged to inform him, but the indignation in her voice was gone. "Mary Beth Morgan...invited me."

Russ's mouth quirked just a fraction. "Remind me to thank her."

His grip tightened, and although Taylor was determined to keep a safe, respectable distance from this man, she found herself relaxing in his embrace. He slid his hand up and down the length of her back, sending hunger shooting through her. She eased closer, reveling in the strength she sensed in the rugged, hard contours of his body. She didn't mean to, didn't even want to, but when he tucked her hand between them and rested his face against her hair, she closed her eyes once again. He smelled of rum and spice, and she breathed in deeply, inhaling his scent.

When the song ended, it was Taylor who swallowed a sigh of regret. Dancing like this was a lost art in the city. The last time she'd danced with a man who'd placed his arms around her so tenderly, she'd been with Mark, early in their relationship. She'd almost forgotten how good it was to feel so cherished.

Russ refused to release her; if anything, he pulled her closer. "Let's get out of here for a few minutes."

Taylor groaned inwardly. She couldn't believe how tempted she was to agree. "I…can't. I just got here. People will talk."

"Let them."

"Russ, no." Using her hands for leverage, she pushed herself free. He didn't offer any resistance, but the effort it had cost her to move away left her weak. And furious. How dare he assume she'd go into the parking lot with him—and for what? She'd bet cold hard cash he wasn't planning to discuss cattle breeding techniques with her.

"I want it understood that I'm not going anywhere near that parking lot with you, Russ Palmer."

"Whatever you say." But a smile tugged insolently at his mouth.

The music started again, and they stood facing each other in the middle of the dance floor with couples crowding in around them. Russ didn't take her in his arms, nor did she make a move toward him.

Amusement flickered in his eyes. There was no re-sisting him, and soon Taylor responded to his smile. He slipped his hands around her waist, drawing her back into the circle of his arms. They made a pretense of dancing but were doing little more than staring at each other and shuffling their feet.

No woman in her right mind would deliberately get involved with an avowed chauvinist like Russ Palmer, yet here she was, a thoroughly modern woman, so attracted to him that she ached to the soles of her feet.

The music came to an end, and his arms relaxed. A careless, handsome grin slashed his mouth. "Enjoy yourself," he whispered. "Dance with whomever you like, but remember this. I'm the one who's taking you home tonight. No one else. Me."

An immediate protest rose in Taylor's throat, but before she could utter a single word, Russ bent forward and set his mouth over hers. She clenched her fists against his gray suit jacket while his lips caressed hers. Taylor could hear the curious voices murmuring around them, and she gave a small cry.

Russ ended the kiss, smiled down on her and whispered, "Remember."

Then he walked off the floor.

Taylor felt like a first-class fool, standing there by herself with half a dozen couples staring at her. When the hushed whispers began, she smiled blandly and all but ran from the dance floor.

Taylor was so mortified that she headed directly for the ladies' room and stayed there a full five minutes, trying to compose herself. If there'd been a sofa, she would have sat down and wept. Wept because she'd been so tempted to let Russ take her outside. Wept because she felt so right in his arms. Wept because she hadn't learned a thing from her disastrous affair with Mark Brooks.

Once she reappeared at the dance, she didn't lack

for attention. She waltzed with Cody Franklin, chatted over punch with Les Benjamin, another rancher, and even managed a second two-step with Harry Donovan. She smiled. She laughed. She pretended to be having the time of her life, but underneath everything was a brewing frustration she couldn't escape. Every now and then she'd catch a glimpse of Russ dancing with someone else. Usually someone young and pretty. Someone far more suited to him than she'd ever be. Yet, each time, she felt a stab of jealousy unlike anything she'd ever experienced.

By the time the evening started to wind down, Taylor decided the best way to thwart Russ was to accept someone else's offer to drive her home.

Only no one asked.

Of the dozen or so men she danced with, not a single, solitary one suggested taking her home. Charles and Mary Beth Morgan had already left by the time Taylor realized she had no option except to find Russ.

He was waiting for her outside, standing at the bottom of the Grange steps, looking as arrogant and pleased as could be.

"I want to know what you said to everyone," she demanded, marching down the steps. It was more than a little suspicious that she'd been virtually abandoned without a ride.

Russ's eyes fairly shone with devilment. "Me? What makes you think I said anything?"

"Because I know you, and I want one thing clear right now. You can take me home, but nothing else. Understand?"

"You insult me, madam!"

"Good. Now, where's Mandy?" Taylor asked.

"She's spending the night with Chris," Russ explained. "However, rest assured, you're perfectly safe with me."

"I'd be safer in a pit of rattlesnakes," she said wryly. "Do you have any idea how humiliating it was when you kissed me on that dance floor and then took off?" Her voice was a low hiss.

"I promise I'll never do it again," he vowed, and led her across the parking lot where he held open the truck door.

This was a newer model than the one she'd ridden in earlier. She paused and glanced inside and was relieved to see it had seat belts. However, the truck stood probably three feet off the ground, and there wasn't any way she'd be able to climb inside without assistance.

"Here," Russ said, "I'll help you up." His hands closed around her waist and he lifted her effortlessly off the ground.

Once she was inside and Russ had joined her, she asked him, "Where do you drive this thing? Through the Rockies?"

Russ chuckled and started the engine. "You'd be surprised the places this truck has been."

"I'll bet," Taylor grumbled.

She didn't say a word during the short drive to her rented house. Russ didn't, either.

He pulled in to her driveway, cut the engine and was out of the cab before she could object. Opening her door, Russ helped her down. But when her feet were firmly planted on the ground, he didn't release her.

His eyes held hers in the dim light from a nearby streetlamp, and a current of awareness flowed between them. "You were the most beautiful woman there tonight."

"I'm surprised you even noticed." The minute the words escaped, Taylor regretted having spoken. In one short sentence she'd revealed what she'd been doing all evening.

Watching him.

She'd counted the number of women he'd danced with and, worse, envied them the time they'd spent in his arms.

Russ didn't answer her. Not with words, anyway. Instead he pulled her into his arms and kissed her. His mouth was hard, his kiss thorough. When he lifted his head, their panting breaths echoed each other.

"Invite me inside," he whispered, his voice husky.

Taylor felt powerless to do anything other than what he asked. Her hands were shaking as she drew the keys from her purse. Russ took them from her and unlocked the door, pushing it open for her to precede him.

She walked through the living room and to the kitchen, turning on the lights. "I'll…make some coffee."

"No," Russ said, stopping her. His arms anchored her against the wall. "I don't want any coffee and neither do you."

Taylor gazed into his face and recognized his hunger, aware that it was a reflection of her own. Closing her eyes, she leaned against the wall, feeling needy and weak.

"Trust me," Russ whispered. "I know what you're thinking. We're both crazy. I should stay as far away from you as possible. You don't want to feel these things for me any more than I want to feel them for you. We argue. We fight. But, lady, when we kiss, everything else pales by comparison."

"What we're experiencing is just physical attraction," she whispered as her fingers sank into his thick, dark hair.

"Physical attraction," he repeated, seconds before his mouth came crashing down on hers. Low, animal sounds came from deep within his throat as his mouth twisted and turned over hers.

Braced against the wall, she could feel every hard, rugged inch of him.

Restlessly she moved against him as her hands clenched fistfuls of his hair.

"Russ," she panted, lifting her head. "I...I think we should stop now."

"In a minute." Grasping her by the waist, he dragged her against him and groaned.

Taylor did, too.

He was so hard. She was so soft.

Man to woman.

Cowboy to lady.

They fit together so perfectly.

Drawing in deep, shuddering breaths, Russ buried his face in the curve of her neck. It took him several seconds to regain control of himself.

It took Taylor even longer.

He raised his head and smoothed the hair from her face. "I've changed my mind," he murmured. "I will take that coffee, after all."

Grateful for something to occupy herself, Taylor moved to the counter where she kept her coffeemaker. While waiting for the aromatic coffee to drip through, she got two mugs and placed them on a tray. She was so absorbed in her task that when she turned around she nearly collided with Russ.

He took the tray from her hands and carried it into the living room. "I think it's time we cleared the air," he said, setting their mugs on the oak coffee table.

"In what way?" Taylor asked, perching on the edge of the sofa cushion.

"Above all else, we've got to be honest with each other."

"Right."

Taylor sipped from her mug, the scalding coffee too hot to savor or appreciate.

"Are you wearing a bra?" he asked unexpectedly.

"What?" She jerked forward, setting her cup back on the tray to avoid spilling hot coffee down her front. It sloshed over the edges of the mug.

Taylor's mouth gaped as she glared at him. "Is *that* the kind of honesty you're interested in?" Unable to sit still, she got up and started pacing, so furious she was tempted to throw him out of her home.

"I'm sorry. Forget I asked. I was holding you and it felt as if you weren't and the question just…slipped out. You're right—that was a stupid question."

He lowered his eyes, and Taylor noted that his ears were red. As red as Harry Donovan's had been when he'd asked her to dance. Russ Palmer embarrassed? The very thought was inconceivable.

Stepping around the low table, Taylor sat back down and reached for her coffee. "As a matter of fact, no."

Russ closed his eyes as though in pain. "You shouldn't

have told me." He took a gulp of coffee, then stood abruptly. "Maybe it'd be best if I left now."

"I thought you wanted to talk. I refuse to answer personal questions like the last one, but I think you're right about us being honest with each other."

Now it was Russ's turn to do the pacing. He stood and stalked across her living room carpet and then back again as if he intended to wear a pattern in it.

"Russ?"

He rammed his fingers through his hair and turned to face her. "If you want honesty, I'll give it to you, Taylor, but I'll guarantee you aren't going to like what I have to say."

She wasn't sure she was up to this. But, on the other hand, she didn't want him to leave, either. "Just say it."

"All right," he said sharply. "Right now, I want you so damn much I can't even think straight." He raked one hand down his face. "Does that shock you?"

"No," she cried softly.

"Well, it should."

Holding the mug so tightly that it burned her palms, Taylor gathered her courage. "Earlier I objected when you called me your lady. The lady part wasn't what offended me. It might be an old-fashioned term, but I *am* a lady. And I'll always be a lady."

Russ frowned. "I know that, Taylor. No one can look at you and not realize the kind of woman you are."

"I have no intention of falling into bed with you, Russ. I wish I understood why we're so attracted to each other, but I don't. I do know we're playing with fire. Unfortunately, if we continue like this, one of us is going to get burned."

Russ closed his eyes and nodded. "You're right, of course." He inhaled deeply. "Does this mean you want me to leave?"

"No," she said, smiling at her own lack of willpower. "But I think you should, anyway."

Five

"Mandy, I'm not going near that horse."

"Taylor, please. I want to do something to thank you for all the sewing lessons you've given me."

As far as Taylor was concerned, the chestnut gelding looked as huge as the Trojan horse. He didn't seem all that friendly, either. Her palms were sweating, and her throat felt dry from arguing with the persistent teen.

"Shadow is as gentle as they come," Mandy assured her, stroking the white markings on the horse's face. "You don't have a thing to worry about."

"That's what they said to Custer, too," Taylor muttered under her breath. This whole episode had started out so innocuously. Taylor had spent an hour after school helping Mandy cut out the pattern for a vest. Then, because Russ was busy with an errand in Miles City, Taylor had dropped her off at the ranch. One of the men had been exercising a horse, and Taylor had innocently inquired about the stock. Before she knew how it had happened, Mandy was insisting on teaching her to ride, claiming she couldn't accept sewing lessons from Taylor without giving her something in return.

"Once you climb into the saddle, you'll feel a whole lot better about it," Mandy told her.

"I'm not much of a horse person," Taylor said.

"That doesn't matter. Shadow's gentle. I promise you."

"Another time perhaps," Taylor murmured.

"But today's perfect for riding."

Before Taylor could answer, she saw Russ's truck speeding down the driveway, leaving a trail of dust in its wake. Taylor hadn't seen Russ since the night of the Grange dance, and she hated the way her pulse immediately started to race.

Russ pulled to a stop and leaped out of the truck, but he paused when he saw Taylor's Cabriolet parked near the barn. Setting his hat farther back on his head, he changed his direction and walked toward them.

"Hello, Taylor," he said, bowing his head slightly.

"Russ."

"Maybe you can talk some sense into her." Mandy gestured toward Taylor, looking wistful. "I think she should learn to ride. Here she is giving me all these sewing lessons, and I want to repay her."

"You've already had me over for dinner," Taylor reminded the girl. "Really, horses just aren't my thing. The last time I sat on a horse was on a carousel when I was ten years old."

"If Taylor's afraid…"

"What makes you say that?" Taylor demanded. "I'm not *afraid* of horses. It's just that I'm unfamiliar with them. I don't think now is the time for me to do more than gain a nodding acquaintance with Shadow here, but I most certainly am not afraid."

"Then prove it," Russ challenged. He patted Shadow

on the rump. The gelding returned the greeting with a nicker and a swish of his thick tail.

"I promise you'll enjoy it," Mandy said.

Grumbling under her breath, Taylor took the reins from Mandy's hands. "Why do I have the sinking suspicion I'm going to regret this?"

"You won't," Mandy vowed.

"This kid is much too free with her promises," Taylor told Russ. Lifting her left foot and placing it in the stirrup, Taylor reached for the saddle horn and heaved herself up.

"You might need some help," Mandy said. "Russ, help her."

"She seems to be doing fine without me."

Taylor had hoisted her weight halfway up when she started to lose her grip. Russ was behind her in an instant, supporting her waist. "All right, Annie Oakley, I'll give you a hand."

Swinging her leg over the back of the horse, Taylor held on to the saddle horn as if it were a life preserver and she was lost at sea.

"See?" Mandy cried triumphantly. "There isn't anything to it. Didn't I tell you?"

Russ adjusted the stirrups for her. "You look a little green around the gills. Are you okay?"

"It's…a little higher up here than I imagined. Can I get down now?"

Mandy giggled. "But you haven't gone anyplace yet."

"Isn't *this* enough to prove I'm not afraid? You didn't say anything about actually moving."

"Josh, bring me Magic," Russ instructed the hand who'd saddled Shadow earlier. A large black gelding was led from the barn, and with Josh's assistance Russ saddled and bridled the horse.

"You go ahead and take Taylor out and I'll start dinner," Mandy suggested. "By the time you two get back, everything will be ready."

"Uh… I'm not so sure this is the best time for me to ride," Taylor said, struggling to hide the panic in her voice. "I've got papers that need to be corrected and a couple of loads of wash…and other things."

"It's Friday," Mandy announced over her shoulder as she strolled toward the house. "You can do all that tomorrow."

"Of course," Taylor muttered. "I should've thought of that."

"Don't look so terrified. This is going to be a good experience for you," Russ told her, his expression far more smug than she liked.

He mounted the black gelding, gave instructions to the hands to unload the pickup, then turned to Taylor. "We'll take it nice and easy. You haven't got a thing to worry about."

"If that's the case, why do I feel like I'm about a mile off the ground?"

Russ's returning chuckle warmed her heart. She'd missed him this week—although she'd had to search her soul to even admit that. With Mandy stopping in after school, three days out of five, Taylor had been kept well-informed about Russ's activities. He'd done the ordering on Tuesday and was grumpy most of the night, and Mandy didn't have a clue why. Thursday he was out on the range, looking for strays, and Friday he'd traveled into Miles City for supplies. Taylor had never openly asked about Russ, but she was always pleased when Mandy slipped her small pieces of information.

Russ, riding Magic, set the pace, and once they were past the barn, he pointed out a trail that led toward rolling hills of fresh, green grass. "We'll head this way."

"Do you mind if we go a bit slower?" She swayed back and forth, beginning to feel a little seasick with the motion.

"If we went any slower, we'd be standing still."

"What's wrong with that?" she muttered. "By the way, if it isn't too much to ask, where are you taking me?"

Russ waggled his eyebrows suggestively. "*Now* she asks."

"And what's that supposed to mean?"

"Nothing." But his dark eyes were twinkling—a look Taylor had seen before, once too often.

She pulled back on the reins several minutes later, mildly surprised when Shadow slowed to a stop. "I don't trust you, Russ. Tell me this minute exactly where we're going."

Russ leaned back in the saddle, nonchalantly throwing one leg around the saddle horn and clasping his hands behind his head. He was as at ease in a saddle as he was in his own living room. "No place in particular. You want to stop and rest a minute? There's a valley about a quarter mile from here."

Taylor hated to admit how sore her posterior already felt. And they hadn't even gone very far. If she squinted, she could just make out the back of the red barn in the distance.

"Yes, let's stop and rest," she agreed. "But no funny business."

Theatrically Russ removed his hat and pressed it over his heart with a roguish grin. "Once again you insult me, madam."

Taylor said nothing, unwilling to take part in his performance.

"Mandy says you're helping her sew a vest," Russ said conversationally a few minutes later. He slowed Magic and swung down with a grace Taylor could only envy. It had taken all her strength just to raise herself into the saddle. If Russ hadn't given her a boost, she would've been caught with one foot in the stirrup and the other madly waving in midair—until she crashed to the ground.

"Need any help?"

"I can do it myself," she announced, not the least bit confident. Surely climbing out of the saddle would be less of a strain than getting into it had been. Besides, if Russ lent her a hand, he'd use it as an excuse to kiss her. Not that she'd mind, but for once she'd enjoy having a relaxed conversation without falling into his arms like a love-starved teenager.

Taylor was pleased at how easy dismounting turned out to be. Her legs felt a little shaky, but once her feet were on the ground and she'd walked around a bit, she decided this horseback riding business wasn't as difficult as she'd assumed.

"I don't expect many more warm days like this one," Russ said. He tilted his hat back on his head and stared into the distance. Several cattle were grazing on a hill across from them.

Taylor joined him, and he slipped an arm around her waist as familiarly as if he'd been doing so for years.

"Thank you for everything you're doing for Mandy."

"It's nothing."

"It's a lot. Teaching her to sew. Encouraging her. She comes home high as a kite after she's been with you, chattering a mile a minute." A boyish grin lifted his mouth. "For that matter, I come home happy, too."

Taylor lowered her eyes. "I think her making the drill team is what boosted her spirits more than anything. She could've walked on water the day she learned she'd been chosen."

"Only three freshmen made the squad," Russ said, smiling proudly.

Linking her hands behind her back, Taylor strolled over to a large tree. Leaning against the trunk, she raised one knee and rested her booted foot behind her. "I've enjoyed working with Mandy this week. She reminds me of my sister, Christy, when she was fourteen. Unfortunately I was sixteen at the time and considered Christy a major pest."

"Mandy told me you came from a large family."

"By today's standards, I guess you could say that. I have three older brothers, Paul, Jason and Rich. Paul's the only one who's married, and believe me, the rest of us are eternally grateful to him because he quickly presented my parents with twin sons. Now that Mom and Dad have grandchildren, the rest of us are off the hook, at least for a while."

"You're close to your family, aren't you?"

Taylor nodded. "I can't believe how much I miss them. They must be feeling the same way because I've heard from them practically every day."

Russ lowered himself to the grass, stretching his legs in front of him and crossing his ankles. "Mandy said something about how your father reminds you of me."

"Is nothing sacred?" she teased. If his sister had been dropping tidbits about him, she'd also done a bang-up job of keeping Russ informed of their conversations. "My dad's a born chauvinist. I don't think he's sure it was a good thing that women were granted the vote."

Russ didn't laugh the way most people would. "I don't mind if women vote. It's holding public office that concerns me."

Taylor shoved away from the tree so fast, she nearly fell. Her mouth worked for several seconds before any words came out. "I can't *believe* you just said that. Why *shouldn't* a woman hold public office?"

"My, my, you're always so touchy."

"Who can blame me when you say something so ludicrous?"

"Think about it, Taylor. A woman is the very heart of a home and family. What kind of wife and mother would she be if she was so deeply involved in politics that she couldn't tend to her family?"

"I'm not hearing this," she muttered.

"Don't you think a woman's place is with her children?"

"What about a father's place?"

"The husband's got to work in order to support the family."

Taylor covered her face with both hands. Even if his opinion was half-meant to be provocative, arguing with him would do no good. She'd tried often enough with her father, but to no avail. The two men were equally out of date in their views, equally stubborn and difficult.

Not knowing what possessed her, she leaped forward, jerked Russ's hat from his head and took off running.

"Taylor?" Russ vaulted to his feet in one smooth

movement and chased after her. "What are you doing with my hat? What's gotten into you?"

Walking backward, keeping a safe distance from him, Taylor hid the Stetson behind her. "You're narrow-minded and the second-worst chauvinist I've ever known."

"You stole my hat because of that?"

"Yes. It was the only way I could make you suffer."

Russ advanced toward her, taking small steps. "Give me back the hat, Taylor."

"Forget it." For a good part of her life, Taylor had been playing keep-away with her brothers. She might not be as big as Russ and not nearly as agile, but she was quick.

"Taylor, give me the hat," he said again. His gaze narrowed as he advanced toward her, holding out his hand.

"No way. Women don't have any business holding public office? I can't let something that outrageous pass without making you pay."

Laughter flashed from his eyes as he lunged for her. Taylor let out a playful shriek and darted sharply to the left. Russ missed her by a yard.

Russ turned and was prepared to make another dive toward her when Taylor tossed the black cowboy hat with all her might into the sky. "Catch it if you can!" she shouted, bobbing past him. She was in such a rush that she stumbled and would have crashed face-first onto the grass if Russ hadn't captured her around the waist and brought her against him. The full force of her weight caught him off balance. He twisted so that he took the brunt of the impact, and they toppled onto the ground.

Within a heartbeat, Russ had reversed their positions, pinning her hands above her head. Taylor looked up into the dark warmth of his eyes and smiled. Her breasts were heaving with excitement.

"Who's making whom pay?" Russ demanded. He pressed his mouth to her neck, running the tip of his tongue over the smooth skin of her throat. Sensation wove its way down her spine, and she moaned softly and bucked. "No..."

"You're going to be doing a lot more begging before I'm through with you," Russ whispered. He kissed her then, his lips teasing and taunting hers with soft nibbles, promising but never quite delivering.

Arching her back, she struggled and was immediately released. With her hands free, she buried her fingers in his hair, raised her head and fused her mouth to his. She could feel herself dissolving, melting against him.

Russ kissed her mouth, her eyes, her throat. Taylor felt as if she were on fire, her whole body aflame with need. His hand found her breast, and Taylor sighed as a fresh wave of fiery sensation engulfed her.

"Oh, Russ," she pleaded, not sure what she was asking of him. The physical urge was strong and compelling, but there had to be so much more before she could freely give herself to him. A merging of their hearts. Commitment. Love.

She had no time to voice her concerns. Russ kissed her, and a swift, acute sensation of hot, urgent desire rose up in her, blocking out everything but her awareness of Russ and her growing need.

She wanted him to continue—and yet...

"Either we stop now or we finish." His breathing was

raspy as he slid his hands from her hips to her shoulders. "The choice is yours."

Taylor squeezed her eyes shut. Her throat was tight as she slowly shook her head. She didn't need to think twice; the decision had been made for her the moment she met Russ. He was as much a part of this landscape as the sycamore trees around them. She was as misplaced as a hothouse flower. But beyond that, Russ was a chauvinist. There was no other word for it. After the years of battling with her father, Taylor had no intention of falling in love with a man who shared the same outdated attitudes toward women.

She gave a shake of her head.

Russ exhaled sharply. "That's what I thought." His breath left him in a defeated rush and he stroked her hair. "Were you hurt when we hit the ground like that?"

She shook her head a second time, wishing she could hide her face in her hands and never look at him again. She certainly hadn't intended to let things go this far. One moment she was teasing him, playfully tossing his hat into the air, and the next...

"Are you sure you're all right?"

"Of course." But that was far from the truth. Taking his cue, she moved away from him and sat on the grass.

"Mandy's probably wondering about us," she said, doing her best to keep her voice from trembling as badly as her hands did.

"Don't worry. She won't send out a search party."

To Taylor's way of thinking, it might have been better if Mandy had.

It seemed everyone was looking at Taylor when she rode back into the yard. The ranch hands' curiosity about her was probably due to her precarious seat atop

Shadow more than anything. As soon as she was able to stop the horse, she tossed the reins over his head and slid ingloriously from the saddle. Her feet landed with a jarring thud when she connected with the ground.

Mandy came out of the house, waving. "Gee, what took you guys so long?" she called, walking toward them. "I've had dinner ready for ages."

"We stopped and rested for a bit," Russ said, sharing a secret smile with Taylor, who was confident the color in her cheeks spelled out exactly what they'd been doing.

"I thought you were going to be back right away, so I fixed soup and sandwiches for dinner. That's all right, isn't it?"

"Actually, I should be getting back to town," Taylor said, eager to make her escape. Only when she was alone would she be able to analyze what had happened. Of one thing she was sure: there wouldn't be a repeat of this.

All her good intentions to take the time to heal her broken heart properly were like dust particles caught in the wind, blowing every which way. She had no business getting involved with Russ.

"Oh, please, don't go yet." Mandy's face fell at Taylor's announcement.

"I really have to," Taylor insisted. Spending any more of this day with Russ would have been agonizing, reminding her of what she couldn't allow herself to have.

Taylor hadn't been in her rental house five minutes when she felt the urge to talk to her mother. But it was her father who answered on the third ring.

"Hi, Dad."

"Taylor, sweetheart, how are you?" No matter what his mood, he always sounded gruff.

"Fine."

The pause that followed was brief. "What's wrong?"

Taylor smiled to herself. She'd never been very good at keeping anything from her parents. "What makes you ask?"

"You don't call home very often."

"Dad," she whispered, closing her eyes, "is Mom around? I'm in the mood for a mother-daughter chat."

"Your mother's shopping. Just pretend I'm her and talk."

"I can't do that." She loved him dearly, but they were constantly arguing. Of all the Manning children, Taylor was the one who didn't hesitate to stand up to him. Her bravery had won her the esteem of her siblings.

"Why can't you talk to me? I'm your father, aren't I? You're the one who's always throwing equality of the sexes in my face. So talk."

"But, Dad, this is different."

"Hogwash. I haven't been married to your mother for the past thirty-five years without knowing how she thinks. Tell me what you want and I'll respond just as if I were your mother."

"It's nothing really, but, well…" She decided to jump in with both feet. "What would you say if I told you I met a cowboy I think I might be falling in love with? The problem is, I'm not sure I could even get along with this man. From the moment we met he set my teeth on edge."

"I take it the situation has changed?"

"Not really," she mumbled, knowing she wasn't making much sense. "He still says things that make me so mad I could scream, but then at other times he'll do something so sweet and sincere I want to cry." Her voice shook. "I realize it probably goes back to Mark, and you're going to say I'm on the rebound. Russ and I are as incompatible as any two people could be. I can't even believe I'm so attracted to him." She pulled in a deep breath once she'd finished. There was silence on the other end. "Dad?"

"I'm here."

"Well, say something."

"You want me to say something?" he repeated, but he didn't sound like himself. He paused and cleared his throat. "In this case I think you might be right—talk this over with your mother. She knows about these things."

Taylor laughed softly into the phone and shook her head. For the first time in recent history she'd won an argument with her father.

On Tuesday afternoon, as Taylor walked home, she stopped at the grocery store, then mailed her electric bill payment at the pharmacy. She loved going into Cougar Point's drugstore. Not only could she have a prescription filled, but she could buy just about anything she needed. A tiny branch of the post office operated there, as well as a liquor store. In Seattle one-stop shopping generally referred to a large mall, but in Cougar Point it meant going to the pharmacy.

As she carried her groceries home, she noticed that the leaves were starting to change and wondered how long this pleasant fall weather would continue. Turning off Main Street and onto Oak, she saw Mandy sitting on her front porch.

"Mandy?" The girl's eyes were red and puffy from crying. "Sweetheart, what's wrong?"

Russ's sister leaped to her feet and wiped her eyes. Her chin was tilted at a proud, indignant angle and her mouth trembled. "I'm leaving."

"Leaving?"

"Running away," she explained in a tight voice. "But before I go, I thought I should tell someone so Russ won't send Cody Franklin out looking for me."

Six

"Come inside," Taylor urged the girl. "I think we should talk about this."

Mandy hedged, keeping her eyes downcast. "I don't really have time."

"It'll just take a few minutes. I promise." Withdrawing the key from her purse, Taylor opened the door, walked inside and deposited her groceries on the kitchen counter.

Mandy followed, clearly anxious to be on her way.

Pulling out a chair, Taylor indicated she should sit down. Then she grabbed them each a can of cold soda as inducement and took the chair opposite Mandy.

"It's Russ," the girl said in a choked whisper. "He's making me quit the drill team."

Taylor struggled to hide her dismay. "Is it your grades?"

"No. I've always been high honor roll. We got our uniforms this afternoon and I tried mine on and Russ happened to come into the house. He saw me and got all bent out of shape, saying the skirt was too short. I tried to tell him the skirts have been the same length for the past hundred years, and that just made him madder."

"I don't think your brother appreciates sarcasm."

"No kidding. He insisted I drop the hem on the skirt five inches. I know I should've been more subtle, but I couldn't help it. I laughed and told him he was being ridiculous."

"I can't imagine that pleased him."

"No," Mandy said, shaking her head. She clutched the can with stiff fingers, but as far as Taylor could see she hadn't taken a sip. "Then he said this wasn't an issue we were going to discuss. He was ordering me, as my legal guardian, to lower the hem of the skirt, and he didn't want any arguments."

"Naturally you refused."

"Naturally. What else could I do?" Mandy yelped. "I'd look totally asinine with a drill team skirt that went to midcalf. I'd be the laughingstock of the entire school district, and all because my bullheaded brother won't listen to reason."

"Is that when he issued the ultimatum?"

"H-how'd you know?"

"I know Russ, or at least someone a whole lot like him. The way I figure it, he suggested that either you lower the hem or you quit the drill team, and then he stalked out of the house."

Mandy blinked, then took a deep swallow of the soda. "That's exactly what happened."

"You've gotten into plenty of arguments with your brother before without deciding to run away. Why now?"

Mandy's green eyes clouded with tears as she lifted one shoulder in a halfhearted shrug. "Because."

"That doesn't tell me much." Taylor stood and reached for a box of tissues, setting it on the table.

"He doesn't want me around."

"That isn't true," Taylor said. "We were talking about you making the drill team just the other day, and Russ was so proud. He loves you, Mandy. I'm sure of it."

"I'm not. At least not anymore. He's so stubborn."

"Opinionated?"

"That, too, and…" She hesitated, searching for another word.

"Unreasonable?"

Mandy slowly raised her eyes to Taylor. "I didn't realize you knew Russ so well."

"I told you before that my father and I had trouble getting along when I was your age, didn't I?"

Mandy nodded and jerked a tissue from the box, as though admitting that she needed one was a sign of weakness.

"Sometimes I swear my father and your brother were cut from the same cloth. It would be easier to change the course of the Columbia River than to get them to alter their opinions." Raising her feet onto the edge of the chair, Taylor looped her arms around her bent knees. "The family money was limited and my parents couldn't afford to pay for all five of us to go to college. So he decided that educating the boys was more important. He assumed they'd be supporting families, while Christy and I would end up with husbands."

"But you went to college."

"Indeed I did, but I paid for every cent of it myself. It took me eight years to complete my education. I worked summers in Alaska when I could, in addition to nights and weekends during the school year. Once I was a senior, I was able to get on as a dorm mother, and that took care of my room and board."

"But, Taylor, that's not fair!"

"In my father's eyes it was. Granted, if Christy and I had been the only two, I'm sure he would have gladly paid for our education, but Dad was financially strapped paying for the boys."

"Yeah, but your brothers will probably end up getting married, too."

Mandy's logic was closely aligned with Taylor's own. "Yes, but as my father said, they won't be having babies, and it's unlikely they'll have to delay whatever career they choose in order to raise a family."

"Women are entitled to a career if they want one!"

"Of course. But it wasn't only college that my father and I argued over. It started with the usual things, like clothes and makeup and friends, but later we found ourselves at odds over just about everything else."

"Wh-what about boyfriends? Did your dad find reasons to dislike them all?"

"No. Just one." Now Taylor lowered her eyes. From the moment her father had met Mark, he hadn't liked the up-and-coming financial planner. When Taylor had questioned him about his instant dislike, Eric Manning had given her the most nonsensical reply. Her father had claimed Mark was too smooth. Too smooth! He'd made Mark sound like a used car salesman. Her father had refused to look past the friendly smile and the easy laugh to the talented man beneath. Mark had tried hard to win him over; Taylor gave him credit for that. The more effort he'd put forth, the more she'd loved him. Taylor and her father had argued constantly over Mark.

Then one day she'd learned that everything her father

had guessed about Mark was true. She'd gone to him and broken into bitter tears. For the first time he hadn't said I told you so. Instead, he'd held her in his arms and gently patted her head while she wept. She'd heard later from her brothers that their father had wanted to confront Mark and tell him what a bastard he was. It had taken some fast talking on their parts to convince him it was best to leave the situation alone.

"You've had arguments with Russ before," Taylor said again, tearing herself away from the memories of a painful past.

Mandy plucked out another tissue, noisily blew her nose and nodded. "Lots of times, especially lately. He's always finding things to gripe at me about."

"But why run away now?"

"I have my reasons."

Her words were so low that Taylor had to strain to hear. "Where will you go?"

"I have an aunt in New Jersey.... I'm not exactly sure where. She was my mother's half sister, and she sent me a birthday present once before my mom died. I think she might let me live with her."

Taylor didn't bother to point out the numerous holes in Mandy's plan. "Wouldn't it be a good idea to contact her first?" she asked.

"I...was hoping to surprise her."

"You mean show up on her doorstep so she can't say no?"

"Something like that," Mandy admitted.

The phone rang, and standing, Taylor walked over to answer it. Apparently Mandy thought this was a good time to use the bathroom and left the kitchen.

"Hello."

"Taylor, this is Russ. I don't suppose you've heard from Mandy, have you?" He sounded impatient and more than a little worried. "I'm at my wits' end with that girl. I've called practically everyone in town. I've got enough to do without playing hide-and-seek with her."

"She's here."

"We had another one of our fights and—" He stopped abruptly. "She's there? In town? With you?"

"That's what I just said."

"How'd she get there?"

"I assume she either walked or hitchhiked."

"Into town?" He groaned. "Listen, keep her there. I'll be at your place in ten minutes. You can warn her right now, she may be on restriction for the rest of her natural life."

"Russ, there seems to be a lack of communication here."

"You're damn right there is. She can't go running to you every time she needs someone to champion her cause. And while I'm on the subject, I refuse to listen to your arguments regarding this skirt issue. I'm not going to have any sister of mine running around half-naked."

"Mandy didn't ask me to champion her cause," Taylor said, having trouble holding back her own quick temper. "She came to tell me she was running away."

Russ's response was a short, harsh laugh. "We'll see about that," he said, and slammed down the receiver.

Stifling a groan herself, Taylor hung up.

"I should be leaving," Mandy said when she returned to the kitchen.

"What about clothes?"

"I packed a bag and hid it in the bushes outside. I wasn't going to tell you I was running away at first.

I only came to thank you for being my friend. I...I think Russ likes you and I hope that you two...well, you know." She smiled bravely, but tears rolled down her face and she smeared them across her cheeks with the back of her hand.

"Money?" Taylor tried next, thinking fast. She had to stall Russ's sister until he arrived, although in his present frame of mind, she wasn't sure he'd help matters any.

"I have enough."

"How much is enough?"

"A couple of hundred dollars. I was saving it for a new saddle, but after I saw the dress you made for the dance I was going to buy a sewing machine. Now I'll need it to get to New Jersey."

"But, Mandy, that won't even pay for a bus ticket."

"I'll...think of something."

"I've got some cash," Taylor said, reaching for her purse. "It's a shame you're leaving. I was asked to be a chaperone when the drill team goes to Reno next month. I was looking forward to seeing you perform."

"You were?" Mandy brightened somewhat. "It's going to be fun. We've been practicing early every morning for this competition, and by next month we should be really good. The larger high schools almost always win, but all the girls who go have such a good time." Some of the excitement left her, and her shoulders sagged. She forced a smile. "At least in Reno you'll be able to use your American Express."

"And order pizza. I would kill for a good pepperoni pizza on a Friday night."

"The bowling alley makes a decent one. You should try it sometime."

"I suppose I will," Taylor said, rummaging through her wallet. "Are you sure you won't change your mind? Mandy, sweetheart, it's a cold, cruel world out there. If you like, you can call your aunt from here and feel her out before you leave Cougar Point."

"I guess maybe I should," Mandy murmured, not looking certain about anything. She hesitated, then turned huge appealing eyes on Taylor. "I was wondering...do you think maybe I could live with you? No, don't answer that," she said quickly. Regretfully. "Russ would never allow it, and, well, it wouldn't work. Forget I asked."

"I'd love it if you did, but, honey, that isn't any solution."

Mandy tucked her chin against her collarbone. "I'll leave in a few minutes, okay?"

"Mandy." Taylor stopped her. She couldn't continue this pretense. "That was Russ on the phone a few minutes ago. He's on his way to talk to you."

The pale green eyes widened with offense. "You told him I was here? How could you, Taylor? I thought you were my friend. I trusted you...."

"I am your friend. I care about you and can't let you ruin your life because you've had a spat with your brother."

"It's more than that."

"I know. Trust me, I know," Taylor said gently, resisting the urge to pull Mandy into her arms. "What I'd like to suggest is that when your brother arrives you stay in the kitchen, and I'll keep him in the living room and try to talk some sense into him."

"He won't listen," Mandy cried. Tears ran unrestrained down her cheeks, and she clenched her fists at her sides. "It would be best if I just left now."

The sound of Russ's truck screeching to a stop outside the house was a welcome relief, at least to Taylor. "Give me ten minutes alone with him," she said.

"All right," Mandy reluctantly agreed. "But that's all the time I've got." She made it sound as if she had a plane to catch.

Taylor was at the front door before Russ could even knock. What she saw didn't give her any hope that this matter could easily be put to rest. His fury was all too evident; his face was red and his steps were quick and abrupt as he let himself in the house. Taylor practically had to throw herself in front of the kitchen door to keep him in the living room.

"Where is she?"

"Before you talk to Mandy, you and I need to discuss something."

"Not now," he said, looking past her. "Running away? That's a laugh. And just where does she intend to go?"

"Russ, would you stop shouting and listen to me." Taylor used her best schoolteacher voice and placed her hands threateningly on her hips as if to suggest one more cross word and she'd report him to the principal.

"I have somewhere to go, so you needn't worry," Mandy yelled from the kitchen.

"Sit down," Taylor said, pointing at her sofa. "We've got a problem here that isn't going to be settled by you hollering threats at your sister."

"They're a lot more than threats." Russ continued pacing the floor, occasionally removing his hat long enough to angrily plow his fingers through his hair.

"Mandy didn't come to me about the length of the drill team uniform—"

"It's a damn good thing because I'm not changing my mind. No sister of mine is going to parade around a field in that skimpy little outfit." His frown informed Taylor that he didn't appreciate her interference in what he considered a family affair.

"I'm leaving!" Mandy shouted from the other room.

"Over my dead body," Russ retaliated. "I'll drag you back to the ranch if I have to."

"Then I'll run away tomorrow. You can't force me to live with you."

"She's right, you know," Taylor whispered.

Russ shot her a look hot enough to boil water.

"Listen to what she's really saying," Taylor pleaded.

Russ advanced a step toward the other room. Taylor's hand on his arm stopped him. He glanced down at her and blinked as though he'd almost forgotten that she was there. "This is between me and my sister," he growled.

"Listen to her," Taylor repeated, more forcefully this time. "Hear the doubt and pain in her voice. She doesn't want to leave any more than you want her to go."

"Then why...?"

"Because she's convinced you don't love her and you don't want her living with you anymore."

Russ removed his hat and slapped it against the coffee table. "Of all the foolish..." Suddenly he seemed at a loss for words. "That's the most ridiculous thing I've ever heard."

"Mandy," Taylor called, "come out here and sit down." She gestured toward Russ, motioning for him to do the same. "The only way I can see that'll do any good is for the two of you to clear the air. You need to talk face-to-face instead of hurling insults at each other."

Mandy hesitantly moved into the living room. She

sank slowly into a chair and picked up a women's magazine sitting on the arm, absently flipping through the pages.

Russ sat on the other side of the room, looking nonchalant and relaxed. He propped his ankle on one knee and spread his arms across the back of the davenport as if they were discussing the abrupt change in weather rather than the future of his only sister and their relationship.

"Mandy, why do you want to move in with your aunt?" Taylor asked.

"Because my pigheaded brother is so unreasonable."

"You've gotten along with him up until now."

"No, I haven't." Her voice grew smaller and smaller. "Besides, I'm just in the way."

"Russ," Taylor said, twisting around to confront him, "is Mandy in the way?"

"Hell, no, I need her."

"Sure, to cook your meals and wash your clothes. You can hire someone to do that. I bet Mary Lu Randall would do it for free. She's had a crush on you forever."

"You're all the family I've got," Russ countered gruffly.

"I'm nothing but a problem," Mandy said, rubbing the tears from her eyes. "You think I don't notice, but I do. There isn't a single thing you like about me anymore. You're always complaining. If it isn't my hair, it's my clothes or I'm wearing too much makeup or spending too much time with my friends."

Russ dropped his leg and leaned forward, hands clasped. He studied Mandy, then started to frown. "I'm just trying to do the best job I can to make sure you turn into a responsible adult."

Mandy looked away. Unable to stand still, Taylor crossed the room, sat on the arm of the chair and placed her own on Mandy's thin shoulders.

"I love you, Amanda," Russ said starkly. "Maybe sometimes I don't show it the way I should, but I do. You're as much a part of my life as the Lazy P. I need you, and not to do the cooking and laundry, either."

Mandy sniffled in an effort not to cry, and Taylor reached inside her pocket for a fresh tissue, handing it to the girl.

"I…didn't realize this drill team thing was so important to you," Russ went on. "I suppose Taylor's going to tell me I should've been more sensitive." Russ paused, shaking his head. "When I saw you all dressed up like that, it made me realize how grown-up you're getting, and I guess I didn't want to face the fact you're going to be a beautiful young woman soon. It kind of scares me. Before long, the boys are going to be swarming around the ranch like ants."

"I-if you really want me to quit the drill team, I will," Mandy offered in a thin, raspy voice.

"No, you can stay on the team. If the other parents are willing to let their daughters prance around a playing field in those little outfits, then I'll just have to get used to the idea." Russ stood up and walked across the room, standing in front of his sister. "Friends?"

Mandy nodded, fresh tears streaking her face. She jumped up and moved into Russ's arms, hugging him tight. "I didn't really want to live with Aunt Joyce in New Jersey."

"That's good because the last I heard she retired someplace in Mexico."

"She did? How come you never told me?"

"Maybe because I was afraid you'd think it was an exotic, fun place to be and decide you'd rather live with her. I meant what I said about loving you, Mandy. You're going to have to be more patient with me, I guess, but I promise I'll try harder."

"I...will, too."

Russ slowly shut his eyes as he hugged his sister close.

Taylor felt her own eyes fill with tears. She hadn't expected Russ to be so open about his feelings for Mandy. When he'd first arrived, she'd been convinced everything was going to go from bad to worse. Russ was so proud and so furious, but once he'd stopped to listen to his sister and heard her fears, he'd set the anger aside and revealed a deep, vulnerable part of himself that Taylor had never even suspected was there.

"Say, how about if I treat my two best girls to dinner?" Russ suggested.

"Yeah," Mandy responded. "Pizza?"

"Anything you want," he said, smiling down on his sister. He raised his eyes to Taylor, and they softened perceptibly.

"I...can't," she said, declining the invitation. "Anyway, this should be a time for the two of you to talk. I'd just be in the way."

"No, you wouldn't. We'd never have been able to do this without you," Mandy insisted. "I really want you to come."

"Another time," Taylor promised. "You two go and have fun."

Russ squeezed Mandy's shoulders. "I don't know about you, but I'm famished. If Taylor wants to turn down an offer for the best pizza in town, there's only one thing we can do—let her suffer."

"It's your loss," Mandy told Taylor on their way out the door.

"Yes, I know," she said, standing behind the screen door. Mandy bounded down the front steps and ran around the side of the house, where she'd apparently hidden her bag of clothes.

While Russ was waiting for his sister to reappear, he turned to Taylor and mouthed the words, "Thank you." Then he touched his fingers to his lips and held his hand out to her. She pressed her open palm against the screen door.

The following evening Taylor sat at the kitchen table with her feet propped on a chair, stirring a bowl of soup. "You're in deep trouble here," she muttered to herself. "If you don't watch it, you're going to fall in love with a cowboy. You're already halfway there. Admit it."

She vigorously stirred her chicken noodle soup until it sloshed over the rim of the bowl. Setting the spoon aside, Taylor leaned her elbows on the table and buried her face in her hands.

The whole purpose of coming to Montana was to avoid relationships. She hadn't been in town a week when she'd met Russ. And from there everything had quickly gone downhill. From the first time he'd kissed her she'd known she was headed for disaster. But had that stopped her? Oh, no. Not even the cool voice of reason—or the memory of Mark's betrayal—had given her pause. Instead she was walking straight into his arms, knowing full well that nothing could ever come of their relationship. She wouldn't have an affair with him. Marriage was out of the question; Russ would agree with her there. So exactly where was their relationship going?

Nowhere.

"Nowhere," she repeated out loud. "Save yourself some heartache," she told herself, then sat back and wondered if she was wise enough to follow her own advice, immediately doubting that she was. The voice in her heart was so much louder than anything her brain was telling her. She'd been a fool once. Hadn't she learned anything? Apparently not!

The phone rang, startling her. She dropped her legs and stood to answer it, afraid it might be Russ and not knowing what she'd say.

It was.

"Hi," she said, forcing some enthusiasm into her voice. The man had no idea of the turmoil he was causing her.

"I'm calling to thank you for what you did for Mandy and me yesterday."

"It wasn't anything," she said lightly. Her hand tightened around the telephone receiver as she supported herself against the kitchen wall. She hated the way her pulse reacted to the sound of his voice. If he had a voice like other men, it wouldn't affect her so strongly. His was deep and so sexy. . . .

"You were right about me not being aware of her doubt and fear," he went on to say. "I don't know what I did to make her think I don't want her around anymore, but she's totally wrong."

"You were wonderful with her." Taylor meant that. She hadn't expected him to be half as understanding or sensitive to his sister's needs. Perhaps it would be easier to walk away from him if she could continue to view him as a difficult male, but he'd shown her another side of his personality, one so appealing that she found her heart softening toward him.

"I felt bad because I'd overreacted to the whole issue of her drill team uniform," Russ explained. "I'd come into the house, and seeing Mandy dressed in that outfit caught me by surprise. My nerves were on edge, anyway. We'd just found a dead calf, and when I saw Mandy, I took my frustration and anger out on her. She didn't deserve that."

"But you apologized. And taking her out to dinner was nice."

"I wish you'd come along. We both owe you."

"Nonsense. That was your time with Mandy."

Taylor could sense Russ's smile. "I will admit that we did have fun. I'd forgotten what a kick my sister can be. She's a sweet kid, but she's growing up too fast." There was a pause. "Listen, I didn't call you just to talk about Mandy. How about dinner Friday night?"

Taylor closed her eyes. The lure of the invitation was as strong as the pull of the tide. Squaring her shoulders, she shook her head.

"Taylor?"

"I don't think it's a good idea for us to see each other again," she said flatly.

Seven

"What the hell do you mean?" Russ demanded. He didn't know what kind of game Taylor was playing, but he wasn't about to become a participant. If there was a problem, he wanted it out in the open.

"Exactly what I said," she returned, sounding shaky and unsure. "I don't think it's wise for us to continue seeing each other."

"Why not?" He tried to keep his voice even, but dammit, Taylor was irritating him, not that this was anything new.

Russ had never met a woman like Taylor Manning before. She could make him madder than anyone he'd ever known, but when he kissed her, the earth moved, angels sang, and whatever else people said about moments of passion. Russ didn't understand it. No one had ever affected him the way Taylor did.

He'd tried staying away from her. Tried exercising a little more self-control, but five minutes with her and his good intentions went the way of all flesh. He wanted her in his bed, her hair spread out over his pillow. He thought about that a lot, far more than he should. Not for the first time, the image brought with it the stirrings of arousal. How could this teacher—and worse, one from a big city—inspire such hunger in him? It made no sense.

He'd run into a cocktail waitress friend when he'd been in Miles City the week before. It had been an uncomfortable encounter. April had expected him to come home with her for what she called "a little afternoon pleasure." Instead, Russ couldn't get away from her fast enough. Not that he didn't crave being with a woman. But deep down he'd known that the only woman he wanted was Taylor.

That afternoon Russ had seen April for what she was, jaded and cold, and he wanted nothing to do with her. He'd escaped and hurried back to the Lazy P, only to discover Taylor there with his sister. He'd wanted her so badly that day. There was no use lying to himself about it. Even now, almost a week later, when he closed his eyes, he could still smell the fragrance of her perfume. Her mouth had parted beneath his, eager for his kisses. Every touch had hurled his senses into chaos.

"I...don't want there to be any misunderstandings between us," Taylor said, cutting into his thoughts.

Reluctantly Russ pulled himself from his musings. "I don't, either. If you won't have dinner with me, I'd like to know why. That's not such an unreasonable request, is it?"

"I...think the reason should be obvious."

"Tell me, anyway."

Russ felt her hesitation, and when she spoke again, her voice was a little raspy, as if she found it difficult to share her thoughts. "Our personality differences should be more than adequate reason for us to use caution."

She sounded exactly like the schoolteacher she was.

"That hasn't stopped us before. Why should it now?" he asked.

"Darn it, Russ Palmer," she cried. "You aren't going to make this easy, are you?"

"All I want is the truth."

Her sigh sang over the wire. "I can't give you anything less than the truth, can I?"

"No," he said softly. "I'll admit we're different. Anyone looking at us could be able to see that. Our opinions on most subjects are completely opposite, but frankly, I'm willing to work around that. I like you, Taylor."

"I know," she whispered dismally. That knowledge seemed to cause her distress rather than celebration.

Russ wasn't pleased, but he refused to make an issue of it. "There are plenty of girls in Cougar Point who'd be mighty pleased if I invited them out to dinner," he added, thinking that might set her back some, help her realize she had competition.

"Ask them out then," she said tartly.

"I don't want to. The only woman who interests me is you."

"That's the problem," she mumbled, and it sounded like she was close to tears.

The thought of Taylor crying did something funny to Russ's stomach. His protective urges ran deep when it came to this woman. "Taylor, maybe I should drive into town and we can talk face-to-face."

"No," she returned abruptly. "That would only make this more difficult." She paused, and Russ had to restrain the yearning to put the phone aside and go to her immediately.

"Is this about what happened the other day?" he asked.

"I know our kissing went further than it should have, but that wasn't intentional. If you want an apology…"

"No, that's not it. Oh, Russ, don't you see?"

He didn't. "Tell me."

"I like you too much. We both know where this is going to lead—one of these days we're going to end up in love and in bed together."

That didn't sound too tragic to Russ. He'd been dreaming about it for weeks. "So?"

"So?" she shouted, and her voice vibrated with anger. "I'm not interested in a permanent relationship with you. You're a wonderful man—and you'll make some woman a terrific husband. But not me."

He let a moment of tense silence pass before he commented. "If you'll recall, the invitation was for dinner. All I was asking for was a simple meal together. I'm not looking for a lifetime commitment."

"You're doing your best to make this difficult, which is all too typical. I will not have an affair with you, and that's exactly where our relationship is headed. People are already talking, especially after the Grange dance. And then we went horseback riding and… Before I know it, you're going to be telling me how to vote and insisting a woman's place is in the home." She paused only long enough to inhale a quick breath. "I'm sorry… I really am, but I don't think we should have anything to do with each other. Please understand."

Before Russ could say another word, the line was disconnected. He held the receiver in his hand for several minutes in disbelief. His first response was anger. He didn't know what Taylor was muttering about. Her words about voting and a woman's place were utterly nonsensical.

He had every right to be upset with her; no one had ever hung up on him before. Instead he felt a tingling satisfaction. Slowly, hardly aware that it was happening, Russ felt a smile creep over his face.

Mandy strolled past him just then. "Hey, what's so funny?"

"Taylor," he said, grinning hard. "She likes me."

Russ was riding the range, looking for strays, when he saw his lifelong friend come barreling toward him in a battered pickup. Removing his hat, Russ wiped his forearm across his brow. He'd been in the saddle since morning, and he was wearier than he could remember being in a long while. He hadn't been sleeping well; Taylor was constantly on his mind, and he still hadn't figured out what to do about her. If anything. He'd delayed confronting her, thinking it was best to give her time. But he was growing anxious. In the past couple of days Russ had faced a few truths about the two of them.

"Cody, good to see you," Russ greeted him, dismounting from Magic. "Problems?"

"None to speak of," Cody said, opening the cab door and getting out.

"You didn't come looking for me to discuss the weather."

Cody wasn't wearing his sheriff deputy's uniform, which was unusual. Instead, he had on jeans and a thick sweater. He was about the same height as Russ, but he kept his dark hair trimmed short.

"It's been nice the past week or so, hasn't it?" Cody said, gesturing toward the cloudless blue sky. He tucked his fingertips into the hip pocket of his Levi's and walked to the front of the truck. Leaning his back against the grille, he raised one foot and rested it on the bumper.

For early October the weather had been unseasonably warm. They'd experienced several Indian summer days, and while Russ appreciated the respite before winter hit, he knew better than to take anything about Montana weather for granted.

"What's up?" he asked. "It isn't like you to beat around the bush."

Cody nodded, looking slightly chagrined. "I came to talk to you about the new schoolteacher."

"What about her?" Russ asked, tensing. He moved over to the truck and put his foot on the bumper, meeting Cody's eyes.

The deputy glanced away, but not before Russ saw the troubled look on his face.

"We've been friends a lot of years, and the last thing I want is for a woman to come between us."

"I take it you want to ask Taylor out?"

Cody nodded. "But only if you have no objection. Word is the two of you aren't seeing each other anymore."

"Who told you that?" Russ demanded, fighting to repress the surge of instant jealousy that tightened around his chest. He'd resisted the temptation to rush into town and talk some sense into Taylor, assuming she'd have second thoughts by now. Apparently that wasn't the case. Truth be known, Russ had been doing some thinking about their situation. They were both mature adults and they weren't going to leap into something that would be wrong for them. Okay, so they were strongly attracted—that much was a given—and not seeing each other wasn't going to change the situation, not one bit.

It came as a shock for Russ to admit he was falling in love with Taylor. There wasn't any use in fighting it—hell, he didn't even want to. Nor was he going to pretend he didn't care about her.

"Mary Beth Morgan said something to me this morning," Cody continued. "Mary Beth said she and Taylor were having coffee in the faculty lounge and she inquired about the two of you. Evidently Taylor told her you'd decided not to see each other again."

"Taylor came right out and said that?"

"I don't know her exact words. Hey, I'm repeating what someone else repeated to me. How close it is to the truth, I wouldn't know. That's why I'm here."

The mental image of Cody holding Taylor in his arms brought a sudden flash of rage so strong that for a moment Russ couldn't breathe. Shoving away from the truck, he returned to Magic, reached for the reins and leaped onto the gelding's back.

"Russ?" Cody asked, frowning.

"Go ahead and ask her out."

Taylor couldn't remember Friday nights being so lonely before moving to Cougar Point. It seemed she'd always had something to do, someplace to go. But that wasn't the case anymore. Her entertainment options were limited. The town sported one old-time theater. One screen. One movie. The feature film for the week was a comedy Taylor had seen six months earlier in Seattle. By now it was probably available on video in most parts of the country.

There had been an offer for dinner from Cody Frank-

lin, which had been a surprise, but she'd turned him
down. In retrospect she wished she hadn't been so quick
to refuse him. He was certainly pleasant. They'd met at
the dance, and she'd found him reserved, and perhaps
a little remote.

If she was looking for some way to kill time, she
could sew, but Taylor simply wasn't in the mood. After
a long week in the classroom, she was more interested
in doing something relaxing.

Well, she could always read, she supposed. Locating
a promising romance, she cuddled up in the armchair
and wrapped an afghan around her legs. She hadn't
finished the first chapter when her eyes started to drift
closed. Struggling to keep them open, she concentrated
on the text. After the third yawn, she gave up, set the
open book over the arm of the chair and decided to rest
for a few minutes.

The next thing she knew someone was pounding at
her front door.

Taylor tossed aside the afghan and stumbled across
the room, disoriented and confused. "Wh-who is it?"
she asked. The door didn't have a peephole; most folks
in town didn't even bother to lock their front doors.

"Russ Palmer," came the gruff reply.

Taylor quickly twisted the lock and opened the door.
"What are you doing here?" she insisted. It took all her
willpower not to throw her arms around him.

Now that Russ was standing in the middle of her
living room, he didn't look all that pleased about being
there.

The wall clock chimed, and Taylor absently counted
ten strikes. It was ten! She'd been "resting" for nearly

two hours. Good grief, she'd been reduced to falling asleep at eight o'clock on a Friday night.

"Russ?" she prodded. He was frowning, and she had no idea why. "Is something wrong?"

"No." He gave her a silly, lopsided grin. "Everything's wonderful. You're wonderful. I'm wonderful. The whole world's wonderful."

"Russ?" She squinted up at him. "You've been drinking."

He pointed his index finger toward the ceiling. "Only a little."

She steered him toward the sofa and sat him down. "How much is a little?"

"A couple of beers with a bunch of guys." His brows drew together as he considered his words. "Or was that a couple of guys and a bunch of beers? I don't remember anymore."

"That's what I thought," she murmured. He'd obviously downed more than two beers! "I'll make you some coffee."

"Don't go," he said, reaching out and clasping her around the waist. "I'm not drunk, just a little tipsy. I had this sudden urge to visit my lady, and now that I'm here, I want to hold you."

He effortlessly brought her into his lap. Her hands were on his shoulders. "I thought we agreed this sort of thing had to stop," she whispered.

His mouth found the open V of her shirt, and he kissed her there, gliding his tongue over her warm skin, creating sensations that were even warmer.

"We weren't going to see each other anymore, remember?" she tried again. Her nails dug into the hard muscles of his shoulders as she exhaled slowly.

"I've been thinking about that," Russ said between nibbling kisses that slid along the line of her jaw. "I haven't thought of anything else all week."

"Russ, please stop," she whimpered.

To her surprise, he did as she asked. Her hands were in his hair, and she reluctantly withdrew them. "You shouldn't be driving."

"I know. I left the truck at Billy's and walked over here. Only I didn't realize where I was headed until I arrived on your doorstep."

Billy's was one of the town's three taverns—the most popular, according to what Taylor had heard. During the summer months, they brought in a band every third Friday, and apparently every adult in town showed up.

"You shouldn't have come," she whispered. Then why was she so glad he had? Taylor didn't want to analyze the answer to that, afraid of what she'd discover.

"You're positively right," Russ concurred. "I have no business being here. Go ahead and kick me out. I wouldn't blame you if you did. Fact is, you probably should."

"If you promise to behave yourself, I'll put on a pot of coffee." She squirmed off his lap and moved into the kitchen. She'd just poured cold water into the automatic drip machine when Russ stole up behind her. He slipped his arms around her waist and buried his face in the curve of her neck.

"Russ...you promised."

"No, I didn't."

"Then...you should leave."

He dropped his arms, walked over to the chair, turned it around and straddled it. He was grinning, obviously pleased. "Cody told me," he announced.

Taylor busied herself bringing down two mugs from the cupboard and setting them on the counter. Apparently there were no secrets in this town. Taylor regretted not accepting Cody Franklin's dinner invitation. She certainly wished she had now.

"You turned him down. Why?" His dark eyes held hers with unwavering curiosity, demanding a reply.

"I...don't think that's any of your business."

He shrugged, his look indifferent. "I'd like to think it *is* my business."

"You don't own me." She pressed her hands into the counter behind her.

He grinned. "Not for lack of trying." He held out his arms to her, beseeching her to walk over. "We've got a good thing going, and I can't understand why you want to throw it away." His eyes continued to hold hers, but he was no longer smiling. "The first time I met you, I recognized trouble. That didn't stop me, and it didn't stop you, either, did it?"

She lowered her gaze rather than answer. When she raised her head, she discovered Russ standing directly in front of her.

"Did it?" he repeated. He grabbed her around the waist, and with one swift movement set her on top of the counter.

She stared at him, wondering about his mood. "Russ?"

He slanted his mouth over hers, kissing her long and hard, and when he'd finished, she was panting. "Did it?" he asked a third time.

He reached for her shoulders again, intent on another kiss—and more.

"Russ, you're drunk." From somewhere she found

the strength to stop him, although it felt like the most difficult task of her life.

Ever so slowly he tilted back his head. His grin was sultry and teasing. "I'm not that drunk."

"You shouldn't have come here."

"Yes, I know." His hands were in her hair. He couldn't seem to leave it alone. Every time they were together, he ran his fingers through it. Carefully he removed the combs, then arranged it over her shoulder, smoothing it with his callused fingertips. Then his hands framed her face and he kissed her once more.

Unable to resist him, she parted her lips in welcome, and they clung to each other.

When he finally dragged his mouth from hers, he smiled at her. "Go ahead and give me that coffee, and then you can drive me home."

Without question, Taylor did as he asked. They drank their coffee in silence, and its sobering effect hit her immediately. After all her intentions to stay away from him, she'd been giddy with happiness when he'd arrived. It hadn't mattered that he'd been drinking. It hadn't mattered that he took liberties with her. All that mattered was seeing him again. Taylor had never thought of herself as a weak person, but that was how Russ made her feel. Spineless and indecisive.

Russ fell asleep on the drive out to the ranch. Taylor was glad to see that the back porch light was on when she pulled in to the yard. She parked the car and hurried around to the passenger side.

"Russ," she said, shaking him by the shoulders. "Wake up."

His eyes opened slowly, and when he recognized her, he grinned, his gaze warm and loving. "Taylor."

"You're home."

His arms circled her waist. "Yes, I know."

Taylor managed to break free. "Come on, let's go inside, and for heaven's sake, could you be a little less noisy? I don't want anyone to know I brought you here."

"Why not?" He inclined his head as if the answer demanded serious concentration.

"There's enough talk about us as it is. The last thing I need is for someone to report seeing my car parked at your house late on a Friday night."

"Don't worry. No one can see the house from the road."

"Just get inside, would you?" She was losing her patience with him. Despite the coffee, his actions were slower than before. He moved with the deliberateness of inebriation, taking unhurried wobbly steps toward the house.

The back door was unlocked, and Russ slammed it shut with his foot. The sound ricocheted through the kitchen like a blast from a shotgun, startling Taylor.

"Shh," Russ said loudly, pressing his finger over his lips. "You'll wake Mandy."

Taylor wished the teenager *would* wake up and come to help her. Russ was increasingly difficult to handle.

"You need to go to bed," she said and prepared to leave.

"I'll never make it there without you." His smile was roguish and naughty, and he staggered a few steps as though that was proof enough. "I need you, Taylor. No telling what might happen to me if I'm left to my own devices."

"I'm willing to chance that."

"I'm not." With his arm around her waist, he led her

toward the stairs. He stumbled forward, bringing Taylor with him. She had no choice but to follow. She didn't know if it was an act or not, but he really did seem to need her assistance.

They were two steps up the stairs when Russ sagged against the wall and sighed heavily. "Have I ever told you I think you're beautiful?"

"I believe the word was *wonderful*," she muttered, using her shoulder to urge him forward.

"You're both. A man could drown in eyes that blue and not even care."

"Russ," she said in a whisper, "let's get you upstairs."

"In bed?" He arched his brows suggestively.

"Just get upstairs. Please."

"You're so eager for my body, you can hardly wait, can you?" he asked, then chuckled softly, seeming to find himself exceptionally amusing. He leaned forward enough to kiss the side of her neck. "I'll try to make it worth your while."

Taylor was breathless by the time they reached the top of the stairs. "Which room is yours?" she asked.

Russ turned all the way around before raising his arm and directing her to the bedroom at the end of the hall. "There," he said enthusiastically, pointing straight ahead as if he'd discovered uncharted land.

With her arm firmly around his middle, Taylor led him to the room. The hall was dark, lit only by the light of the moon visible through an uncurtained window. She opened the door, and together the two of them staggered forward, landing on the bed with a force that drove the oxygen from her lungs.

Russ released a deep sigh and rolled onto his back,

positioning Taylor above him. His unrelenting dark eyes stared up at her.

"I...should be going."

"Not yet," he whispered. "Kiss me good-night first."

"Russ, no." She tried to move, but his hands were on her hips, holding her fast.

"All I'm asking for is one little kiss. So when I wake up in the morning I'll remember you were here and that'll make me feel good."

She rolled her eyes. "The only thing you're going to feel in the morning is a world-class headache."

"If you won't kiss me, then you leave me with no option but to kiss you."

He began to kiss her lips, tiny nibbling kisses that promised so much more than they delivered. Then he changed tactics, drugging her with prolonged kisses that chased away all grounds for complaint.

For some reason he stopped. Suddenly. He threw back his head and dragged in several deep breaths.

"Does this prove anything?" he asked urgently.

"That...that I should have left you to your own devices. You didn't need my help."

"I did. I do. I always will."

She shook her head, but Russ ignored that.

"In case you haven't figured it out yet," he informed her, "you belong in my bed, and that's exactly where you're going to end up."

With what remained of her shredded dignity, Taylor pushed herself free. She bolted off the bed and paced the room. As she did, Russ sat up on the bed, leaning against the bunched pillows, looking smug and arrogant. "You're so beautiful."

It was all Taylor could do not to throw her hands in

the air and scream. "This doesn't change a thing," she insisted. "Not a thing."

His answering grin was filled with cocky reassurance. "Wanna bet?"

Eight

"Hi, Taylor," Mandy said as she stepped into Taylor's classroom early the following week.

"Howdy."

Mandy grinned. "You're beginning to sound like a country girl."

That gave Taylor cause to sit back and take notice. "I am?"

Mandy nodded. "Russ told me just the other day that he's going to make a country girl out of you yet." Mandy walked over to the front row of desks and sat on the edge of one as she spoke.

At the mention of Russ, Taylor began to fiddle with the pencils on her desk.

"Do…you remember the day I was thinking about running away?" Mandy asked, and her voice lowered.

"Of course," Taylor said.

"I asked you what your father thought about the boys you dated, and you told me he'd generally approved of your boyfriends." She pressed her books close to her chest, and Taylor noted how tense her hands were. "There was…a reason I asked about that. You see, there's this boy in school—he's a junior and his name is Eddie and…well, he's really nice and my family knows his family and we've known each other almost all our lives and—"

"You like Eddie?"

Mandy's responding nod was fervent. "A whole lot, and I think he likes me, too. We've only talked in the hall a couple of times, but this morning when I was putting my books in my locker, he walked up and we started talking…not about anything in particular, at least not at first, then all of a sudden he asked if I wanted to go to the movies with him Saturday night."

"I see." Taylor did understand her dilemma. All too well. Mandy was only fourteen, and Russ would surely consider a high school freshman too young to date. In fact, Taylor agreed with him, but she'd been fourteen once herself and attracted to a boy who'd liked her. He'd been older, too, and had asked her to a party, which her father had adamantly opposed her attending. The memory of the argument that had followed remained painfully vivid in her mind.

"I really, really want to go to the movies with Eddie, but I'm afraid Russ will get upset with me for even asking. I mean, he's been trying hard to listen to my point of view, but dating is something that's never come up before and…well, I have a feeling we aren't going to be able to talk about me having a boyfriend without… an argument." She sighed heavily. "What should I do, Taylor?"

Taylor wished she had an easy answer. "I really don't know."

"Will you talk to him for me?"

"Absolutely not."

"Oh, please! You don't know how much this would mean to me. Don't you remember what it's like to be fourteen and have a boy like you?"

That was the problem; Taylor *did* remember. "When I was your age, a sixteen-year-old boy invited me to a party. My father made it sound as if he wanted to drag me into an opium den. More than anything in the world, I wanted to go to that party."

"Did you?"

Taylor shook her head sadly. "I was too young to date."

Mandy's shoulders sagged with defeat. "It's only a movie, and I don't understand why it would be so bad if Eddie and I went to a show together."

Crossing her arms, Taylor started to pace her classroom, her thoughts spinning. "What about a compromise?"

"H-how do you mean?"

"What if Russ were to drop you off at the theater, you paid your own way and then you sat next to Eddie? With Russ's approval, of course."

Mandy looked more perplexed than relieved. "Eddie could buy me popcorn, though, couldn't he?"

"Sure. It wouldn't be like a real date, but you'd still be at the movies with Eddie."

Mandy's hold on her schoolbooks relaxed. "Do you think Russ would go for it?"

"He's a reasonable man." Taylor couldn't believe she was actually saying this, but in some instances it was true, and he was trying hard with his sister. "I'm sure he'd at least take it into consideration."

Mandy nodded, but her lips were still pinched. "Will you talk to him about it?"

"Me?" Taylor returned spiritedly. "You've got to be joking!"

"I'm not. Russ listens to you. You may not think so but I know he does. It's because of you that I'm allowed to wear makeup and buy my own clothes. Russ and I are trying hard to get along, but I'm afraid this thing with Eddie will ruin everything. Oh, Taylor, please. I'll do anything you want. Cook your meals, do your laundry... all year, anything. *Please.*"

"Russ will listen to you."

"Maybe," Mandy agreed reluctantly, "but this is too important to mess up. I told Eddie I'd have to talk it over with my brother, and he said I should let him know tomorrow. I'm afraid if I put him off he'll ask some other girl, and I'd die if he did."

Against her better judgment, Taylor felt herself weakening. She hadn't seen Russ since Friday night when she'd dropped him off at the house, taken him up the stairs and put him to bed. That whole episode was best forgotten as far as Taylor was concerned.

"Please," Mandy coaxed once more.

"All right," Taylor muttered. When she was growing up, she'd been able to go to her mother, who'd smooth things over with her father. Mandy didn't have anyone to run interference for her. Taylor didn't really mind—although she worried that Russ would use this opportunity to press her with a few arguments of his own, ones that had nothing to do with his sister.

Russ had been having a bad day from the time he'd woken up that morning. The minute he'd stepped out of the house he'd encountered one problem after another, the latest being a calf standing two feet deep in mud.

After an hour of fruitless effort, Russ had lost his patience and accepted the fact that he was going to need help. He'd contacted a couple of his hands by walkie-talkie and was waiting for them to arrive.

Every calf was valuable, but this one, trapped and growing weaker, had been marked for his breeding herd. Like most of the ranchers in Cougar Point, Russ kept two herds. One for breeding purposes, which he used to produce bulls that he often sold for a handsome profit. Bull calves that didn't meet his expectations were turned into steers and raised for beef. His second herd was strictly grade cattle, sold off at the end of the season.

This particular calf had been the product of his highest quality bull and his best cow. Russ had great expectations for him and sure didn't want to lose him to a mud hole.

Russ checked the sun and wondered how much longer he'd have to wait. He'd sent his two best hands out to mend fences, a tedious but not thankless task.

There was still a lot of work left to complete before winter set in, and he didn't have time to waste. Miles of fence to inspect and mend, which was no small chore. If the fences weren't secure, Russ would soon be dealing with the elk that come down from the mountains in winter. If elk could get through his fence, they'd eat his oats and hay. No rancher could afford to feed elk, and a good fence was the best protection he had.

If Russ had to choose his favorite time of year, it would be autumn. The sun was still warm, but the air was crisp, and morning frost warned of encroaching winter. When he drove his cattle into the feed ground, it was like a homecoming, a culmination of the year's efforts.

The calf mewled, reminding Russ of his predicament.

"I know, fellow," Russ muttered. "I've tried everything I can think of. I'm afraid you're stuck here until one of the other men swings by and lends me a hand."

No sooner had the words escaped his mouth than he saw a truck heading slowly in his direction. He frowned, wondering who'd be coming out this way, knowing all his men were on horseback. Maybe there'd been trouble at the house.

After the day he'd been having, Russ didn't look forward to dealing with any more problems. As the blue ranch truck approached, Russ realized it was Taylor at the wheel.

He walked out of the mud and stood with his hands on his hips, waiting for her. He hadn't seen her since the night she'd driven him home. The truth was, he didn't feel proud of the way he'd finagled her into his bedroom. Yes, he'd had too much to drink, but he hadn't been nearly as drunk as he'd led her to believe.

"Hello," Taylor said as she climbed awkwardly out of the cab. She was dressed in jeans, but they were several inches too short and a tad too small. The sweater looked suspiciously like one of Mandy's.

Russ pulled off his gloves. "What brings you out here?" He didn't mean to sound unfriendly, but he was frustrated, tired and hungry. Despite that, he was damn glad to see her.

She didn't answer him right away, but instead focused her attention on the calf, which mewled pitifully. "Mandy suggested I drive out so I could talk to you," she muttered, then pointed at the mud hole. "That calf's stuck."

"No kidding."

"There's no need to be sarcastic with me," she announced primly. As she stood there, he couldn't help noticing just how tight those jeans were.

"Aren't you going to do something?" she demanded.

Undressing her occurred to him.... Russ brought his musings to an abrupt halt. "Do something about what?" he asked.

"That cow. She needs help."

"She's a he, and I'm well aware of the fact."

"Then *help him,*" Taylor ordered, gesturing toward the calf as though she suspected Russ was simply ignoring the problem.

"I've spent the past hour helping him."

"Well, you certainly didn't do a very good job of it."

He raised his eyebrows. "Do you think you can do any better?"

She looked startled for a moment, then said, "I bet I could."

"Here we go again." He took off his hat long enough to slap it against his thigh and remove the dust. "Because you're a woman, an independent, competent woman, you're convinced you can handle this problem, while I, a chauvinist and a drunk, am incapable of even assessing the situation."

"I...I didn't exactly say that."

"But it's what you implied."

"Fine," she agreed. "I'll admit I can't see why you aren't helping that poor animal."

"I guess I just needed you. Go to it, lady."

"All right, I will." Cautiously she approached the

edge of the mud hole. She planted her boots just outside the dark slime and leaned forward slightly. In a low voice she started carrying on a soothing, one-sided conversation with the calf as if she could reason him out of his plight.

"You're going to have to do a lot more than talk to him," Russ couldn't resist telling her. He walked over to the truck, crossed his arms and leaned against the side. Already he could feel his sour mood lifting. Just watching Taylor deal with this would be more entertainment than he'd enjoyed in a long while.

"I'm taking a few minutes to reassure him," Taylor returned from between clenched teeth. "The poor thing's frightened half out of his wits."

"Sweet-talkin' him is bound to help."

"I'm sure it will," she said, giving him a surly look.

"Works wonders with me, too," Russ had to tell her, although he couldn't keep the humor out of his voice. "However, it's my belief that actions speak louder than words. When you're finished with the calf, would you care to demonstrate your concern for me?"

"No."

Russ chuckled softly. "That's what I thought."

Taylor cast him a furious glance before walking around the edges of the mud-caked hole. The calf continued to mewl, not that Russ could blame him. The fellow had gotten himself into one heck of a quandary.

"It appears he's completely trapped," Taylor announced in formal tones.

It had taken Russ all of three seconds to come to that conclusion.

"Can't you put a rope around his neck and pull him out?" She motioned toward Russ's gelding. "You could loop one end around the calf and the other around the saddle horn and have Magic walk backward. I saw it done that way in a TV rerun. Trigger, I think it was Trigger, saved Roy Rogers from certain death in quicksand doing exactly that."

"It won't work."

Taylor gave an indignant shrug of her shoulders. "Why won't it? If it worked for Roy Rogers, it should work for this poor little guy."

"With a rope around his neck, he'd probably strangle before we budged him more than a few inches."

"Oh." She gnawed on her lower lip. "I hadn't thought of that."

Russ hated to admit how much he was enjoying this. She'd outsmarted him once before with that flat tire business, but Taylor was on his turf now, and Russ was in control. "I don't suppose you'd care to make a wager on this?"

"No more bets."

"What's the matter? Are you afraid you'll lose?"

Taylor firmly shook her head. "I'm just not interested, thanks."

"How about this? If you get the calf out, I'll come willingly to your bed. If you don't, then you'll come willingly to mine."

"Does everything boil down to *that* with you?"

"*That,* my sweet lady, is exactly what we both want."

"You're impossible."

"If you were honest with yourself, you'd admit I'm right."

Her mouth was pinched so tightly that her lips were pale. "You're disgusting."

"That isn't what you said the other night," Russ murmured.

"If you don't mind, I'd prefer it if we didn't talk about Friday night."

"As you wish," he said with a grin.

Taylor frowned, studying the calf. "Couldn't we prod him out?"

"*We?* It was my understanding that you could do this all on your own."

"All right," she flared, "if you won't help me, then I'll do it myself." She took two tentative steps into the thick, sticky mud and wrinkled her nose as she moved warily toward the distressed calf. "For being such a great rancher, you certainly seem to be taking this rather casually," she accused him, glancing over her shoulder. Her arms were stretched out at her sides as though she was balancing on a tightrope.

Russ shrugged. "Why should I be concerned when you're doing such a bang-up job?"

Taylor took two more small steps, her face wrinkled with displeasure.

"You're doing just great," Russ called out to her. "In another week or so you'll have reached the calf."

"I never realized how sarcastic you were before now," she muttered.

"Just trying to be of service. Are you sure you're not willing to stake something on the outcome of this?"

"I'm more than sure," she said. "I'm absolutely, totally positive."

"That's a shame."

She glared at him. "It seems you've forgotten that this calf belongs to you. The only reason I'm doing anything is because I find your attitude extremely callous."

"Extremely," Russ echoed, and laughed outright. He tried to disguise it behind a cough, but the irate look she shot him told him he hadn't succeeded.

The sound of pounding hooves caught his attention, and Russ turned to see two of his men galloping toward him.

"Who's coming?" Taylor demanded. She twisted around to glance over her shoulder and somehow lost her balance. Her arms flailed as a look of terror came over her. "Russ…"

Russ leaped forward, but it was too late. He heard her shriek just as she tumbled, hands first into the thick slime. For a shocked second he did nothing. Then, God forgive him, he couldn't help it, he started laughing. He laughed so hard, his stomach hurt and he clutched it with both arms.

A long string of unladylike words blistered the afternoon air when he waded into the mud. Taylor was sitting upright, her knees raised, holding out her hands while the gunk oozed slowly between her fingers. At least the upper portion of her body had been spared.

"Get away from me you…you—" She apparently couldn't think of anything nasty enough to call him. "This is all your fault." Taking a fistful of black mud, she hurled it at him with all her strength, using such force that she nearly toppled backward with the effort.

The mud flew past Russ, missing him by several feet. "Here, let me help you," he said, wiping tears of mirth from the corners of his eyes.

"Stop laughing," she shouted. "Stop right this second! Do you understand me?"

Russ couldn't do it. He'd never seen anything funnier in his life. He honestly tried to stop, but he simply couldn't.

Taylor was so furious that despite several attempts she couldn't pull herself upright. Finally, Russ moved behind her and, gripping her under the arms, heaved her upward.

The second they were out of the mud, Taylor whirled around, talking so fast and so furiously that he couldn't make out more than a few words. From those he recognized, he figured he was better off not knowing what she had to say.

Russ's two hands, Slim and Roy, stood by, and when Russ met their eyes, he saw that they were doing an admirable job of containing their own amusement. Unfortunately Russ wasn't nearly as diplomatic.

"You two can handle this?" he said, nodding toward the calf.

"No problem," Slim said.

"Taylor didn't think she'd have a problem, either," Russ said, and started laughing all over again.

Both Slim and Roy were chuckling despite their best efforts not to. They climbed down from their horses and leaned against the side of the truck, turning away so Taylor couldn't see them. It wasn't until then that Russ noticed she was missing. He discovered her walking in the direction of the house, which by his best estimate was a good three miles north. Her backside was caked with mud, and her arms were swinging at her sides.

"Looks like you got woman problems," Roy said, glancing at Taylor.

"Looks that way to me, too," Slim said, reaching for his kerchief and wiping his eyes. "I'd be thinking about what Abe Lincoln said if I were you."

"And what's that?" Russ wanted to know.

"Hell hath no fury like a woman scorned."

"That wasn't Abe Lincoln," Roy muttered. "That was Johnny Carson."

Whoever said it obviously knew women a whole lot better than Russ did. The way he figured it, if he ever wanted Taylor to ever speak to him again, he was going to have to do some fast talking of his own.

Taylor had never been angrier in her life. That mud was the most disgusting thing she'd ever seen, and having it on her clothes and skin was more horrible than she even wanted to contemplate. She was cold and wet, and all Russ had done was laugh.

He'd laughed as if she was some slapstick comedian sent to amuse him with her antics. To add to her humiliation she couldn't find the key to the stupid truck. She'd thought she'd left it in the ignition. One thing she did know: she wasn't going to stand around and listen to those men make fun of her.

The least Russ could've done was tell her he was sorry! But he hadn't. Oh, no! He'd roared so loud she swore she'd hear the echo for all eternity.

The sound of the pickup coming toward her did nothing to quell her fury. She didn't so much as turn and look at him when Russ slowed the truck to a crawl beside her.

"Want a ride?"

"No." She continued, increasing her pace. She was already winded, but she'd keel over and die before she'd let Russ know that.

"In case you're wondering, we're about three miles from the ranch house."

She whirled around. "What makes you think I'm going there?"

He shrugged. "Would it help if I said I was sorry?"

"No." Her voice cracked, and her shoulders started to shake while she tried to suppress the tears. Her effort was for naught, and they ran down her face, hot against her skin. Forgetting about the thick mud caked on her hands, she tried to wipe off the tears and in the process nearly blinded herself. The sobs came in earnest then, and her whole body shook with them.

She heard Russ leap out of the pickup, and before she could protest, he was wiping the mud from her face, using a handkerchief. She only hoped it was clean, and once she realized how preposterous that was, she cried harder.

"I hate you," she sobbed, and her shoulders heaved with her vehemence. "I hate Montana. I hate everything about this horrible place. I want to go home."

Russ's arms came around her, but before she could push him away, he'd picked her up and carried her to the truck.

"I...can't sit in there," she wailed. "I'll ruin the up-holstery."

Russ proceeded to inform her how little he cared about the interior of his truck. He set her inside the cab, with her feet hanging out the door, then reached into the back and grabbed a blanket and placed that around her shoulders.

"You're cold," was all he said.

"I'm not cold. I'm perfectly—" She would've finished what she was going to say, but her teeth had started to chatter.

Russ brushed the hair from her face, his fingers lingering at her temple. "I am sorry."

"Just be quiet. I'm in no mood for an apology."

Russ moved her legs inside, then closed the door. The blast of heat coming from the heater felt like a warm breeze straight from paradise, and tucking the blanket more securely around her, Taylor hunched forward. She didn't want to know where this tattered old blanket had been.

Russ hurried around the front of the truck and climbed in beside her. "Hold on," he said. "I'll have you at the house in two minutes flat."

"Where did you find the truck key?" she asked grudgingly.

"I always carry one on my key chain."

"What about the poor little calf?"

"Don't worry. The guys'll get him out. And they'll bring Magic back for me."

If Taylor had thought the ride from town the day they'd met had been rough, it was a Sunday School picnic compared to the crazy way Russ drove across the pasture.

Mandy must have heard them coming, because she was standing on the back porch steps when Russ pulled in to the yard and screeched to a halt. He turned off the engine and vaulted out of the cab.

Taylor couldn't seem to get her body to move. Russ opened the door and effortlessly lifted her into his arms.

"What happened?" Mandy cried, racing toward them.

"Taylor fell in the mud. She's about to freeze to death."

"I...I most certainly am not going to freeze," she

countered. "All I need is a warm bath and my own clothes."

"Right on both counts," Russ said, bounding up the back steps with her in his arms. He paused at the top and drew in a deep breath. "How much do you weigh, anyhow?"

"Oh," Taylor cried, squirming in his arms, struggling to make him release her.

Her efforts were in vain as Mandy held open the door and Russ carried her through the kitchen and down a narrow hallway to the bathroom.

"How'd it happen?" Mandy asked, running after them.

Russ's eyes met Taylor's. "You don't want to know the answer to that," Taylor informed the teenager.

"I'll tell you later," Russ mouthed. When they reached the bathroom, Mandy opened the door wider so Russ could haul Taylor inside.

"Boil some water and get the whiskey bottle from the top cupboard," he instructed.

Mandy nodded and dashed back to the kitchen.

"Put me down," Taylor insisted. If it wasn't for this egotistical, stubborn, *perverse* man, she wouldn't be in this humiliating position in the first place.

Russ surprised her by doing as she asked. Gently he set her feet on the tile floor, then leaned over the tub to adjust the knobs, starting the flow of warm water.

For the first time Taylor had an opportunity to survey the damage. She looked down at her legs and gasped at the thick, black coating. A glance in the mirror was her second mistake.

Her lower lip trembled and she sniffled, attempting to hold back the tears.

"You're going to be just fine in a few minutes," Russ said in an apparent effort to comfort her.

"I'm not fine," Taylor moaned, catching her reflection in the mirror again. "I look like the Creature from the Black Lagoon!"

Nine

"Taylor!" Russ shouted from the other side of the bathroom door, "close the shower curtain. I'm coming in."

Resting her head against the back of the tub until the warm soothing water covered her shoulders, Taylor turned a disinterested glance toward the door. She felt sleepy and lethargic. "Go away," she called lazily, then proceeded to yawn, covering her mouth with the back of her hand.

"If you don't want to close the curtain, it's fine with me. Actually, I'd be grateful if you didn't."

The doorknob started to turn and, muttering at the intrusion, Taylor reached for the plastic curtain and jerked it closed.

"Damn," Russ said from the other side, not bothering to hide his disappointment. "I was hoping you'd be more stubborn than this."

"Why are you here?" she demanded.

"I live here, remember?"

"I mean in the bathroom! You have no business walking in on me like this." Actually Taylor should have been out of the bathtub long ago, but the water was so warm and relaxing, and it felt good just to sit there and and soak.

"I'm taking these clothes out so Mandy can put them in the washing machine," he said, and his voice faded as he went down the hall.

All too soon he was back. "Stick out your arm."

"Why?"

"You'll find out."

Taylor exhaled sharply, her hold on her temper precarious. "May I remind you that I'm stark naked behind this curtain."

"Trust me, lady, I know that. It's playing hell with my imagination. Now stick out your arm before I'm forced to pull back this shower curtain."

Grinding her teeth, Taylor did as he asked, knowing full well he'd follow through with his threat given the least provocation. Almost immediately a hot mug was pressed into her palm. She brought it behind the curtain and was immediately struck by the scent of whiskey and honey mixed with hot water. "What's this for?"

"It'll help warm you."

"I wasn't really that chilled." Actually she'd been far too angry to experience anything more than minimal discomfort.

"If you want the truth," Russ said in low, seductive tones, "I was hoping the drink would help take the edge off your anger."

"It's going to take a whole lot more than a hot toddy to do that."

"That's what I thought," he muttered. "I've left a couple of Mandy's things here for you to change into when you've finished. There's no hurry, so take all the time you want."

"Are you leaving now?" she asked impatiently.

"Yes, but I'll be waiting for you."

"I figured you would be," she grumbled.

Taylor soaked another ten minutes until the water started to turn cool, then she reluctantly pulled the plug and climbed out of the tub.

A thick pale blue flannel robe that zipped up the front was draped over the edge of the sink, along with a pair of fuzzy pink slippers. After Taylor had finished drying, she slipped into those, conscious that she wore nothing underneath.

Russ was sitting at the kitchen table. "Where's Mandy?" she asked, doing her best to sound casual and composed, as if she often walked around a man's home in nothing more than a borrowed robe.

"She's on the phone, talking to Travis Wells's boy."

This must be the famous Eddie who'd caused Taylor so much grief. Not knowing what she should say or do, she walked over to the counter and filled her empty mug with coffee. She'd just replaced the pot when Russ's hands settled on her shoulders. He turned her around and gazed into her eyes.

"I shouldn't have laughed." His voice was husky, his expression regretful.

She lifted one shoulder in a delicate shrug. "I don't think you could've helped it—laughing was a natural reaction. I must have looked ridiculous."

"Do you forgive me?"

She nodded. Her sojourn in the bath had washed away more than the mud; it had obliterated her anger. She acknowledged that she hadn't been completely guiltless in this fiasco, either. "You weren't really to blame. I did it to myself with my stubborn pride. You're the rancher here, not me. I was a fool to think I could free that poor calf when you couldn't. I brought the whole thing on myself, but you were handy and I lashed out at you."

Russ lifted her chin with his index finger. "Did you mean what you said about hating Montana?"

Taylor didn't remember saying that, although she'd muttered plenty about Russ and his stupid cows and everything else she could think of.

"Not any more than I meant what I said about everything else."

"Good." Russ obviously took that as a positive answer. He raised his finger and traced it slowly over her cheek to her lips. His touch was unhurried and tender as if he longed to ease every moment of distress he'd caused her, intentionally or otherwise. His eyes didn't waver from hers, and when he leaned forward to kiss her, there wasn't a single doubt in Taylor's mind that this was exactly what she wanted.

His mouth settled over hers, and she sighed softly in hopeless welcome. His kisses, as always, were devastatingly sensual. Taylor felt so mellow, so warm.

"I could get drunk on you," Russ murmured in awe.

"It must be the whiskey," she whispered back.

He shook his head. "I didn't have any." His hands were in her hair, his lips at her throat, and the delicious, delirious feelings flooded her.

Sliding her hands over the open V of his shirt, she wound her arms around his strong neck. He leaned her against the counter and pressed himself against her, creating a whole new kaleidoscope of delectable sensations. Taylor let her head fall back as he continued to kiss her. He was so close she could feel the snap of his jeans. He was power. Masculine strength. Heat. She sensed in him a hunger she'd never known in any man. A hunger and need. One only she could fill.

Then, when she least expected it, Russ stilled his body and his hands and roughly dragged his mouth from hers. Not more than a second had passed when…

"Oops…oh, sorry," Mandy said as she walked into the kitchen. "I bet you guys want me to come back later. Right? Hey, no problem." She backed out of the kitchen, hands raised.

Russ's arms closed protectively around Taylor, but she broke free and managed a smile, then deftly turned toward the teenager. "There's no reason for you to leave."

"Yes, there is," Russ said. "Taylor and I have to talk."

"No, we don't," she countered sharply. "We've finished…talking."

Russ threw her a challenging glance that suggested otherwise, and Taylor, who rarely blushed, did so profusely.

"We haven't even started *talking,*" Russ whispered for her ears alone. Taylor wasn't going to argue with him, at least not in front of his sister.

Mandy stared down at the linoleum floor and traced the octagonal pattern with the toe of her tennis shoe. "You've already talked to Russ?" she asked, darting a quick glance at Taylor. Her soft green eyes were imploring.

"Not yet," Taylor said pointedly.

"Disappear for a while, Mandy," Russ urged, turning back to Taylor.

"No," Taylor said forcefully. The minute the girl was out of the room, the same thing would happen that always did whenever they were alone together. One kiss and they'd burst spontaneously into a passion hot enough to sear Taylor's senses for days afterward.

"No?" Mandy echoed, clearly confused.

"I haven't talked to Russ yet, but I will now."

The fourteen-year-old brightened and nodded eagerly. She pointed toward the living room. "I'll just wait in there."

"What's going on here?" Russ demanded once Mandy was out of the room.

"Nothing."

"And pigs fly."

"Sit down," she coaxed, offering him a shy smile. She got a second mug and filled it with coffee, then carried it to the round oak table where Russ was waiting for her. His arm slipped around her waist, and she braced her hands against his shoulders.

"You're supposed to talk to me?" he asked.

She nodded.

"This has to do with Mandy?"

Once more Taylor nodded.

Russ frowned. "That was why you drove out to see me earlier, wasn't it?"

"Yes," she answered honestly. He kept his arms securely around her waist, but he didn't look pleased. Taylor felt the least she could do was explain. "Mandy came to talk to me after school, and she asked me to approach you about…something."

"She isn't comfortable coming to me herself?" Russ muttered, looking offended. "I've been trying as hard as I can to listen to her. I can't be any fairer than I've already been. What does she want now? To get an apartment in town on her own?"

"Don't be silly," Taylor answered, riffling his hair,

seeking some way to reassure him. "Mandy knows you're trying to be patient with her, and she's trying, too. Only this was something special, something she felt awkward talking to you about, so she came to me. Don't be offended, Russ. That wasn't her intention and it isn't mine."

He nodded, but his frown remained. From the first, Taylor hadn't been sure she was doing the right thing by approaching Russ on Mandy's behalf. She'd only wanted to help, but regretted her part in this now. Look where it had led her! Two feet deep in mud.

Positioning herself on his lap, she rested her arms over his shoulders, her wrists dangling. "You're right," she said, and kissed him long and leisurely by way of apology.

His eyes were still closed when she'd finished, his breathing labored.

"Mandy," Taylor called, embarrassed by how noticeably her voice trembled.

The teenager raced into the kitchen so fast she nearly skidded across the polished floor. "Well?" she asked expectantly. "What did he say?" She seemed a little startled to see Taylor sitting on her brother's lap, but didn't mention it at all.

"I haven't said anything yet," Russ growled. "I want to know what's going on here. First of all, Taylor drives out to talk to me, and from what I can tell she's wearing your clothes."

"I couldn't very well send her out there in the dress she was wearing at school. I'm certainly glad I insisted she put on something of mine, otherwise look what would've happened!" Mandy declared.

"What's that got to do with this?"

"You were supposed to be back early today, re-member?" Mandy reminded him pointedly. "You said something about driving over to Bill Shepherd's this afternoon—"

"Oh, damn," Russ muttered, "I forgot."

"Don't worry. He phoned while you were out with Taylor, and I said you'd probably run into some trouble. He's going to call you back tonight."

Russ nodded. "Go on."

"Well, anyway, I thought it might even be better if Taylor talked to you when I wasn't around, so I suggested she take the truck and—"

"How'd you know where I was?" Russ asked his sister, clearly confused.

"I heard you speaking to Slim this morning about checking the south fence lines. I just headed Taylor in that direction. I knew she'd find you sooner or later."

Russ's gaze shot to Taylor. "She found me all right. Now tell me what you were going to talk to me about." The tone of Russ's voice suggested he was fast losing patience.

"Mandy, I'm holding him down, so you do the talking," Taylor said, smiling at Russ.

"You ask him, Taylor. Oh, please…" the girl begged.

"Nope, you're on your own, kiddo."

"Will the two of you stop playing games and tell me what's going on here?"

"Okay," Mandy said, elevating her shoulders as she released a deep breath. She pushed up the sleeves of her sweater, not looking at her brother, and launched into her request. "You know Travis Wells, don't you?" She didn't give Russ time to respond. "His son Eddie goes to school with me."

"Eddie's older than you."

"He's sixteen," Mandy returned quickly. "Actually he's only twenty-two months and five days older than I am. If he'd been born in October and I'd been born in August we might even have been in the same class together, so there's really not that big a difference in our ages." She paused as though waiting for Russ to comment or agree.

"All right," he said after an uncomfortable moment.

Mandy looked at Taylor pleadingly, silently asking her to explain the rest. Taylor shook her head.

"Eddie's been talking to me lately…in the halls and sometimes at lunch. Yesterday he sat with me on the bus." This was clearly of monumental significance. "Eddie was the one who encouraged me to try out for the drill team, and when I made it, he said he knew I would."

"That was him on the phone earlier, wasn't it?"

A happy grin touched the girl's mouth. "Yes—he wanted to know if I'd talked to you yet."

"About what?" Russ asked, then stiffened. His eyes narrowed. "You're not going out with that young man, Amanda, and that's the end of it. Fourteen is too young to date, and I don't care what Taylor says!"

If she hadn't been sitting on his lap, Taylor was sure Russ would have jumped to his feet. Framing his face with her hands, she stroked the rigid muscles of his jaw. "There's no need to yell. As it happens, I agree with you."

"You do?"

"Don't look so shocked."

"Then why were you coming to talk to me about it?

Because I'll tell you right now, I'm not changing my mind."

"I'm not, either," she said softly, "so relax."

"Mandy?" Russ turned to his sister, his frown threatening.

"Well…as you've already guessed, Eddie asked me out on a date. Actually he just wanted me to go to the movies with him."

"No way," Russ said without so much as a pause.

Mandy's teeth bit her trembling bottom lip. "I thought you'd feel that way. That's the reason I went to Taylor, but she said she agreed with you that fourteen's too young to date. But while we were talking she came up with a…compromise. That is, if you'll agree."

"I said no," Russ returned resolutely.

Taylor felt she should explain. "When I was fourteen, my father—"

"You're from the city," he said in a way that denigrated anyone who lived in a town with a population over five hundred. "Folks from the country think differently. I don't expect you to understand."

His harsh words were like a slap in the face to Taylor. She blinked back the sharp pain, astonished that he would offend her so easily.

"Russ," Mandy whispered, "that was a terrible thing to say."

"What? That Taylor's from the city? It's true."

"You're right, of course." She slipped off his lap and looked at Mandy. "Are my clothes in your room?"

The girl nodded. "I hung them in my closet."

Drawing in a deep breath, Taylor looked at Russ. "I apologize. I should never have involved myself in something that wasn't my affair. I went against my better judgment and I was wrong. Now, if you'll excuse me, I'll change clothes and get out of here." The way she felt at the moment, she never intended to come back. What Russ had said was true; he was only repeating what she'd been saying to him from the first. They were fooling themselves if they believed there was any future in their relationship.

Mandy's bedroom was on the main floor, next to the bathroom. Taylor shut the door and walked over to sit on the bed. Her hands were trembling, and she felt close to tears. Raised voices came from the kitchen, but Taylor couldn't make out the words and had no intention of even trying. If anything, she was regretful that she'd become yet another source of discord between brother and sister.

Taylor was dressing when someone tapped politely on the door. "I'll just be a minute," she said, forcing a cheerful note into her voice.

Slipping the dress over her head, Taylor walked barefoot across the room and opened the door. Mandy came inside, her face red and stained with tears. Sobbing, she threw both arms around Taylor's waist.

"I'm sorry," she whispered. "I'm really sorry…it was so selfish of me to involve you in this. Look what happened. First you fell in that terrible mud—"

"But, remember, I was wearing your clothes."

"I don't care about that." She lifted her head to wipe the tears from her face. "You could take all my clothes and put them in a mud hole if you wanted."

"If you don't mind, I'd prefer to avoid any and all mud holes from now on."

Mandy's responding chuckle sounded more like another sob. "Russ should never have said what he did."

"But it's true," Taylor said lightly, pretending to dismiss the entire incident.

"Maybe so, but it was the way he said it—as if you're not to be trusted or something. You're the best thing that's ever happened to my brother—and to me. All the kids in school are crazy about you and…and for Russ to say what he did was an insult."

"Don't be so hard on him. You can take the girl out of the city, but you can't take the city out of the girl," she joked.

"He'll be sorry in a little bit," Mandy assured her. "He always is. He's the only man I know who slits his own throat with his tongue."

"There's no need for him to apologize," Taylor said, hugging the teenager close. She broke away, slipped on her shoes and reached for her jacket. She draped her purse over her shoulder. "Chin up, kiddo. Everything's going to work out for the best."

Mandy bobbed her head several times.

Russ wasn't around when Taylor walked through the kitchen and out the back door. For that she was grateful. She opened her car door, but didn't get inside. Instead she found herself studying the house and the outbuildings that comprised the Lazy P, giving it a final look. Sadness settled over her and she exhaled slowly.

This was her farewell to Russ and to his ranch.

If the day Taylor fell in the mud hole had been full of problems, Russ decided, the ensuing ones were just as impossible. Only now the difficulties he faced were of his own making.

Taylor had been on his mind for the past three days. Not that thinking about her constantly was anything new, but now, every time he did, all he could see were her big blue eyes meeting his, trying so hard to disguise the pain his words had inflicted. He'd been angry with Mandy for going to Taylor, and angry with Taylor for listening.

Unfortunately Russ didn't have time to make the necessary amends. Not yet, anyway. Slim and Roy had set up cow camp in the foothills, and Russ and two of his other hands were joining them. They were running cattle, branding the calves born on the range, vaccinating and dehorning them. It would be necessary to trim hoofs, too; otherwise the snow, which was sure to arrive sometime soon, would clump in their feet.

There'd been snow in the mountains overnight, and there was nothing to say the first snowfall of the season couldn't happen any day. With so much to do, he didn't have time for anything but work. The cattle buyers would show up right after that, and Russ would be occupied with them, wheeling and dealing to get the best price he could for his beef.

He'd contact Taylor later and apologize.

When Russ returned to the house, it was after seven and he was exhausted. Mandy was sitting at the kitchen table, doing her homework.

"Any calls?" he asked hopefully. Maybe Taylor had finally decided to forgive him, although he doubted it.

"None."

Russ frowned. That woman was too stubborn for her own good—or his.

"Dinner's in the oven," Mandy said, not looking at him. She closed her book and inserted pages into her binder.

Russ took the plate from the oven with a pot holder,

then set it on the table. "I've been thinking over what you suggested about this thing with Eddie," he said while he took a glass from the cupboard and poured himself some milk.

Mandy's eyes rose to search his. "It wouldn't be like a real date. I'd be paying for my own ticket and all Eddie and I would be doing is sitting together. It'd be just as if we'd accidentally met there. If Eddie wants, I'd let him buy me some popcorn—but only if you think it would be all right."

"I'd drop you off and pick you up at the theater?"

"Right."

Russ pulled out a chair and sat down. "This is a sensible compromise," he said as he spread the paper napkin across his lap. "This idea shows maturity and insight on your part, and I'm proud of you for coming up with it."

"I didn't."

Russ finished his first bite and studied his sister, who was standing across the table, her hand resting on the back of the chair. "Taylor's the one who suggested it first. She tried to explain it to you.... Actually, we both did, but you wouldn't listen."

The bite of chicken-fried steak stuck halfway down Russ's throat, and he had to swallow hard before he could speak normally. "Taylor came up with the idea?"

"I think her parents were the ones who thought of it because she was telling me that's what they did with her and her sister when they were fourteen and boys began asking them out."

"I see."

"Just think, Russ," Mandy murmured sarcastically. "Taylor's parents are from the big city, and they managed to come up with this all on their own. Naw, on second thought, I bet someone from the country suggested it."

Normally Russ wouldn't have tolerated his sister talking to him in that tone of voice. The kid sure knew all the right buttons to push. But this time Russ didn't react as he usually did. The pressure that settled on his chest made it difficult to concentrate on anything else.

His appetite gone, Russ pushed his plate away, propped his elbows on the table and stared straight ahead.

He'd done it now. Taylor would never speak to him again. Unless...

Another lonely Friday night, Taylor mused as she sat at the kitchen table with paper and pen. She owed everyone letters, and it wasn't as though she had anything pressing to do.

She leaned back in the chair and reread the long letter from Christy, chuckling over her youngest sibling's warmth and wit.

Someone knocked at the door and, laying aside the letter, Taylor went to answer it. A smiling Mandy stood on the other side.

"Mandy? Is everything all right?"

"It's perfect. Well, almost..." she said, beaming. She seemed in a hurry and glanced over her shoulder.

Taylor's gaze followed hers, and she noticed Russ's truck parked alongside the curb. He was sitting in the cab.

"Russ said I could meet Eddie at the movies and sit with him under one condition, and I'm afraid that involves you."

Taylor couldn't have heard Mandy correctly. "I beg your pardon?"

"Russ seems to feel that Eddie and I are going to need a couple of chaperones."

"That's ridiculous."

"No, it isn't," Mandy insisted much too cheerfully to suit Taylor. "At least I don't mind if you guys sit on the other side of the theater from Eddie and me."

"You guys?"

"You and Russ. He said I can only do this if you agree to sit with him during the movie so he doesn't look like a jerk being there all by himself."

"You can tell your brother for me——"

"Taylor," Mandy cut in, leaning forward to whisper as if there was a chance Russ might overhear. "This is the *only* way Russ could think of to get you to talk to him again. He's really sorry for how he acted and the things he said."

"Sending you to do his apologizing for him isn't going to work," Taylor said matter-of-factly. "Neither is this little game of blackmail."

Mandy thought about it for a moment, then nodded. "You know what? You're absolutely right!" Placing her hands on her hips, she whirled around to face the street. *"Russ!"* she yelled at the top of her lungs.

Russ leaned across the cab of the pickup and rolled down the window.

"If you want to apologize to Taylor, you're going to have to do it yourself!" Mandy shouted. Taylor was certain half the neighbors could hear. Her worst fears were confirmed when she saw the lady across the street pulling aside her drape and peeking out.

"*And* Taylor says she refuses to be blackmailed."

Taylor was mortified when the doors to several more homes opened and a couple of men stepped onto their porches to investigate the source of all the shouting.

"What are you going to do about it?" Mandy yelled.

By this time Russ had climbed out of the truck. He was wearing the same gray suit jacket with the suede yoke he'd had on the night of the Grange dance.

"Hey, Palmer, what's going on with the school-teacher?" one of Taylor's neighbors heckled.

Two or three others came off their porches and onto the sidewalk. A low murmur followed Russ's progress toward Taylor.

"Hey, Russ, apologize, would you?"

"Yeah," another chimed in. "Then we can have some peace and quiet around here."

Russ paid no attention. When he reached the end of the walk, he looked straight at Taylor, then leaped up the steps. "You want a formal apology?" he asked. "Fine, I'll give you one, but after that we're going to the movies."

Ten

"I'm not going to the movies with you, Russ Palmer. That's all there is to it," Taylor said, and gently closed the door. She turned the lock just to be on the safe side and went back to the kitchen where she'd started a letter to her sister.

A few minutes later, she heard the faint strains of a guitar and someone singing, badly off key. Good grief, it sounded like… Russ. Russ singing?

Deciding the only thing she could do was ignore him, Taylor returned to her letter-writing project.

Apparently Russ wasn't going to be easily foiled, and when she didn't immediately appear, he countered by singing and playing louder. His determination was evident in each word of his ridiculously maudlin song. He was completely untalented as a singer, and his guitar-playing abilities weren't anything to brag about, either.

Covering her ears, Taylor slid as low as she could in her chair. The man's nerve was colossal. If she'd learned anything during her time in Cougar Point, it was that cowboys didn't lack arrogance. To assume that she'd be willing to forget everything simply because he serenaded her was downright comical.

It was then that the phone rang. Taylor answered it on the second ring, grinning at Russ's impertinence, despite her irritation.

"For heaven's sake," her neighbor shouted over the line, "do something, will you? His singing is making my dog howl."

No sooner had Taylor replaced the phone than it rang again. "My china's starting to rattle. Would you please kiss and make up before my crystal cracks?" Taylor recognized the voice of Mrs. Fergason, the lady from across the street.

Grinding her teeth with frustration, Taylor tore across the living room and yanked open the door. "Stop!"

Russ took one look at her and grinned broadly. He lowered the guitar, obviously delighted with himself. "I see you've come to your senses."

"Either stop singing or I'm calling the police. You're disturbing my peace and that of my neighbors. Now leave."

Russ blinked, apparently convinced he'd misunderstood her. "I wish I could, but I owe you an apology and I won't feel right until I clear the air."

"Okay, you've apologized. Now will you kindly go?"

He rubbed his hand down his jaw. "I can't do that."

"Why not?" Taylor jerked back her head hard enough to give herself whiplash. "I don't believe it. Why are you doing this?"

"Because I'm falling in love with you."

A lump immediately formed in Taylor's throat. This was the last thing she'd wanted. Living in Cougar Point was supposed to give her a chance to heal from one disastrous relationship, not involve her in another.

"Russ," Mandy called, leaning out the window of the truck, "hurry or we'll be late for the movie."

"Are you going or not?" Mrs. Fergason shouted. "Decide, will you? *Jeopardy!*'s about to start, and I don't want to miss Alex Trebek."

Taylor was still too stunned to react. "Don't love me, Russ. Please don't love me."

"I'm sorry, but it's too late. I knew the minute you went headfirst into that mud hole that we were meant for each other. Now, are you going to ruin Mandy's big night with your stubbornness, or are you going to the movie with me?"

If she'd had her wits about her Taylor would never have agreed to this blatant form of blackmail, but Russ had taken all the wind from the sails of her righteousness. Before she realized exactly how she'd gotten there, she was inside the Cougar Point Theater, sitting in the back row with Russ, munching on hot buttered popcorn.

"We've got to talk," she whispered as the opening credits started. She'd seen the movie months earlier, and although she'd enjoyed it, she wasn't eager to see it a second time—especially now, after Russ's shocking declaration.

His large callused hand reached for hers, closing around her fingers. "We can talk later."

How she managed to sit through the entire film, Taylor didn't know. Her mind was in a chaotic whirl. All too soon the closing credits were rolling and the house lights came up. The theater began to empty.

Mandy dashed down the aisle, the famous Eddie at

her side. "Would it be all right if we went over to the bowling alley? Chris's mom and dad offered to buy everyone nachos. Lots of other kids are going."

"How long will you be?" Russ asked.

Mandy looked at Eddie. "An hour," the boy said firmly, perhaps expecting Russ to argue with him. He was over six feet tall and as lean as a telephone pole, yet Mandy gazed at him as if he were a Hollywood heartthrob.

"All right," Russ said, apparently surprising them both. "I'll pick you up in exactly one hour."

"Thanks," Mandy said, and impulsively kissed his cheek.

"That gives us forty-five minutes to settle our differences," Russ said, smiling over at Taylor, his eyes filled with silent messages.

By now Taylor felt more than a little disoriented. It was as if her entire world resembled the flickering frames in a silent movie. Everything had a strange, staccato feeling, and nothing seemed real.

"Where are we going?" she asked when Russ opened the truck door for her.

"Back to your place. Unless you object."

Russ had ignored every one of her objections from the moment they'd met, and there was no reason to assume he was going to change at this stage.

When Russ parked his truck, Taylor half expected her neighbors to file out of their homes and line the sidewalk, offering advice. But all the excitement earlier in the evening had apparently tired everyone out. It was only nine, and already most of the houses were completely dark.

"I'll make us some coffee," Taylor said, finding her

voice. She unlocked the door, but before she could flip on the living room lights, Russ gently turned her around and pulled her into his arms.

He closed the front door with his foot and pressed her against the wall. Their eyes adjusted to the dark, and met. "You're so beautiful," he whispered reverently. He lifted his hands to her hair, weaving the thick strands through his fingers. Taylor felt powerless to stop him. She closed her eyes and savored the moment. Savored the exquisite sensations Russ evoked within her.

"Please don't fall in love with me," she pleaded, remembering the reason for this discussion. "Don't love me."

"I can't help myself," he whispered, kissing the taut line of her jaw. "Trust me, Taylor, I wasn't all that happy about it myself. You belong in the city."

"Exactly," she said, breathing deeply. It never seemed to fail: Russ would hold her and she'd dissolve in his arms. Her breathing became labored, and her heart went on a rampage. She tried to convince herself that they were simply dealing with an abundance of hormones, but no matter how many times she told herself that, it didn't matter.

Russ *couldn't* love her. He just couldn't. Because then Taylor would be forced to examine her own feelings for him. She'd be compelled to face what she intuitively knew would be better left unnamed.

"You're a West Coast liberal feminist."

"You're a small-town Montana redneck."

"I know," he agreed, continuing to kiss her jaw, his mouth wandering down the side of her neck.

Listing their differences didn't seem to affect their reactions to each other. Russ raised his head and traced his thumb across her lower lip. It was all Taylor could do not to moan. No man had ever incited such burning need.

Taylor took Russ's finger between her teeth and slowly drew it into her mouth, sucking lightly. He closed his eyes and smiled, then sighed from deep within his chest.

With his hands cupping her face, he kissed her, and it was incredibly sweet, incredibly sexy. Every time Russ took her into his arms, he eliminated all the disparities between them, took everything in their lives and reduced it to the simple fact that they were man and woman.

She gripped his wrists and held on tightly. "Russ, no more…please." With a strength she didn't realize she had, Taylor broke off the kiss.

"I've just begun," he warned.

His lips remained so close to hers that she inhaled his moist, warm breath.

"Why does everything come down to this?" she murmured. Her knees were slightly bent as she struggled to hold on to what little strength she still possessed.

"I don't know," he answered honestly. "I can't seem to keep my hands off you." As though to prove his point, he trailed a row of kisses across the curve of her shoulder.

"Russ…"

"Not here… I know." His voice was so husky Taylor barely recognized it. Without any difficulty, he lifted her into his arms.

"What are you doing?" she demanded.

"Carrying you into the bedroom."

"No," she whispered, close to tears.

"Rhett Butler carried Scarlett—I can't do any less for you. I thought all women, even you feminist types, went for this romantic stuff."

"We can't do this…. Russ, listen to me. If we make love, we're both going to regret it later." She was nearly frantic, desperate to talk some sense into him. Talk some sense into herself. All the while, Russ was walking along the hallway to her bedroom.

Her weight must have gotten to be too much for him, because he paused and leaned heavily against the wall. Before she could argue, insist that he put her down, his mouth sought hers, his lips sliding back and forth over hers with mute urgency. Whatever objection Taylor was about to raise died the instant his mouth took hers. She entwined her arms around his neck and boldly kissed him back.

"I thought that would shut you up," he murmured triumphantly as he shifted her weight in his arms and carried her directly into the bedroom.

There was ample time to protest, ample time to demand that he stop, but the words, so perfectly formed in her mind, were never spoken. Instead she leaned her head against his shoulder and sighed heavily. She couldn't fight them both.

Russ placed her on the bed. Taylor closed her eyes, hating this weakness in her. At the same moment, savoring it. "I can't believe we're doing this."

"I can," he said. "I haven't stopped thinking about it since the day we met. I haven't been able to stop thinking about *you*," Russ murmured, "day and night, night and day."

She smiled softly up at him and slipped her arms around his neck. "You've been on my mind, too."

"I'm glad to hear it. But it's more than that," he continued between kisses. "I can't seem to rid myself of this need for you. I want to make love to you more than I've wanted anything in my life."

Taylor felt his moist breath against her cheek and sighed audibly as he began kissing her again, creating magical sensations. Scorching need.

Her arms and legs felt as if they were liquid, without strength. Russ continued to hold her, to rain kisses over her face. Then he nuzzled her neck. Taylor tried to immerse herself in his tenderness, but as hard as she tried, she couldn't seem to block out the fact that their lovemaking would only lead to pain. It had been months since she'd seen Mark, and she was still suffering. How could she do this to herself a second time when she was all too aware of the emotional aftermath?

She'd tried so hard to fight her attraction to Russ. Yet here she was, inviting even more pain, more doubts, more questions. She wasn't the type of woman who leaped into bed with a man just because it felt good.

"Russ...no more," she pleaded, pushing with all her strength against the very shoulders she'd been caressing only moments earlier. "Stop...oh, please, we have to stop."

He went still, and slowly raised his eyes. They were darker than she'd ever seen them. Hotter than she'd ever seen them, but not with anger.

"You don't mean that." Lovingly, tenderly, he ran his hands over her face and paused when he discovered the moisture on her cheeks.

"You're crying."

Taylor hadn't realized it herself until he'd caressed

her face. His eyes questioned hers, filled with apprehension, misgivings. "What's wrong?"

She placed the tips of her fingers on his cheek. "I can't make love with you.... I can't."

"Why not?" His voice was little more than a whisper, and gruff with anxiety. "I love you, Taylor." As if to prove it, he kissed her again, but even more gently this time.

Twisting her head away, Taylor buried her face in the curve of his neck, dragging in deep gulps of air as Russ held her close.

"I don't want you to love me," she sobbed. "If we continue like this, it'll only cause problems—not just for me, but for you, too."

"Not necessarily."

How confident he sounded, how secure, when she was neither.

"I've been in love before...and it hurts too much." She raised her head and swallowed a sob, then wiped the tears from her face. "His name was Mark—and he's the reason I moved to Montana. I had to get away...and heal.... Instead, I met you."

The sobs came in earnest then. Huge heaving sobs that humiliated and humbled her. She wasn't crying for Mark; she was over him. Yet the tears fell and the pain gushed forth in an absolution she hadn't expected. Pain she'd incarcerated behind a wall of smiles, and then lugged across three states.

Russ obviously didn't know what to think. He stroked her hair, but he didn't say anything, and she knew her timing couldn't have been worse. Bringing up the subject of Mark now, tonight, was insane, but she'd had to stop Russ. Stop them both. She'd had to do *something*.

Still sobbing, she rolled off the bed. Finding her footing, she gestured in his direction, miming an apology and at the same time pleading with him to go. She needed to be alone.

"I'm not leaving you."

Unable to find the strength to go on standing, Taylor lowered herself to the edge of the bed. "Do you always have to argue with me? Just for once couldn't you do what I want?"

"No." He eased himself behind her and wrapped his arms around her shoulders, holding her carefully. "I love you," he told her again.

"Please don't."

"The choice was taken from me long ago."

"No…don't even say it. I can't bear it if you love me—I can't deal with it now. Please, try to understand."

His arms tightened slightly, pulling her back against him. "I wish it wasn't so, for your sake, but my heart decided otherwise. I can't change the way I feel."

"I refuse to love you! Do you understand?" Taylor cried. "Look at us! We're a pair of fools. It won't work, so why should we put each other through this? It doesn't make sense! Oh, Russ, please, won't you just leave me alone?"

"Loving you makes sense. We make sense. I love you, Taylor. Nothing will change that."

"Don't tell me that. I refuse to love you," she repeated. "Do you understand? Nothing has changed. Nothing!"

"It doesn't matter."

If Russ had been angry or unreasonable, it would've helped her. Instead he was gentle. Loving. Concerned.

While she was angry. Angrier than she'd ever been.

"Leave me alone. Go!" She pointed to the door in case he wasn't convinced that she meant what she said. "Stay away from me. I don't want to get involved with you."

Russ studied her for several nerve-racking minutes, then sighed and stalked out of the room.

The whole house went quiet, and it reminded her of the hush before a storm. Russ had left; he'd done exactly what she'd asked. She should be glad. Instead, the ache inside her increased a hundredfold and the emptiness widened.

Clutching her stomach, Taylor sobbed while she sat on the bed and rocked. Back and forth. Side to side. She wept because of one man she no longer loved. She wept for another she was afraid of loving too much.

She lost track of time. Five minutes could have been fifty-five; she had no way of telling.

A noise in her kitchen alerted her to the fact that she wasn't alone. Curious, she righted her clothes, wiped her face with a corner of the sheet and walked out of the bedroom.

Russ was sitting in the kitchen, his feet balanced on a chair, ankles crossed. He was drinking a cup of coffee. Apparently he'd made it himself.

"You didn't leave?"

"Not yet."

"What about Mandy?"

"I called the bowling alley and told her to kill another hour." Dropping his legs, he stood and poured Taylor a mug, then set it down for her. "Feeling any better?"

Embarrassed, she looked away and nodded. She would rather he'd left when she'd asked, but that would have created other problems. Eventually she'd need to explain, and the sooner the better. "I'm…sorry. I shouldn't have yelled at you."

"Do you want to talk about it?"

"Not really, but…" She shrugged, then pulled out a chair, sat down and reached for the coffee. Cradling the mug, she warmed her hands with it.

"I suppose I should've suspected something," Russ said after a moment. "Someone like you wouldn't accept a teaching position in this part of the country without a reason. You didn't come to Montana out of a burning desire to learn about life in the backwoods of America."

Her gaze continued to avoid his, but she did manage a weak smile.

"So you were in love with Mark. Tell me what happened."

She sighed. "How much do you want to know?"

"Everything. Start at the beginning, the day you met him, and work through to the day you moved to Cougar Point. Tell me everything—don't hold back a single detail."

Taylor closed her eyes. He wouldn't be satisfied with anything less than the truth, the whole truth. He wanted names, places, dates, details. Gory, painful details. The man was wasted on a cattle ranch, she thought wryly; he should've been working for the Internal Revenue Service. Or the FBI.

"I can't," she whispered as the ache in her heart increased with the memories. "I'm sorry, Russ. If I talked to anyone about Mark, it would be you, but he's behind me now and I'm not about to dredge up all that pain."

"You wouldn't be dredging it up," he told her. "You've been carrying it with you like a heavy suitcase all the way to Cougar Point. Get rid of it, Taylor."

"You think it's that easy?" she responded tartly. "You're suggesting I casually take what little remains of my pride and my dignity and lay it out on the table for you to examine. I can't do it."

The heat in the kitchen felt stifling all of a sudden. Taylor stood abruptly and started pacing. "I wanted to get away—that's understandable, isn't it? I read everything I could find about Montana, and the idea of living here for a year or so appealed to me. I thought... I hoped I could use these months to recharge my emotions, to mend."

"It hasn't worked, has it?"

She hung her head. "No."

"Do you know why?"

"Of course I know why!" she cried. "Meeting you has messed up everything. I wasn't in town a week and you were harassing me. Goading me. I'd be a thousand times better off if we'd never met. Now here you are, talking about loving me, and I'm so afraid I can't think straight anymore."

"Are you looking for an apology?"

"Yes," she cried, then reconsidered and slowly shook her head. "No."

"That's what I thought."

She reached for her coffee, downed a sip and set the mug back on the table. The hot liquid burned her lips and seared its way down the back of her throat. "I met Mark while I was student-teaching." She folded her arms around her waist and resumed pacing. "Between working and school I didn't have a lot of time for relationships. For the first four years of my college education, I might as well have been living in a convent."

"Why was Mark different?"

"I…don't know. I've asked myself the same question a hundred times. He was incredibly good-looking."

"Better-looking than me?" Russ challenged.

"Oh, Russ, honestly, I don't know. It isn't as if I have a barometer to gauge the level of cute."

"Okay, go on."

"There isn't much more to tell you," she said, gesturing with her hands. "We became…involved, and after a couple of months Mark brought up the idea of us living together."

Russ frowned. "I see."

Taylor was sure he didn't; nevertheless she continued. "I loved him. I truly loved him, but I couldn't seem to bring myself to move in with him. My parents are very traditional, and I'd never come face-to-face with something that contradicted my upbringing to such an extent."

"Mark wanted you to be his 'significant other'?"

"Yes. He wasn't ruling out the idea of marriage, but he wasn't willing to make a commitment to me, either, at least not then."

"Did you agree to this?"

It took Taylor a long moment to answer, and when she did, her voice was low and husky. "No. I needed time to think over the decision, and Mark agreed it was a good idea. He suggested we not see each other for a week."

"So what did you decide?"

Russ's question seemed to echo through the room. "Yes… I reached an intelligent, well-thought-out decision, but it didn't take me a week. In fact, five days was all the time I required. Having made my choice, I planned to contact Mark. I'd missed him so much that I went over to his apartment the following evening after work...." The floor seemed to buckle, and she reached out and grabbed the back of a chair. "Except that Mark wasn't alone—he was making love with a girl from the office." The pain, the humiliation of that moment, was as sharp now as it had been several months earlier. "Correction," she said in a breathy whisper. "In his words, he was 'screwing' the girl from the office. But when he was with me, he was making love."

Russ stood and walked over to her side, then drew her into his arms.

Clenching her hands in tight fists, Taylor resisted his comfort. The burning tears returned. Her breath seemed to catch in her throat and released itself with a moan. "You don't understand," she sobbed. "You don't know...no one does. No one ever asked."

"I do," Russ whispered, brushing the tendrils from her face. "You'd decided to move in with him, hadn't you?"

Sobbing and nearly hysterical, Taylor nodded.

Eleven

Every part of Russ longed to comfort Taylor. He wasn't immune to pain himself. His mother had run off and abandoned him when he was still a child. He'd been unable to understand what had driven her away, unable to understand why she hadn't taken him with her. Then, several years later, his father met and married Betty. Mandy was born and Russ was just beginning to feel secure and happy when Betty died. His father had buried himself in his grief and followed not long afterward. Russ had been left to deal with his own anguish, plus that of his young sister, who was equally lost and miserable.

Emotional pain, Russ had learned during the next few years, was a school of higher learning, a place beyond the instruction of ordinary teachers. It was where heaven sagged and earth reached up, leaving a man to find meaning, reconciliation and peace all on his own.

Taylor sobbed softly, holding him close. Russ shut his eyes. The ache he felt for this woman cut clear through his heart. Taylor had loved another man, loved him still. Someone who didn't deserve her, someone who didn't appreciate the kind of woman she was. The overwhelming need to protect her consumed him.

Lifting her head, Taylor brushed the confusion of hair from her face. "I think you should go now," she said in a voice thick with tears.

"No," he answered, his hands busy stroking her back. He couldn't leave her. Not now. Not like this.

"Please, Russ, I want to be alone. I need to be alone."

"You'll never be alone again," he promised her.

Her head drooped, and her long hair fell forward. "You don't understand, do you? I can't... I *won't* become involved with you. I'm here to teach, and at the end of my contract I'm leaving. And when I do, I don't want there to be any regrets."

"There won't be. I promise you." Russ tried to reassure her, but when he bent to kiss her, she broke away from him and skittered over to the other side of the kitchen, as if that distance would keep her safe.

"It would be so easy to let myself fall in love with you," she whispered. "So easy..."

Witnessing her pain was nearly Russ's undoing. He moved toward her, but for every step he advanced, she retreated two. He hesitated. "All I want to do is love you."

"No," she said firmly, holding out her arm as if that should stop him. Russ found little humor in her pathetic attempt. *He* wasn't the one who'd cheated on her. He wasn't the one who'd abused her love and her trust. And he damn well refused to be punished for the sins of another.

"Taylor, listen to me."

"No," she said with surprising strength. "There isn't anyone to blame but me. From the moment you and I met I realized we were in trouble, and we've both behaved like fools ever since. Me more than you. I've said it once, and apparently you didn't believe me, so I'm saying it again. I don't *want* to become involved with you."

"You're already involved."

"I'm not—not yet, anyway. Please, don't make this any more difficult than it already is. I'm not asking you this time. I'm telling you. If you care about me, if you have any feelings toward me whatsoever, you'll forget you ever knew me, forget we ever met."

Her words seemed to encircle his heart and then tighten like barbed wire. If he cared for her? He was crazy in love with her! His breath felt frozen in his chest.

"Am I supposed to forget I held you and kissed you, too?"

She nodded wildly. "Yes!"

Russ rubbed the back of his neck while he contemplated her words. "I don't think I can forget."

"You've got to," she said, and her shoulders heaved with each pleading syllable. "You have to."

Walking out on her then would have been like taking a branding iron and burning his own flesh. Despite everything she'd claimed, and asked for, Russ walked to her side, took her by the shoulders and pulled her against him. She fought him as though he was the one responsible for hurting her so terribly. As if he was the one who'd betrayed her.

Her fists beat against him, but he felt no pain. None. Nothing could hurt him as much as her words.

Gripping her by the wrists, he pinned her hands behind her back. She glared up at him, her eyes spitting fire. "Why do you have to make this so difficult? Why?"

"Because I don't give up easily. I never have." He raised his hand and glided his fingertips over the soft contours of her face. He traced her stern, unyielding mouth, and with his hand at the small of her back, pressed her forward until her body was perfectly molded to his. Then he buried his face in her sweet-smelling hair and inhaled deeply.

"Russ," she pleaded, bending her head to one side, "don't do this."

He answered by sliding his mouth over hers. His hand freed her wrists as he held her against him. The fight had gone out of her, and her arms crept up his chest, pausing at his shoulders, her nails digging hard into his muscles. But Russ still felt no pain.

A moment later, she pulled away from him, looking into his eyes. "Do I have to walk out on my contract, pack my bags and leave town to convince you I mean it?" she asked. "Is that what it's going to take?"

"If you want me out of your life, just say so," Russ said, shoving his hands in his pockets.

"What do you think I've been trying to do for the past weeks? Stay away from me, Russ! I've got to get my head straightened out. I'm not ready to fall in love again, not with you, not with anyone. I can't deal with this—with you—right now. I may not be able to for a long time."

"All right," he said gruffly. "I get the message. Loud and clear." He stalked out of the kitchen, paused long enough in the living room to reach for his hat and then he was gone.

But as he closed the door, he heard Taylor's sobs. He

forced himself to walk away from her, but he hesitated on the porch and sagged against the pillar. Regret and pain worked through him before he was able to move.

Once more he had to find meaning, reconciliation and peace in the aftermath of pain.

"Cody Franklin just pulled into the yard," Mandy told Russ as though that was earth-shattering news.

Russ grumbled something in reply, and his muscles tensed involuntarily. If Cody was stopping by to talk, Russ knew what—who—the subject was bound to be.

Taylor.

"I don't understand you," Mandy said, clearly at the end of her wits. "Why don't you just call Taylor and put an end to this nonsense? You've been walking around like a wounded bear all week."

"When I need your advice, I'll ask for it," Russ bit out, and stood up so fast, he nearly toppled the kitchen chair. "Stay out of it, Amanda. This is between me and Taylor."

"She obviously isn't doing any better. She called in sick twice this week."

"How many times are you going to tell me that?" Russ muttered. "It doesn't change the situation. She doesn't want anything to do with me. If and when she does, she'll contact me. Until then it's as if we never met."

"Oh, that's real smart," Mandy said, her fists digging into her hips. "You're so miserable, it's like having a thundercloud hanging over our lives. You love Taylor and she loves you, so what's the problem?"

"If Taylor feels anything for me, which I sincerely doubt, she'll let *me* know. Until then I have nothing to say to her." It gnawed at him to admit it, but the truth was the truth, no matter how many different ways he chose to examine it. Taylor had claimed she wanted nothing to do with him often enough for him to believe her. He had no other choice.

"Save me from stubborn men," Mandy groaned, as she headed for the door, pulling it open for Russ's friend.

"Howdy, Amanda," Cody Franklin said as he walked into the kitchen. He removed his cap and tucked it under his arm. He was dressed in his uniform—green shirt and coat and tan slacks. His gunbelt rode low on his hips.

"Hello, Cody." Mandy craned her neck toward Russ. "I hope you've come to talk some sense into my bull-headed brother."

Cody seemed uneasy. "I'll try."

Mandy left the two of them alone, a fact for which Russ was grateful. He didn't need a letter of introduction to deduce the reason for his friend's latest visit. One look at Cody confirmed what Russ had already guessed. The deputy had stopped by as a courtesy before going out with Taylor himself.

"So you intend to ask her for a date?" Russ forestalled the exchange of chitchat that would eventually lead to the subject of Taylor.

Cody's eyes just managed to avoid Russ's.

"Frankly, Cody, you don't need my permission. Taylor is her own woman, and if she wants to date you that's her business, not mine."

Having said as much, Russ should have felt relieved, but he didn't. He'd been in a rotten mood from the moment he'd left Taylor's nearly a week before, and Cody's coming by unannounced hadn't improved his disposition any.

Cody must have sensed his mood, because he gave Russ a wide berth. He walked over to the cupboard, brought down a mug and poured himself coffee before he turned to face Russ.

"Sit down," Russ snarled. "I'm not going to bite your head off."

Cody grinned at that, and it occurred to Russ that Cougar Point's deputy sheriff wasn't bad-looking. Handsome enough to stir any woman's fickle heart. Plenty of women were interested in him, but he took his duties so seriously that no romantic relationship lasted more than a couple of months. Cody Franklin didn't smile very often, and Russ thought he knew why.

The two men went back a long way, and Russ didn't want their friendship to end because of one stubborn woman. "You're planning on asking Taylor out, aren't you?" he demanded when Cody didn't immediately respond.

Cody joined Russ at the table. "Actually, I wasn't going to do anything of the kind. I asked her once already, and she turned me down. I figured she wasn't interested, so I was willing to leave it at that."

"Then why are you here?"

"Because she phoned the other day and asked *me* to dinner Friday night." He paused to rub the side of his jaw. "I don't mind telling you, I was taken aback by that. I've never had a woman ask me for a date."

"What did you tell her?"

Cody looked uncomfortable. "I said I needed some time to think it over."

"So Taylor's the one who called you?" Russ was surprised his voice sounded so normal.

"I've never had a woman approach me like this," Cody went on to say a second time. "I'm not sure I like it, either. It puts me in one hell of a position." He twisted the mug around in his hands, as though he couldn't locate the handle. "From what she said, I assume she intends to pay, too. I've never had a woman pay for my meal yet, and I'm not about to start now."

"Don't blame you for that," Russ felt obliged to say, although he couldn't help being slightly amused. He didn't need a script to realize what Taylor was doing. She'd asked Cody Franklin to dinner to prove something to herself and possibly to him.

"You've got feelings for her, haven't you?" Cody asked, eyeing him suspiciously.

"You could say that," Russ confirmed, understating his emotions by a country mile. He had feelings, all right, but he wasn't willing to discuss them with his friend.

Cody grinned, revealing even white teeth. Crow's-feet crinkled at the corners of his eyes. "So, what do you want me to say to her?"

"That you'll be happy to let her buy you dinner."

Cody hesitated before taking a sip of his coffee. "You don't mean that," he finally said.

"Yes, I do. In fact, I've never been more serious in my life."

"But—"

"Taylor Manning doesn't want anything to do with me."

"And you believe her?"

Russ shrugged. "The way I see it, I don't have any

choice. If she wants to go out with you, fine. That's her decision."

Cody shook his head. "I can't believe I heard you right."

"You did. Trust me, dealing with this woman isn't easy."

Cody set his half-finished coffee on the table and stood. "Okay, but I have the feeling you're going to regret this."

Cody Franklin was as nice a man as Taylor had ever met. And a gentleman to boot. He arrived promptly at seven, dressed in a suit and tie. He really was handsome. Considerate. And Taylor was badly in need of some tender loving care. She'd just spent the most miserable week of her life, and an evening with a man who didn't pose the slightest emotional threat was exactly what she needed to pull herself out of this slump. At least that was what she kept telling herself.

"I hope I'm not too early," Cody said, stepping inside and glancing around. Apparently he approved of what he saw, because he gave her a smile.

"No, this is perfect." She reached for her coat, but Cody took it from her hands and held it for her so she could slip it on. With a murmured thanks, she picked up her purse.

"Before we leave," he began, then cleared his throat, "there's something I'd like understood. If we go to dinner, I pay the tab."

"But I invited you," Taylor reminded him, somewhat surprised at the vehemence with which he spoke.

"I pay or we don't go."

Taylor couldn't see any point in arguing. She'd en-

countered enough stubborn male pride with Russ to
know it wasn't going to do her any good. "If you insist."

"I do."

Once that was resolved, they managed to carry on a
pleasant conversation while Cody drove to the restaurant. He'd chosen Larry's Place, the one halfway decent
eating establishment in town. Taylor hadn't eaten there
before, but she'd heard the food was good—and the
company was exemplary. For the first time in a week
she found herself smiling and talkative.

The hostess escorted them to a table, and they were
handed menus. It took Taylor only a moment to decide.
Her appetite had been nonexistent for days, and she
was determined to enjoy this evening no matter what.

"Hello, Cody. Taylor."

Russ's voice came at her like a blast of cold air. She
drew in a deep breath before turning toward the man
who'd dominated her thoughts all week. "Hello, Russ,"
she said coolly.

"Russ," Cody said, standing. The two exchanged
handshakes. "Good to see you again, Mary Lu."

"Have you met Taylor Manning?" Russ asked his
date. His hand was casually draped over the other woman's shoulder as he smiled down on her. "Taylor's the
new schoolteacher."

"Pleased to meet you," Mary Lu said, and she actually sounded as if she was.

Taylor smiled and nodded. The woman didn't reveal
a single shred of jealousy, she mused darkly. Surely by
now everyone in town knew there was something going
on between her and Russ. The least the other woman
could do was look a little anxious. But then, why should

she? Mary Lu was the one with Russ. Taylor was with Cody Franklin.

Cody reclaimed his seat. "Would you two care to join us?"

Taylor's heart shot upward and seemed to lodge in her throat. Seeing Russ accompanied by another woman was painful enough without having to make polite conversation with them for the rest of the evening.

"Another time," Russ said. His thoughts apparently reflected her own.

Taylor was so grateful, she nearly leaped from her chair to thank him with a kiss. It wasn't until he'd left the table that she realized how tense she was. Smiling in Cody's direction, she forced herself to relax. Elbows on the table, she leaned toward her date. "So how long have you been in law enforcement?"

"Since I graduated from college," he answered, but his concentration wasn't on her. Instead, his gaze followed Russ and Mary Lu to the other side of the restaurant.

His frown disturbed her. "Is something wrong?" she asked.

"I don't know yet."

Taylor sighed. This whole evening was a mistake. She'd phoned and asked Cody to dinner for two reasons. The first and foremost was simply because she was lonely, and the thought of spending another weekend alone was more than she could bear. The second was to prove that... She was no longer sure what she'd hoped to accomplish.

Cody sipped his water. "You're in love with him, aren't you?"

This man certainly didn't pull any punches. The

least he could've done was lead into the subject of Russ
Palmer with a little more tact. Taylor considered pretending she didn't know what he was talking about, but
that would've been ridiculous.

She lowered her gaze to the tablecloth. "I don't know
if I love him or not."

"What's there to know? I saw the look in your eyes
just now. Russ walked in with Mary Lu, and I swear
you nearly keeled over."

"You're wrong. I was mildly surprised, that's all."

"It doesn't bother you that he's with Mary Lu?"

She managed a casual shrug. "Not really. I wasn't
expecting to see him. If I reacted, which I don't think
I did, it was due to that and that alone."

"So what are you going to do about it?"

"Do about what?"

"The way you feel for Russ."

"I'm not going to do anything." She didn't need time
to make that decision; it had been made weeks earlier. All the arguments she'd put forth, time and again,
crowded her mind. All the reasons a relationship with
him couldn't work... Yet she couldn't turn her eyes
away from Russ, couldn't stop gazing at him with an
emotional hunger that left her trembling.

"He loves you, too," Cody whispered. He reached
across the table and took hold of her hand. "I don't know
what drove you two apart, but I'm here to tell you right
now, it's eating him alive." His smile was gentle, concerned. "It seems to be having the same effect on you."

"It's not that simple," she whispered.

A long moment passed before Cody spoke again.
"Nothing worthwhile ever is."

* * *

"Taylor, do you realize what time it is?" her sister, Christy, groaned after she answered the phone on the fifth ring.

"I'm sorry... I should've checked," Taylor said, feeling utterly foolish and completely miserable.

Christy yawned loudly. "It's three in the morning! Why are you phoning at this hour? Are you all right? You're not in trouble, are you?"

If only Christy knew! "I...was calling to see if you were going to be free next weekend."

"Are you flying home? Oh, Taylor, it would be so good to see you. I can't believe how much I miss you. Paul, Jason and Rich, too. Mom and Dad don't say much, but know they feel the same way."

"No, but I'll be in Reno, and I thought that, well... I was hoping I could talk you into joining me. There are a bunch of cheap flights out of Sea-Tac and I thought maybe you could meet me in Nevada."

Christy slowly released her breath. "I can't. I'm really sorry, but I can't possibly swing it at this late date. What will you be doing in Reno?"

"Nothing much. The drill team is competing there, and I volunteered to be a chaperone—but apparently the team will be busy for two days and I'm going to have a lot of time to kill. I thought it would be fun if we got together."

"All right, Taylor," Christy said after a moment. "What's wrong? And don't try to tell me *nothing*. The last time you called me at three in the morning was when... I'm sure you remember."

"This doesn't have anything to do with Mark."

"Thank God for that." Her voice lowered slightly with concern. "What's wrong, then?"

Taylor reached for a tissue and blew her nose loudly. "I…think I'm in love."

Christy groaned again. "You've got to be kidding. Who?"

"His name is Russ Palmer and he owns a cattle ranch."

"I was afraid of that. I read your last letter to Mom and Dad and it was full of that cowboy! It was Russ this and Mandy that. Taylor, get control of yourself. You don't want to spend the rest of your life on a ranch out in the wilds of Montana, do you?"

"Of course not!" Taylor sobbed. "The last thing I intended to do was fall in love—especially with someone who thinks just like Dad."

"Your cowboy believes women shouldn't have the right to vote?" Christy asked, aghast.

Taylor started to laugh even while she was crying. "He said he doesn't care if we vote. It's females holding public office that bothers him." She paused. "He knows how much I hate it when he says stuff like that. He does it to get a rise out of me and it works every time."

She could hear Christy taking a deep breath and imagined her mentally counting to ten. "Listen, Taylor, you're my sister and my dearest friend. What you feel isn't love. It's a natural and common emotion following the breakup of any romance."

"That's what I thought…at first."

"You were right. For most of your life your judgment was totally sound. Nothing's changed all that much. So you made a mistake with Mark. So what? But when you come out of a long-term relationship, there's an emptiness and the normal reaction is to immediately find someone to fill it."

"I don't think that applies in this case," Taylor argued. In the beginning she'd assumed the same thing, but not anymore. This ache she felt went deeper than anything she'd ever experienced.

"You've spent the past six weeks in a town where no one even accepts American Express," Christy reminded her. "Taylor, this thing with the cowboy is all due to what happened with Mark. You're away from your family. You're lonely and vulnerable, and it's only natural to find yourself attracted to another man. I know I would be if the situations were reversed."

"You would?"

"Of course," Christy said smoothly and with conviction. "Just hold on for another week, and once you're in Reno, where there are real stores and real people, you can reevaluate your feelings. I'm sure being there will help clear your mind."

"Do you honestly think so?"

"I know so," Christy said without the least qualm. "Now take two aspirin, go to bed and call me next week when you get back from Reno. Ten to one, you're going to feel a lot different than you do tonight."

"Okay," Taylor said. After a few more minutes she replaced the receiver, convinced her sister was right.

The next week flew past, the days blending as Taylor threw herself into her job. Friday afternoon, her suitcase packed, she headed for the school bus and the twenty girls who comprised the Cougar Point High School Drill Team.

The first girl she saw was Mandy, who flew across

the yard and hugged Taylor close. "I'm so glad you're going with us."

"Me, too," Taylor said, meaning it.

Mandy reached for Taylor's suitcase, setting it beside the others. "Everyone's here except the driver." She paused and rolled her eyes. "But then he's always late."

The girls gathered around Taylor, and soon they were chatting away like old friends. Taylor knew many of the team members as well as their coach.

"Everyone ready?" a male voice called out.

Taylor recognized it immediately as Russ's. She swallowed and turned toward him, frowning. "What are you doing here?" she demanded.

He tossed one suitcase into the compartment on the side of the bus and then another. "The same thing as you," he said without the least animosity. "You're a chaperone, and I happen to be driving the bus."

Twelve

It wasn't the twenty boisterous, exuberant high school girls who were driving Russ crazy. They sang, they cheered and they shouted as he drove the school bus across three states.

No, it wasn't the girls—it was Taylor. Taylor, who laughed and sang. Taylor, who joked and teased as if she hadn't a care in the world.

Each and every one of those girls adored her. The problem was, so did Russ.

Other than their brief exchange before they'd boarded the bus, she hadn't said more than a handful of words to him. True, there hadn't been a lot of opportunity. They'd stopped in Billings for something to eat and she'd sat in a booth surrounded by teenagers. Russ had eaten with Carol Fischer, the drill team coach, and another of the chaperones. Carol and he had exchanged a few pleasantries, but the entire time they were eating, Russ had found his gaze drawn again and again to the table next to his where Taylor was seated.

He would've liked nothing better than to get Taylor alone for a few hours. Then, and only then, would he have the chance to talk some sense into that stubborn head of hers.

Okay, she'd gone and fallen in love with the wrong man. Everyone made an error in judgment at some point, but that was in the past and Russ was very much part of the present. Although he told himself this a hundred different times and in as many different ways, the thought of Taylor aching, wanting, crying over another man felt like a knife slicing deep into his heart. It hurt so much that for a moment he couldn't breathe normally. Hell, he hadn't been breathing normally from the second he'd stumbled upon Taylor in the five-and-dime last September.

The long, lonely miles sped past. The girls gave up singing even before they left Montana. Around midnight the only one on the bus who wasn't sleeping was Russ.

"Do you want some coffee?"

Taylor's soft voice behind him sounded like an angel's, Russ thought gratefully.

"Russ?"

"Please." He waited to speak until she'd poured him some from the thermos she carried and he'd sipped it, appreciating the way it revived him. "I figured everyone was asleep."

"They are."

"What's keeping you awake?" He'd love it if she admitted he'd been in her thoughts for two desolate weeks and that she couldn't let another hour pass, or even another second, without telling him how she felt.

"I never could sleep in a moving vehicle."

"Oh," he said, trying to disguise his disappointment. He should know by now that Taylor wasn't going to fulfill his fantasies by saying all the things he longed to hear.

"How have you been?"

They'd barely said a word to each other in two weeks, he mused darkly, frowning, and she was asking about his health!

Briefly he wondered what she'd say if he told her he wasn't sleeping well, his mood was sour and he couldn't sit down to a single meal without suffering indigestion afterward. All these ailments he attributed entirely to her stubbornness.

"I'm fine," he said instead. "How about you?"

"Fine, just fine."

"Now we've got that settled, what else would you like to talk about? The weather seems a safe enough subject, doesn't it?"

"I...I think I'll go back and check on the girls."

"You do that," he muttered, then immediately wanted to kick himself for being such an idiot. At least Taylor had been willing to talk to him, which was a lot better than the strained silence that had existed between them up to this point.

It wasn't until midafternoon the following day that they pulled into the congested streets of Reno. The girls were leaning out the windows, shouting at tourists, while Carol and the other adults attempted to calm their rampant enthusiasm.

Carol and Russ had traded off driving, but like Taylor, Russ didn't sleep well in a moving vehicle. He leaned back, shoved his hat low over his face and did a fair job of pretending, but he hadn't slept a wink in over twenty-four hours.

When Russ pulled in to the parking garage at Circus

Circus, the hotel where they were booked, he heaved
a giant sigh of relief. He was exhausted, mentally and
physically. With the help of two bellboys, he unloaded
the ton of luggage the girls had found indispensable
for this short trip. While he was busy with that, Carol
and the other chaperones, accompanied by the entire
drill team, checked in. As soon as he was finished,
Carol handed him his room key and suggested he get
some sleep.

Russ didn't need to be told twice. He practically fell
asleep in the elevator on the way up to his floor. Taylor
and several of the girls rode with him, and just before
he entered his room, Russ saw that she'd been assigned
one on the same floor.

Some of his tiredness vanished when he discovered
that Taylor would be sleeping down the hall from him.
Not bothering to unpack his bag he tossed his hat onto
the small table and collapsed on top of the bed. Bunching up the pillow, he closed his eyes and savored the
quiet, the peace. It wasn't until sleep began to over-
take his mind that he realized he had two whole days
in which to convince Taylor she loved him.

Taylor couldn't remember a time when she'd been
more exhausted. Other than brief stops, the bus had
spent nearly twenty hours on the road, and she hadn't
gotten more than a catnap the entire distance. Carol,
bless her heart, had insisted Taylor go upstairs to bed
while she and the assistant coach managed the girls.
Taylor didn't offer a single argument.

From the moment they pulled in to the hotel, the
girls' schedule was packed. In less than two hours they
were meeting several other out-of-state teams, who

would also be competing the following day, for a social. Then, first thing the next morning, Carol would be
driving the drill team to a local high school and they'd
be there the entire day until their performance, which
was scheduled late that evening. After a good night's
sleep, they'd be back on the road again, heading home
to Montana.

Yawning, Taylor ran a tub of hot bathwater and
soaked in it, struggling to stay awake. When she got
out, she crawled between clean, crisp sheets, already
half-asleep.

There was noise and confusion around her for part of
the time, since her room adjoined one with teenagers,
but she hardly noticed. She woke at eight the next morning, just in time to see the team off and wish them well.

"You're coming to watch us, aren't you?" Mandy
pleaded.

"Wild horses couldn't keep me away," Taylor promised.

"Do you think Russ will want to come?"

Taylor nodded. "I'm sure of it."

Beaming, Mandy hugged Taylor and then rushed to
join her teammates.

Once the Cougar Point High School Drill Team had
departed the hotel, Taylor wandered downstairs to the
casino, where most of the gambling took place. Bells
jingled incessantly and smoke rose like a sacrificial offering to the unpredictable gods of chance and good fortune. Row upon row of slot machines lined the brightest,
reddest carpeting Taylor had ever seen.

She'd never gambled much, but the excitement that
crackled through the room lured her toward the slot
machines.

Trading her hard-earned cash for several rolls of nickels, she grabbed a plastic container and picked out a one-armed bandit at the end of a long row of identical machines.

"A fool and her money are soon parted," she muttered, seating herself on a stool.

She inserted three nickels and gingerly pulled down on the handle. Oranges, plums and cherries whirled past in a blur, then came to an abrupt halt.

Nothing.

She tried again and again and was rewarded by several minor wins. Two nickels here, ten there.

Someone slid onto the stool next to hers, and when she glanced over, a ready smile on her lips, her eyes clashed with Russ's. He looked well-rested and so devastatingly handsome that her breath jammed in her throat. The lazy grin he gave her was more potent than any of the free drinks she could have ordered.

"How are you doing?" he asked.

"Fine…good, really good." She plopped three more coins into the appropriate slot and pulled the lever with enough energy to dismantle the machine.

"How much have you won?"

She looked down at the small pile of nickels.

"Actually, I think I'm out a couple of bucks."

He grinned. "I'm down about the same. I don't suppose I could talk you into having some breakfast with me? You wouldn't consider that a breach of protocol, would you?"

"I… That would be fine." Taylor didn't know how a grown woman, a college graduate and teaching professional, could be so flustered around one man. The way her heart was jitterbugging inside her chest, anyone might assume Russ had asked her to join him in bed instead of in a restaurant.

Neither of them appeared to have much to say until they'd been seated by the hostess and handed menus.

Russ chose quickly and set his aside. "So how did your dinner with Cody Franklin go last weekend?"

"Cody's a wonderful man," she answered, glancing over her menu. Their eyes met briefly and she quickly switched her gaze back to the list of breakfast entrées.

"So you plan on seeing him again?" Russ demanded. Then he shook his head. "I'm sorry. I didn't have any right to ask you that. Whom you choose to date is your business."

Actually, she'd decided against dating Cody again, but not because she hadn't enjoyed his company. He'd been polite and gentlemanly all evening. After they'd left the restaurant, she'd invited him in for coffee and he'd accepted, but to her dismay their entire conversation then, as it had through most of dinner, centered on Russ. Cody hadn't kissed her good-night, nor had he asked her out again. Why should he? Taylor mused. She'd spent the evening with one man, while longing to be with another.

The waitress came by for their order and filled their coffee cups. Taylor took a sip of hers, and decided if Russ could question her, she should feel free to inquire about his own evening out. She carefully returned her cup to the saucer. "How was your dinner with Mary Lu Randall?"

"Great," Russ answered. "She's a lovely woman. Interesting, fun to be with, thoughtful…"

Taylor's throat constricted painfully as she nodded.

Everything Russ said was true. Mary Lu Randall was known as a generous, unassuming woman.

"I won't be seeing her again, though," Russ muttered, drinking his coffee.

Despite everything she'd hoped to prove to this man, Taylor sighed with relief. "You won't? Why not?"

Russ set his coffee cup down hard enough to attract attention, and several heads turned in their direction. Russ glanced apologetically at those around him.

"Why?" he asked in a heated whisper. "Do you honestly need me to explain the reason I won't be dating Mary Lu again?" He threw his head back and glared at the ceiling. "Because I'm in love with you is *why*. In addition, you've ruined me for just about any other woman I might happen to meet."

"I've ruined you?" she echoed vehemently. She leaned toward him, managing to keep her voice low enough not to attract further attention.

The waitress delivered their meals, and Russ dug into his fried eggs as though he hadn't eaten in a week. He'd eaten both eggs before Taylor had finished spreading jelly across her toast, which she did with jagged, awkward movements.

"I would've thought Mary Lu was perfect for you," she said, unwilling to let the subject drop. "She's sweet and gentle and *deferential,* and we both know how important that is to a man of your persuasion."

"I used to think that was what I wanted until I met you." He stabbed his fork into his fried potatoes. "I'll be damned if you didn't ruin me for decent women."

"Ruined you for decent women?" Taylor cried, not caring whose attention she drew.

"That's right. *You.* This is all your fault. No woman

ever challenged me and dared me the way you do, and I'm having one heck of a hard time adjusting. Compared to you, every other woman has the appeal of watered-down soup." He jammed his index finger against the top of the table before continuing. "Mary Lu's one of the nicest women in Cougar Point, and any man she married would consider himself lucky."

"But it won't be you," Taylor stated, hating the way her heart gladdened at that.

"How can it be when I'm crazy about you?"

The irritation drained out of Taylor as quickly as it had risen. She set her slice of toast aside and dropped her eyes, suddenly close to tears. "I wish you wouldn't say that."

"Why? Because you don't like hearing it? Fine, I won't say it again, but that isn't going to change a thing. If you want to put us both through this hell, then go ahead. There's nothing I can do to stop you. But I love you, Taylor, and like I said, that's not going to change."

"But I don't *want* you to love me."

"Don't you think I know that? Trust me, lady, if I had any choice in the matter, you'd be the last woman I'd fall in love with. Do you honestly believe I need this aggravation in my life? If so, guess again."

"There's no need to be angry."

Russ pushed his near-empty plate aside and downed the last of his coffee in a single gulp, apparently doing his best to ignore her.

"Thank you for breakfast," Taylor said, pushing her own plate aside after a moment. She'd only managed a few bites of egg. The toast she'd so carefully spread with jelly remained untouched.

"You're welcome." Leaning back in his chair, Russ

rubbed a hand over his eyes. When he dropped his hand, it was clear that he was forcing himself to put their disagreement behind him. He smiled. "What are your plans for today?"

"The first thing I'm going to do is shop. There's a fingernail hardener with epoxy that I need to find," she said, glancing down at her carefully groomed nails. "Not a single store in Cougar Point carries it."

"Don't they use epoxy in glue?" Russ frowned as he stared down at her hands. "If you want to go putting that stuff on your pretty nails, far be it from me to stop you."

"Thank you," she said graciously, resisting the urge to roll her eyes. "After that, I thought, since I was in town, I'd pick up a few other things for the sheer joy of using my American Express card."

Russ chuckled. "Would you mind if I tagged along?"

"Of course not," she said promptly. She didn't mind. In fact—perversely—the prospect delighted her.

Over the past few weeks and all the disagreements, Taylor had forgotten what pleasant company Russ could be. He was good-natured and patient to a fault as she dragged him from one store to the next. He was more than tolerant while she tried on a series of dresses, and after she chose one, he went with her to the shoe department and helped her pick out a comfortable pair of heels.

Taylor tried to return the favor and help him choose new work shirts. Russ seemed to be of the opinion that if he found one shirt that suited him, he might as well buy five exactly like it. Taylor made a concerted effort to convince him otherwise.

"Where would you like to go for lunch?" Russ asked four hours later. His arms were loaded with a large number of bags and packages as he led the way down the street.

"Since you asked," Taylor said, smiling up at him, "I'm dying for a good pepperoni pizza, only—"

"Only what?"

"Only my favorite pizza chain doesn't have inside seating."

Russ looked at her as if she were deranged. "How do they do business then?"

"It's take-out and delivery only."

"All right," he said, mulling over this information. "Then I suggest we go back to the hotel. You can drop off the packages in your room while I phone and order a large pepperoni pizza."

Taylor agreed without realizing what she'd done until it was too late. After returning to her room, she piled her shopping on the double bed, then sat on the edge while she considered this latest development. She'd agreed to join Russ in his room. In the middle of the day. With no one else around.

Walking into the bathroom, she ran a brush through her hair. She toyed with the idea of finding an excuse, phoning Russ's room and canceling the whole thing. The hotel was filled with restaurants. The food was good and so reasonably priced it was a shame to order out.

Taylor slumped against the bathroom sink and closed her eyes dejectedly. Who was she kidding? Certainly not herself. She was in love with Russ and had been for weeks. They had no business falling in love, but it had happened, and instead of fighting it she should be grateful. Her attitude should be one of thanksgiving that she'd come across a man as fundamentally honest as Russ. There was no comparison to Mark, none whatsoever.

Five minutes later, she knocked on Russ's door. He let her in but had obviously been having second thoughts of his own. He marched to the other side of the room as though he feared she was carrying some dangerous virus.

"I phoned that pizza place and ordered," he said, apparently trying to sound casual. He tucked his hands into his pockets as if he suddenly didn't know what to do with them. "They said they'd be here in thirty minutes or less." He checked his watch. "That gives them nearly twenty-five minutes."

"Good," Taylor said, walking farther into the room. His was almost identical to her own. One queen-size bed, a dresser, one small table and two chairs.

"Make yourself at home," he said, pulling over a chair. Then he walked around the bed, averting his eyes.

"That was quite a morning we had, wasn't it?" he asked, rubbing his palms together. Heaving a sigh, he whirled around and faced her. "Listen, Taylor, this isn't going to work. If you want to have your pizza, fine, but I've got to get out of here."

"You don't have to leave," she said as she sauntered across the room, making sure her hips swayed just a fraction more than normal. When she turned to look at Russ, she was well rewarded for the little extra she'd put into her walk. His jaw was tight, and the edges of his mouth had whitened. His hands were knotted into fists at his sides.

"I…don't think you understand," Russ said faintly.

She moved close so that she was almost directly in front of him. Standing on her toes, she raised her arms and slid them around his neck, then molded her body against his.

Russ held himself completely rigid. Then he brought up his hands and closed them around her wrists, ready to pull her away from him. For some reason he hesitated. His gaze was hot and questioning when it locked with hers. "Just what kind of game are you playing?"

"The seductress. How am I doing?"

His gaze narrowed, and she noted that his breathing had become ragged. "Good. Too good."

He gazed down on her, his look a mixture of doubt and wonder. "Do you love me?" he asked.

She found herself lost, the words confusing her before they even reached her lips. Before she could tell him everything, before she could explain what was in her heart, Russ sighed and hauled her back in his arms.

His hands were in her hair, and his mouth was seeking hers. "It doesn't matter," he whispered brokenly. "I love you enough for both of us. It doesn't matter," he said again, just before his hungry lips claimed hers.

The passion between them was explosive. Tears clouded her eyes and fell down her face without restraint. But these were tears of joy, tears of thanksgiving and discovery, surging from deep within.

"I love you, I love you," she chanted silently as she felt the tremors that went through Russ. He pulled her against him and held on as if he'd jerked her from the jaws of death and feared losing her a second time.

For the longest moment he didn't move.

"Russ?" she whispered. "What's wrong?"

The merest hint of a smile turned up the corners of his mouth. He leaned forward and with infinite care he brushed the hair from her brow. His callused, work-roughened hands had begun to shake.

"Russ?" she repeated, growing alarmed. Her hands framed his face, and he dragged one palm across his cheek to his lips and kissed the inside of her hand.

"I need to explain something first," he whispered, and the words seemed to be pulled from the farthest reaches of his soul. "If we make love now, there'll be no turning back."

Taylor blinked. She heard the desperation in his voice and read the havoc in his handsome face.

Her own mind was reeling, her thoughts jumbled. Had she been able to speak, her words would have made no sense.

Russ lowered his mouth to hers, but his kiss was featherlight. "Look at me," he whispered. "I want you so much I'm shaking like a newborn calf. All these weeks I've dreamed of this moment, of making you mine, and when the time arrives, I discover… I can't."

Not according to the evidence pressing against her thigh. Taylor didn't know a delicate, or even indelicate, way of mentioning the fact.

"I know your career is important to you, and it should be. You worked too hard for your education to give it up now," he said.

"That's r-right," Taylor returned, puzzled.

Holding her hand in his own, Russ whispered, "And another thing…"

"There's more?"

"Lots more," he said, grinning down at her. His mouth brushed hers in a lazy, affectionate kiss. "I know you haven't come to appreciate Cougar Point yet, but that's all right. I promise you will in time. There's something about standing outside on a crisp autumn night and seeing the moonlight through the branches. Or hearing the crunch of snow under your boots in winter. In spring it's newborn animals, the smell of the earth and the rush of wind as it blows over the treetops. Those are the things I love most."

Taylor frowned in confusion. Her hands went back to his face and she studied him, seeking some meaning to his words. "Why are you telling me all this?"

"Because I want you to love my home as much as I do. I want you to love the country. Cougar Point will never rival Seattle. It won't even rival Reno, but it's a good place to live, a good place to raise a family."

Taylor had no argument with that. None. From the first, she'd seen how strong the sense of family was in this small community. "In the beginning I was so lost. Moving to Montana was like visiting a foreign country. Time seemed to have been turned back thirty years."

"What about ranch life?"

Again she wasn't sure what he was asking. "In many ways it's beautiful. I never thought I could say that and mean it. At first all I saw was the harshness of the land, and how unforgiving it could be. I saw how hard you and the others work. How busy you are. I learned a little about the problems and wondered why anyone would bother when ranching's such a demanding way of life."

"And now?"

"Now…there's still a great deal I don't understand about your kind of life, and I probably never will, but I see the contentment of knowing you've worked hard." She hesitated, surprised at how well-formed her thoughts actually were since she'd never voiced them before. "I moved to Cougar Point looking for one thing and found something else entirely. In the past few weeks I've learned what's important in life and what isn't."

Russ smiled and rewarded her with a lengthy kiss. "Now that we've got that subject all cleared up, I want you to know that I consider babies a woman's business...."

Bracing her hands against his chest, Taylor lifted her head. "What are you talking about? Honestly, Russ, I have no idea where this conversation is going."

His mouth dropped open. "You don't?"

She shook her head.

"Good grief, I thought you knew all along. I'm asking you to marry me."

Thirteen

"Marriage!" Taylor said, stunned. "You're joking."

"Trust me, a man doesn't joke about something like this."

All at once Taylor's knees didn't feel as if they would support her anymore, and she slumped onto the bed. Breathless and light-headed. She held her hand over her heart in an effort to calm its erratic beating, but that didn't seem to help.

"Taylor, what's wrong?" Russ knelt in front of her and took both her hands in his own. "You look like you're about to faint."

"Don't be ridiculous."

"What's wrong?"

She pointed at his door. "When I walked into this room, I wasn't thinking about getting married. Not for a second."

"Do you mean to say you came here after my body? Well, and the pizza, of course," he added with a laugh.

"Your body? Don't go all righteous on me," she muttered. "You've been after mine for weeks."

"I've reconsidered," Russ said with infuriating calm.

"I want more than an occasional tumble with you. A whole lot more."

"Isn't marriage carrying this a little too far?"

"No. Is it so wrong to want to wake up with you at my side?"

"You shouldn't hit a woman with this kind of talk. I'm not prepared for it." She pulled her hands from his and waved them dramatically. "Out of the blue he starts talking about marriage."

Russ ignored her outburst and sat beside her on the bed. "When I come into the house after a hard day's work, it's you I want to find."

Taylor's gaze narrowed. "I suppose it's me you want cooking your dinner and laundering your clothes!"

"Yes," he said matter-of-factly. "Because I'll have spent the past twelve or more hours building a good life for us. But if washing a load of clothes bothers you so much, I'll bring someone in. I'm not marrying you for your domestic talents."

He was serious. "Russ," she whispered, running her hands down his face, "marriage isn't something we should discuss now. Let's talk about it later...much, much later." Leaning forward, she slanted her mouth over his. Russ resisted her at first but quickly surrendered. His response was gratifying.

He wrapped his arms around her, and his returning kiss was urgent, charged with unleashed passion. As their kissing intensified, Russ eased her onto the bed and positioned himself above her.

"Taylor..." He lifted his head and groaned. He looked like a man who didn't know what to do, a man trapped in one world, seeking entrance to another. His eyes were shut.

Taylor had no answers to give him. All she knew was that she was tired of fighting this feeling, tired of living a life filled with denial. She hadn't meant to fall in love with Russ Palmer, but she had. Her fingers tangled in his hair as she directed his lips back to hers.

She yearned for more of him. He kissed her again, and she felt it in every part of her body, from the crown of her head to the soles of her feet.

When she least expected it, he started kissing her in a fierce and raging storm of his own, and then without warning, he moved away from her.

With shaking hands, Taylor said, "Russ?" She kissed him lightly. "Why did you stop?"

"I already told you. If we're going to make love, even once, there's no turning back. I've got to have more from you than your body.... I want you for my wife."

"Does it have to be all or nothing?"

"Yes," he said forcefully.

"But why talk about marriage now?" she asked gently. "Isn't that something we could consider later?"

"No...it'll be too late to think about it afterward," he said fervently. "If we're going to make love, there's got to be a commitment between us."

"But, Russ..." She wasn't sure why she was fighting him so hard; the reasons had escaped her. She'd already admitted she loved him, and if she'd gone that far, then accepting responsibility for their feelings was the next logical step. Only she felt as if she'd just learned to walk and Russ was signing her up for a marathon.

Russ took her by the shoulders. "I realize things are done differently in the city. Men and women change partners as often as they do their sheets. I've read about 'swinging singles' and 'hooking up.'"

"That's not true," Taylor argued. "At least not for me. There's only been one other man in my life, and it was the biggest mistake I've ever made."

"Then don't repeat it. I'm offering you what Mark never would have, because I don't want anything less. When we make love, there won't be any doubt in your mind about my commitment to you. It's complete and total. When I told you I loved you, that wasn't a momentary thing based on physical attraction or a case of overactive hormones. It's something that's been growing from the first moment we met. It's not going to change or go away. I love you, and it's the first time I've ever said that to a woman and truly meant it."

A lump formed in Taylor's throat, and tears brimmed in her eyes. "But we're so different...."

"Of course we are," Russ said, tucking both her hands between his. "That's the crazy part in all this. At first I thought those differences would doom any chance of a lasting relationship between us. I figured we didn't have any business joining our lives together when our views are so far apart. Then I realized that being with you, fighting with you, has brought balance into my life. You've shown me and taught me things I needed to know. There's a lot I still disagree with, but we can face those issues when they arise. Basically I'm coming around to your way of thinking."

That was news to Taylor. He still seemed as obstinate as ever in several areas. But then again, he'd allowed Mandy to wear makeup and he'd changed his opinion about the drill team uniform and even agreed to her compromise on the dating issue. There'd been other changes, too. Subtle ones. When she argued with him now, Russ listened and weighed her argument, which was something she'd never gotten her father to do. Her mother had always lent a willing ear, but never her father.

"I can see the changes in you, too," Russ continued. "Remember how you felt when you first moved to Cougar Point? As I recall, you said it was the farthest corner of the known world. Yet just a moment ago you were telling me you've come to appreciate some of the qualities of small-town living. True, no merchant in town accepts American Express, but who knows? And if you really get a craving to use that card, Billings isn't all that far."

"It's three and a half hours," she muttered, resisting the urge to laugh. She was actually considering this crazy proposal of his! What he'd said about Mark had hit home. The months apart had given her perspective. Russ was right; Mark would never have married her.

"Billings is only three hours, and that isn't far," he explained eagerly. "If you like, we'll make a regular weekend trip of it and spend our days shopping and our nights making love. I'm willing to compromise. If doing housework offends you—"

"That's not it!"

"Then what is?"

For the life of her, Taylor couldn't think of a single argument that made sense. She stuck with one that was tried and true. "It's the idea of a woman working for a wage and then being expected to do everything else at home, too. If a wife works outside the home, her husband should do his share of the housework and rearing the children."

"I agree," Russ murmured, although it looked as if

he'd had to swallow a watermelon to say so. "But that's also why I feel a mother's place is in the home."

"Oh, please, let's not get into that again."

"Right," Russ said emphatically. "We could inadvertently start another war, and the last thing I want to do is fight with you. I love you, Taylor. Heaven help me, but it's true."

She raised her hand and caressed the side of his face. "I love you, too."

Russ pressed his own hand over hers and sighed deeply. "I knew you did. I couldn't believe anything else because it hurt too damn much. I swear to you, Taylor, I've never been a jealous man, but when you were having dinner with Cody Franklin last weekend, it took every ounce of restraint I possess not to march across that restaurant, pick you up and carry you out of there."

Taylor smiled and leaned forward until their foreheads touched. Her lips brushed his. "I'm not much for the green-eyed monster myself, but Mary Lu Randall should consider herself a lucky woman. I felt like tearing her hair out."

"Does this mean you'll marry me?"

Taylor closed her eyes and waited for a list of sound, rational arguments to convince her otherwise. To her surprise there were none. "Yes...."

With a triumphant shout loud enough to crack the windows, Russ bolted to his feet, taking her with him. With his arm at her waist, he whirled her around until Taylor, laughing, begged him to stop.

Instead, he lifted her higher and higher until she supported her hands on his shoulders and threw back her head.

The knock on the door caught them both by surprise. Taylor's eyes found Russ's. She didn't even want to imagine who was on the other side.

"Who is it?" Russ demanded, carefully lowering her to the floor.

"Pizza delivery."

Taylor hurriedly arranged her clothes and paused to smile when she heard that. She'd completely forgotten about the pizza.

Russ paid for their meal and brought the cardboard box and a stack of napkins inside. The scent of pepperoni and melting cheese filled the room.

Taking the box from Russ, Taylor placed it on the table and immediately opened it, inhaling deeply. She was grateful for the napkins the delivery boy had included, and pulled a slice free for Russ. Next she helped herself, savoring the first delicious bite.

"Taylor," Russ groaned, sitting in the chair across from her, "we're having the most important discussion of our lives. How can you eat at a time like this?"

"The pizza is hot *now*," she said, and gobbled down two extra bites, in case he convinced her to put it aside.

"I suppose we're going to have to figure out how to get your pizza fix, too, aren't we?"

She nodded. "At least once a month, please." She closed her eyes. "Oh, my goodness, I'd forgotten how wonderful a pizza can taste. Russ, I'm sorry, but I can't marry you unless we arrange to have a decent pepperoni pizza every few weeks."

"The bowling alley—"

"Makes a great breakfast, but someone has to let those people know that good pizza is made fresh and doesn't come out of the freezer."

Russ jammed his fingers through his hair. "I'll do what I can. Anything else?"

"When are we going to announce the engagement? Christmas time?"

Russ stood abruptly and started pacing. He didn't look at her and seemed to be composing his thoughts.

"Russ?"

He turned to face her. "Taylor, I want us to get married this afternoon. I know you're entitled to a big wedding with the fancy dress and the dinner and dancing and everything else, but dammit all, we could be married within the hour if you'd agree."

The pizza that had seemed so important a few minutes before was forgotten. "You want us to get married *now? Today?*"

"We're in Reno, aren't we? What else do folks do in this town?"

She shrugged, and when she started to speak, her voice sounded as though she'd suddenly been struck with laryngitis. "I understand gambling is a big interest."

"Okay," Russ said, rubbing the side of his jaw, clearly calling upon all his powers of self-control. "Rushing you wouldn't be fair. I've been thinking for weeks about us getting married, but for you it's coming out of the blue. If you want to wait until Christmas, then fine. I can accept that. I don't like it, and I don't know how I'm going to keep my hands off you till then, but I'll try."

"You know what they say: marry in haste, repent at leisure," she felt obliged to remind him.

"Right," he returned with a complete and total lack of conviction. "When we look back on our wedding day, I don't want there to be any regrets. None."

"I certainly wouldn't want you to have any, either."

"The best thing to do is take this nice and slow," he said, raising both hands. "You're a teacher, so you tend to be methodical, and although you've seen evidence to the contrary, I'm not normally one to act on impulse, either."

"I don't think you heard me correctly," Taylor murmured, because he really had misunderstood her. "I thought we'd *announce* our engagement this Christmas."

Russ whirled around and stared at her, looking even more disgruntled. "Are you saying you'd like to be a traditional June bride?"

"School will be out, and it makes sense, doesn't it? But then, I'm not really much of a traditionalist."

He grinned at that and bent to kiss her. "You're more of one than you realize, otherwise you wouldn't have had any qualms about moving in with Mark." Once more he knelt in front of her. "I plan to do everything right for you, Taylor. Set whatever date you want for the wedding."

His eyes were filled with such intensity that Taylor saw herself mesmerized by the love she saw there. "I don't know..." she whispered, feeling overwhelmed by his willingness to commit his life to her. "We're both in Reno now. We're in love, but there are problems...."

"Nothing we can't settle," he suggested with an eagerness that brought a smile to her lips.

Closing her eyes, Taylor leaned forward and slipped her arms around Russ's neck. "Are you *sure* you want to marry me? You haven't met a single member of my family, and my father's opinionated enough to test the patience of a saint."

"It's not your family I'm marrying—it's you." He drew her hand to his mouth and kissed her knuckles. "As for whether I'm sure about marrying you, I've never felt more confident of anything in my life."

Despite everything, Taylor felt equally certain. "Now that you mention it, today does have appeal, doesn't it?"

"Yesterday had appeal, too, as does tomorrow and all the rest of my tomorrows."

"Oh, Russ, sometimes you say the most beautiful things."

"I do?" He seemed completely surprised by that. "I wasn't trying." With his hands at the small of her back, he drew her forward until she was perched on the very edge of the chair. "I love you, Taylor, and I'm going to love you all the days of my life." His mouth captured hers, and he worshiped her in a single kiss.

When he pulled away, Taylor felt like clay in his arms, her will shaped and molded by his. "I'll wear my new dress."

"One more question," he whispered close to her ear. "Are you on birth control?"

Her eyes flew open. "No. Are you?"

He jerked his head back and stared at her, open-mouthed. Then his face relaxed into a lazy smile. "I'm beginning to know you, Taylor Manning, soon to be Taylor Palmer. You're telling me birth control isn't just a woman's responsibility."

She rewarded him with a long, slow, leisurely kiss.

"I'll stop at the drugstore," he murmured when she'd finished.

"No," she whispered between nibbling kisses. "I don't want you to."

"But you might get pregnant."

"Yes, I know." She found his earlobe and sucked it gently. "I'd like it if I did. What about you?"

"I'd like it, too…. Taylor," he moaned, "stop now while I've still got my sanity."

She pressed her breasts against him, loving the feel, savoring the sensations the action aroused.

"Taylor," Russ groaned once more. "Stop…please."

"In a moment."

"Now." He clasped her around the waist and stepped back.

He stood, clutching the back of the chair. "I'll go find us a preacher," he said, and his voice was shaking. "Can you be ready in an hour?"

Taylor stood in the foyer of the wedding chapel, holding a bouquet of small pink rosebuds. The minister who'd married her pointed out the line on the wedding certificate where she was supposed to sign. Taylor did so with a flair, then smiled at her husband and handed him the pen. Russ in turn gave the pen to the receptionist and clerk who'd served as their witnesses.

Russ hurriedly signed the document, and when he'd finished, he shook the minister's hand and guided Taylor out of the chapel.

"I don't think I've ever seen you more beautiful," he said, sliding his hand around her waist and drawing her close. His eyes shone with a light that had been transmitted straight from his heart, a message of joy.

"I don't think I've ever seen you more handsome," Taylor told him.

His eyes didn't stray from her. "What would you like to do next? Have dinner? See a show?"

Taylor chuckled. "You've got to be kidding. You

know what I want because it's the same thing you want. Besides, we've only got a few hours."

"A few hours. Why?"

"Because," she said, leaning forward to press her mouth over his, "the drill team is scheduled to perform at eight, and Mandy would never forgive us if we weren't there for her big moment."

Russ grumbled something under his breath and quickened his pace, leading her back to the hotel.

"You seem to be mighty eager, Mr. Palmer," she said as they entered into the hotel elevator.

"Move your hips like that one more time and I'll show you how eager I can be."

"And I'd let you."

Russ reached for her then, dragging her against him. His mouth took hers, and he gave her a glimpse of the pleasure that awaited her. The elevator had stopped at their floor, and the doors had glided open before either of them was aware of it.

As soon as they stepped into the long, carpeted hallway, Russ lifted her in his arms. "You didn't get the big fancy wedding, with the bridesmaids and orange blossoms and the organ music, but there are some traditions I can and will provide."

However, opening the door with Taylor in his arms proved to be awkward, and after a frustrating moment, Russ tossed her over his shoulder like a bag of grain.

"Russ," Taylor cried, "put me down this minute."

"Be patient," he said, crouching down in an effort to insert the key into the lock. Apparently he was having trouble, because it was taking him forever.

A middle-aged couple strolled past and, mortified, Taylor covered her face with both hands.

"Dear," the woman whispered to Taylor, "do you need help?"

"Not really," she answered. "Just don't ever let your daughters grow up to marry cowboys."

"You're recently married?" the woman asked as if that was the most romantic thing she'd ever heard. "Did you hear that, John? They just got married."

The door finally opened, and Russ walked inside with Taylor still dangling over his shoulder. "We've been married for all of about fifteen minutes," Russ told the couple. "Now, if you'll excuse us, we're going to have our honeymoon." With that he shut the door.

"Russ Palmer, put me down," she ordered him again.

"With pleasure."

He walked to the bed and released her. Taylor went flying backward, a cry hovering on her lips. Chuckling, Russ lowered himself over her.

"Was that really necessary?" she asked, feigning indignation.

"If I wanted to get you inside this room, it was. And trust me, I wanted you in this room."

A smile twitched at the edges of Taylor's mouth.

"Oh, Taylor," Russ groaned, "I'm so crazy about you." He set his long fingers in her hair and pulled up her head to receive his kiss. His mouth was hard over her own, hard with passion and with need.

"Oh, sweet Taylor," he murmured as he tore his mouth free and nestled his face in the delicate curve of her neck. He kissed her there, his lips hot and moist. His hands were gentle as he helped her stand and slip out of her dress. It fell to the floor in a pool of silk and lace. He picked it up and set it aside.

Their mouths met once more in another kiss, a kiss

that promised passion about to be assuaged—and a love that would last through all the seasons of their lives.

An hour later, just before they left for the drill team performance, Taylor used the phone in Russ's room to call her family.

Russ stood behind her, his hands caressing her shoulders. Without her ever having said a word, Russ seemed to know how difficult this discussion would be for her.

"Mom?" she said excitedly when her mother answered. "If Dad's home, get him on the other phone. I've got some important news."

Taylor heard her mother's hurried call. Within a minute, Eric Manning was on an extension.

"Taylor," her father's voice boomed over the long-distance line, "what is it? Is anything wrong? Listen, I've been reading between the lines in your letters, and I'm worried about you and this cowpoke. Christy said you called and talked to her, but she never told us exactly why. Just said you were having trouble with that cowboy."

"Dad...stop a minute, will you?"

"Now you listen to me. If he gives you any more problems, I want you to let me know because your brothers and I will deal with him."

"Eric," her mother interrupted, "Taylor called because she has some news."

It took Taylor a tense moment to compose herself.

"Mom and Dad," she said after swallowing hard, "congratulations are in order.... I was married today." A second of stunned silence followed her announcement. "I'm afraid I married that cowboy." She handed the receiver to Russ.

Fourteen

Russ took the telephone receiver, worried about the way she was frowning, wondering what her parents had said. It looked as if she wanted to advise him, but there wasn't time.

"Hello," Russ said. "I'm Russ Palmer."

"What the hell have you done?" a loud male voice shouted at him.

Russ moved the phone away from his ear. "I married your daughter," Russ explained, doing his best to keep his tone even and controlled. He didn't much take to being yelled at, but he could understand Eric Manning's feelings.

"Taylor's just broken off one relationship, and the last thing she should do is get involved in another, especially with—"

"A cowboy," Russ finished for him. Taylor was sitting on the edge of the bed, her hands clasped tightly in her lap, her blue eyes staring up at him.

"That girl of mine should have her head examined. She doesn't understand what she's done and—"

A soft, feminine voice interrupted the tirade. "Eric,

dear, all this shouting isn't going to settle anything. They're already married. Didn't you hear Taylor tell you that?"

"And we intend to stay married," Russ added, in case there was any doubt in the older man's mind.

"It's too soon," Taylor's father continued, his voice less menacing. "Surely you realize she married you on the rebound. You may be a perfectly fine young man, but my daughter—"

"Is twenty-six and old enough to know her own mind."

"She's always been a hothead. No doubt her sister told her I was dead set against her having anything to do with you."

"I can understand your concern," Russ said, now that his anger had worn off. "You don't know me from Adam."

"What about your family?" Eric thundered anew. "What do they have to say about this?"

"The only family I have is a younger half sister. We haven't told her yet, but Mandy will be delighted."

"You don't have any family?" Eric shouted. "How are you supposed to know what's right? By the way, how old are you?"

"Thirty-five."

"Thirty-five! You're nine years older than Taylor—that's too much."

"Now, Eric," Elizabeth Manning broke in. "You're being ridiculous. If you recall, you're seven years older than I am. Russ, you'll have to excuse my husband's temper. It's just that he loves Taylor and is terribly proud of her, except he has trouble letting her know that."

"You don't need to go telling *him* that."

"Russ is family, dear."

"Not if I have anything to say about it."

"Frankly, Mr. Manning," Russ said firmly, "you don't. The deed is done. Signed, sealed and delivered."

"We'll see about that."

"Stop it now, the pair of you. Eric, either you be civil to Taylor's husband or you can get off the phone. I won't have you speaking to him that way." Her words were followed by the click of a telephone receiver.

Russ waited a moment to compose himself. Taylor had mentioned the type of man her father was more than once, but butting heads with him had been even more of a challenge than Russ had anticipated.

"Mrs. Manning, believe me, I can understand your concern, and I can't say I blame you. But I want you to know I love Taylor, and I have every intention of being a good husband."

"I'm sure you do. Please forgive my husband. Personally I think he was disappointed that he didn't get to walk Taylor down the aisle. Only one of our sons is married, and I think Eric was looking forward to taking part in a wedding for one of his daughters."

"I'm sorry to have cheated him out of that."

"Don't worry about it. There's always Christy, and we expect she'll be engaged to an attorney friend of hers soon. Now, before you think the worst of us, I want to offer you a hearty welcome to the family, such as it is."

"Thank you," Russ said, and smiled reassuringly at Taylor, who was looking more anxious by the minute.

"Would you mind putting Taylor back on the line?"

"Of course not." Russ's eyes found Taylor's as he held the receiver out to her. "Your mother wants to talk to you."

"Was it bad?" she whispered, sounding guilty when there was no reason for it.

"No, I think your father and I will get along just fine."

"The two of you are quite a bit alike."

Russ figured it was probably a good thing that he'd first been introduced to Taylor's father over the phone. Had they met in person it was entirely possible that they would have swung at each other.

Taylor took the phone and relaxed visibly as she started talking to her mother. Russ was relieved to see her good spirits return. This was their day, the one he'd been thinking about for weeks, and he didn't want anything or anyone to ruin it.

The problem, Russ decided an hour later, was that he'd reckoned without Mandy, his cantankerous younger sister.

"You did *what?*" the teenager shrieked in outrage.

"We got married," Taylor explained softly, holding out her ring finger, adorned with a simple gold band, as proof. He could tell that she was equally surprised by his sister's response. "I thought you'd be pleased."

"You did it without even talking to me?" Mandy cried. She stood with her hands on her hips as though she were the adult and they were recalcitrant children. "I can't believe the two of you." She whirled around and confronted Carol Fischer. "Did you hear what they just did?" Mandy demanded.

Carol had trouble containing a grin. "Yes, I did," she said, and stepped forward to hug Taylor. "Congratulations."

"You didn't so much as consult me," Mandy reminded him, her eyes narrowing. "Can you imagine how I feel? I'm your sister, and I should've been in on this! Good grief, you wouldn't have even *met* Taylor if it hadn't been for me!"

"Do you mind our getting married so terribly much?" Taylor asked softly.

"Of course I don't mind. Marrying you is the smartest thing Russ has done in his whole sorry life. It's just that…" She paused, and tears clouded her pretty green eyes. "I would like to have been there. You couldn't have waited until after the drill team performance?"

"Yes, we could have. We should have," Russ agreed, stepping closer to his sister. "I'm sorry if we offended you. That wasn't our intention."

"We were so lost in each other that we forgot everyone else," Taylor said.

"I can't believe it. When we left this morning, you were barely talking to each other, and the next thing I know, you're married. I just don't understand it."

Taylor placed her arm around Mandy's shoulders. "I've been in love with your brother from the first, but I was fighting it because…well, because I didn't think I'd fit into his life. Then we started talking and I realized I couldn't even remember why I was fighting him so hard when I love him so much. This probably doesn't make a lot of sense to you, and I'm sorry."

Mandy lifted one shoulder in a halfhearted shrug. "In a way it does make sense. I just wish you'd waited a little longer. I would've liked to throw rice or birdseed or something."

"We were just thinking about going out for a wedding dinner. We'd like it if you came."

With her arms folded, Mandy cocked her head to one side. "Are you sure I wouldn't be intruding?"

"More than sure," Russ told her. "I'm going to order a bottle of champagne and you can have a virgin daiquiri if you want. It isn't every day a brother can share his wedding dinner with his sister, and we have a lot to celebrate, don't we? In fact, Taylor's and my wedding day wouldn't be complete if you weren't here to share part of it with us."

"You're just saying that," Mandy said with a regal tilt to her chin. "However, I'm going to let you get away with it because I really am pleased." She dropped her arms and threw herself against Russ with such force that he nearly toppled backward. "Hey," she cried, wiping tears from her cheeks with the back of her hand, "did you see how great the team did? Aren't we fabulous?" She didn't wait for a response, but reached for Taylor, slipping an arm around her waist and the other around Russ. "Now listen," she said, serious once more. "A wedding is one thing, but if you're going to start having babies, I want to be consulted. Understand?"

Three weeks later, early on a Saturday morning, Taylor nestled close to her husband under a layer of quilts, seeking his warmth. When she'd first arrived in Montana, Russ had warned her about the winters, but nothing could have prepared her for the bitter cold that had descended upon them in the past ten days.

Russ stirred, rolled over and pulled her into his arms. Taylor smiled contentedly as she repositioned herself so that her head rested on his shoulder. She settled her hands over his chest. Married life certainly seemed to agree with him—and she knew it agreed with her. From the moment they'd said their vows in Reno, Russ had been a devoted and loving husband, with the accent on the word *loving*. He couldn't seem to get enough of her, which was fine with Taylor, since she couldn't get enough of him, either.

With Mandy living with them, it sometimes became embarrassing. More than once after their wedding, Russ had insisted he was exhausted and dragged Taylor upstairs practically before they'd finished clearing the dinner dishes. Mandy loved to tease Russ about his sudden need for extra sleep since he'd returned from Reno.

At one point Taylor had felt it was necessary to talk to Russ's sister. Her fear was that Mandy would feel excluded, and that was the last thing Taylor wanted.

"Are you kidding?" Mandy had said, exchanging a smile with Taylor. "I think getting married is the best thing that's happened to Russ. He should've done it years ago. He's too mellow to fight with me anymore. Keep him happy, okay? Because when he's happy, I'm happy."

Keeping Russ happy made Taylor feel delirious with satisfaction herself. Every now and then they clashed over some issue, but that was to be expected. Both seemed willing, however, to listen to the other's point of view.

"Good morning," Russ whispered. His hand found her breast, and she sighed at the instant surge of pleasure.

"They seem fuller," he whispered.

"I know what you're thinking," she said, snuggling closer. "But it's much too soon to make that kind of assumption."

"Taylor," Russ groaned, kissing her hungrily. "We haven't used any kind of protection. Not once. Have you...you know, started yet?"

"Not yet, but I'm often a few days late."

Russ smoothed the hair about her face. "You know the problem, don't you?"

"The problem is you and your sexy ways," she muttered.

"You've never complained before."

"I'm not complaining now. I'm just telling you."

"Actually, the problem I'm talking about is your parents. They'll be here next week for Thanksgiving, and you don't want to have to tell them you're pregnant."

"My father will assume the worst."

"Let him. We know the truth."

"My father's always been ridiculously protective of us girls, and if he even suspects I was pregnant before we were married, he's going to raise the roof."

"Do you think I care?" Tenderly he rested his hand on her abdomen, and the smile that came to his face was filled with an abundance of pride. "I bet this baby's a boy."

"What a terrible, chauvinistic thing to say."

"I can't help it. Every time I think about you having my son I get all warm. I still have trouble believing we're really married. It seems like a dream."

"We could very well have a girl. In fact, I'd be pleased if we did."

"So you're willing to admit you might be expecting."

Taylor was expecting, all right, but not the way Russ meant. She was waiting for trouble, and the minute her parents arrived there was bound to be plenty of it. Not once since she'd phoned to tell her mom and dad that she and Russ were married had Taylor spoken to her father. Her mother had phoned about the possibility of visiting for Thanksgiving, and Taylor had readily agreed. But she knew the real reason for this visit, and that was so her father could confront Russ about their rushed marriage. Several times in the past three weeks Taylor had tried to prepare Russ for the meeting, but he seemed to let everything she said roll off him. Either he really wasn't concerned or he was living in a world of his own. After doing battle with her father for most of her life, Taylor was nervous. Seldom did she back down from Eric Manning, but this was different. She wanted her family to love and appreciate Russ the way she did.

It wasn't that her father was such a monster, but he tended to be opinionated and hotheaded, especially when it came to his daughters. After Taylor had broken up with Mark, her father had taken pains to introduce her to a handful of eligible young men. All of them were professionals. Taylor didn't doubt for a moment that her father would consider Russ an inappropriate husband for her.

"And for another thing," she said stiffly, reminding him of the ridiculous statement he'd made when they were discussing marriage, "babies are *not* just a woman's business."

"Oh? And what am I supposed to do?"

"Plenty!"

"Come on, Taylor, be sensible. There's not a lot I can do with a baby. They're too…tiny."

"You can change a diaper."

"You've got to be joking."

She rolled away from him and buried her face in the pillow, embarrassed by the tears that sprang to her eyes. Even if she was pregnant, it would be months before the baby was born, and there was plenty of time to deal with the issue of Russ's role as a parent.

"Taylor?" Russ asked softly, his hand on her shoulder. "Are you crying?"

She refused to admit it. "Of course not."

"I've been doing a little reading on pregnancy and birth, and I understand that tears are perfectly normal. Women become highly emotional during this time."

"I suppose you're going to be quoting facts and statistics to me for the next eight months," she said, then immediately regretted her waspish tone. Turning back to Russ, she sobbed and threw her arms around his neck. "I'm sorry... I didn't mean that. It's just that I'm worried about you meeting Dad."

Russ gently kissed the tip of her nose. "There isn't going to be a problem, sweetheart. I promise you."

"You can't say that—you don't know my dad."

"I won't let there be a problem. We have one very important thing in common. We both love you. Two men of similar persuasion are going to get along famously. So stop borrowing trouble, all right?"

She nodded. "Okay, but I don't think we should say anything about the possibility of me being pregnant until after Christmas. Agreed?"

"If that's the way you want to handle it." He eased her more fully into his arms. "But I'm afraid I might inadvertently give it away. I'm so happy about it I have trouble not shouting every time I think about us having a son."

"Or daughter."

"I still think it's a boy."

"Whichever it is, I'd better tell Mandy. Otherwise we'll be subjected to her wrath—just like after the wedding. Weren't we given specific instructions to clear the idea of having kids with her first?"

"I already told her."

"Russ?" Taylor levered herself up on one elbow.

"I hadn't intended to, but we were sitting at the table one afternoon and apparently I was wearing a silly grin and—"

"It was probably more of a satisfied smirk," Taylor interrupted. Then she said, "Go on."

"Anyway, I was sitting there minding my own business and she wanted to know what I found so funny. Of course, I said I didn't find anything funny, and before I knew it, I was telling her about the book I'd picked up at the library about pregnancy and birth and how I thought you were going to have a baby. She was delighted. By the way, I told her the baby's probably a boy."

"Russ, you don't know that!"

"Somehow I do. Deep in my heart I feel he's a boy. Do you think your father will settle down if we promise to give the baby some family name of yours?"

"We've got to get him accustomed to the fact that we're married first. That might take some time." She made a wry face. "You know, like approaching a wild animal slowly..."

"Right," Russ grumbled. "I forgot." He reached for her and pulled her close. "If you're looking for ways to tame *this* wild beast, I might be able to offer a few suggestions." He wiggled his eyebrows provocatively.

Giggling, Taylor encircled his neck with her arms. "I tamed you a long time ago."

"That you did," he whispered as his mouth sought hers. "That you did."

The Wednesday before Thanksgiving Eric and Elizabeth Manning pulled their thirty-foot RV into the yard of the Lazy P.

Since school had been dismissed at noon, Taylor was home. The instant she recognized the vehicle, she called out to Russ, threw open the back door and flew down the steps, hardly taking time to button her coat. Russ followed directly behind her.

Standing by the door, Russ felt Eric Manning's eyes on him. The two men quickly sized each other up, and Russ descended the steps. He waited until Taylor had welcomed each of her parents before he placed his arm protectively around her shoulders.

If her parents didn't immediately guess she was pregnant, he'd be surprised. Taylor positively glowed—just like they said in the books. And he felt no less happy himself. Only rarely had he been this content. This *complete.* Taylor had filled all the dark, lonely corners of his life.

He hadn't been joking when he told her he felt all warm whenever he thought about the child growing inside her. At odd moments of the day he'd think about his wife and how much he loved her, and he'd actually feel weak with emotion. Some nights he'd lie awake and cherish these peaceful moments with Taylor sleeping at his side. She'd been sleeping a lot more lately. The books had told him she'd be extra-tired. He would prefer it if she'd quit work, but the one time he'd suggested it, she'd almost bitten his head off. Moodiness. That was something else the books had addressed. Russ decided he'd let Taylor decide when and if she should stop teaching. She knew her own limits.

"Mom and Dad," Taylor said, slipping her arm around Russ's waist, "this is my husband, Russ Palmer. You'll meet his sister, Mandy, this evening."

Russ stepped forward and extended his hand to Taylor's father. The older man muttered something unintelligible, and the two exchanged hearty handshakes.

"Come inside," Russ invited, ushering everyone into the warmth of the kitchen. He took their coats and hung them in the hall closet while Taylor settled her parents in the living room.

There had been lots of small changes in the house since she'd moved in. She had a natural flair for decorating and had rearranged the furniture and done other things that gave the living room a fresh, comfortable feel.

"Would you like some coffee?" she asked.

"No, thanks. We just had some, honey," her mother said.

Elizabeth Manning was an older version of her daughter. They both had the same intense blue eyes and long, thick dark hair. Eric Manning was as big as a lumberjack, tall and muscular, intimidating in appearance. It was important to Russ to win over this man. Important for Taylor. She'd fought with her father for most of her life. She'd often gone against his will, but she loved him, and his approval meant a great deal to her.

"Eric," Elizabeth Manning said softly, looking at her husband.

The older man cleared his throat. "Before I say anything more to get myself in hot water, I want to apologize for the way I behaved when we last spoke. It's just that finding out my daughter had married without a word to either of her parents came as a surprise."

"I understand," Russ said, "and I don't blame you. If my daughter had done that, I don't think I would've behaved any differently."

The two men shared a meaningful look.

"There's something you should both know," Taylor said, sitting on the arm of Russ's chair. She gave him a small smile, her eyes wide. "I'm pregnant. Now, Daddy, before you assume the worst," she added in a rush, "this baby was conceived in love with a wedding band on my finger. I swear to you it's the truth."

Russ stared up at his wife in shock. For days she'd been schooling him on the importance of keeping their secret until the Christmas holidays. Again and again she'd insisted the worst thing they could do was announce her pregnancy the moment her parents rolled into the Lazy P. Then, with barely a second's notice, Taylor had spilled it all.

"Oh, Taylor, that's absolutely wonderful." Her mother was clearly delighted. One look told Russ that wasn't the case with her father.

"Daddy?" Taylor turned expectantly to her father. She took Russ's hand and held it tightly. "I love him, Dad, more than I ever dreamed it was possible to love a man."

"He's good to you?"

"Damn right I'm good to her," Russ muttered. He wasn't sure what was going on between father and daughter, but he resented being left out of the conversation.

"That true?" Eric asked, tilting his head toward Russ.

"Yes, Dad."

Eric opened his arms to her, and Taylor flew across the room, to be wrapped in a bear hug by her robust father. The older man's gaze found Russ's. "She's more trouble than a barrel of monkeys. Opinionated and strong-willed, and has been from the day she was born. I suggest you keep her barefoot and pregnant."

"Daddy!" Taylor tore herself away from her father, hands on her hips. "What century are you living in?"

"The same one I am," Russ said, and chuckled boisterously when Taylor whirled around to glare at him.

The two men smiled at each other. Taylor understood what Russ was doing but couldn't help reacting anyway.

"If the two of you think you can run my life, I want you to know right now that—"

She wasn't allowed to finish. Russ gently turned her around, draped her over his arm and kissed her soundly.

"I can see our daughter married the right man," Russ heard Eric Manning inform his wife. "The right man indeed."

* * * * *

MY FUNNY VALENTINE

One

Dianne Williams had the scenario all worked out. She'd be pushing her grocery cart down the aisle of the local grocery store and gazing over the frozen-food section when a tall, dark, handsome man would casually stroll up to her and with a brilliant smile say, "Those low-cal dinners couldn't possibly be for you."

She'd turn to him and suddenly the air would fill with the sounds of a Rimsky-Korsakov symphony, or bells would chime gently in the distance—Dianne didn't have that part completely figured out yet—and in that instant she would know deep in her heart that this was the man she was meant to spend the rest of her life with.

All right, Dianne was willing to admit, the scenario was childish and silly, the kind of fantasy only a teenage girl should dream up. But reentering the dating scene after umpteen years of married life created problems Dianne didn't even want to consider.

Three years earlier, Dianne's husband had left her and the children to find himself. Instead he found an SYT (sweet young thing), promptly divorced Dianne and moved across the country. It hurt; in fact, it hurt more than anything Dianne had ever known, but she was a survivor, and always had been. Perhaps that was the reason Jack didn't seem to suffer a single pang of guilt about abandoning her to raise Jason and Jill on her own.

Her children, Dianne had discovered, were incredibly resilient. Within a year of their father's departure, they were urging her to date. Their father did, they reminded Dianne with annoying frequency. And if it wasn't her children pushing her toward establishing a new relationship, it was her own dear mother.

When it came to locating Mr. Right for her divorced daughter, Martha Janes knew no equal. For several months, Dianne had been subjected to a long parade of single men. Their unmarried status, however, seemed their sole attribute.

After dinner with the man who lost his toupee on a low-hanging chandelier, Dianne had insisted enough was enough and she would find her own dates.

This proved to be easier said than done. Dianne hadn't gone out once in six months. Now, within the next week, she needed a man. Not just any man, either. One who was tall, dark and handsome. It would be a nice bonus if he was exceptionally wealthy, too, but she didn't have time to be choosy. The Valentine's dinner at the Port Blossom Community Center was Saturday night. *This* Saturday night.

From the moment the notice was posted six weeks earlier, Jason and Jill had insisted she attend. Surely their mother could find a date given that much time! And someone handsome to boot. It seemed a matter of family honor.

Only now the dinner was only days away and Dianne was no closer to achieving her goal.

"I'm home," Jason yelled as he walked into the house. The front door slammed in his wake, hard enough to shake the kitchen windows. He threw his books on the counter, moved directly to the refrigerator, opened the door and stuck the upper half of his fourteen-year-old body inside.

"Help yourself to a snack," Dianne said, smiling and shaking her head.

Jason reappeared with a chicken leg clenched between his teeth like a pirate's cutlass. One hand was filled with a piece of leftover cherry pie while the other held a platter of cold fried chicken.

"How was school?"

He shrugged, set down the pie and removed the chicken leg from his mouth. "Okay, I guess."

Dianne knew what was coming next. It was the same question he'd asked her every afternoon since the notice about the dinner had been posted.

"Do you have a date yet?" He leaned against the counter as his steady gaze pierced her. Her son's eyes could break through the firmest resolve, and cut through layers of deception.

"No date," she answered cheerfully. At least as cheerfully as she could under the circumstances.

"The dinner's this Saturday night."

As if she needed reminding. "I know. Stop worrying, I'll find someone."

"Not just anyone," Jason said emphatically, as though he were speaking to someone with impaired hearing. "He's got to make an impression. Someone decent."

"I know, I know."

"Grandma said she could line you up with—"

"No," Dianne interrupted. "I categorically refuse to go on any more of Grandma's blind dates."

"But you don't have the time to find your own now. It's—"

"I'm working on it," she insisted, although she knew she wasn't working very hard. She *was* trying to find someone to accompany her to the dinner, only she'd never dreamed it would be this difficult.

Until the necessity of attending this affair had been forced upon her, Dianne hadn't been aware of how limited her choices were. In the past couple of years, she'd met few single men, apart from the ones her mother had thrown at her. There were a couple of unmarried men at the office where she was employed part-time as a bookkeeper. Neither, however, was anyone she'd seriously consider dating. They were both too suave, too urbane—too much like Jack. Besides, problems might arise if she were to mingle her social life with her business one.

The front door opened and closed again, a little less noisily this time.

"I'm home!" ten-year-old Jill announced from the entryway. She dropped her books on the floor and marched toward the kitchen. Then she paused on the threshold and planted both hands on her hips as her eyes sought out her brother. "You better not have eaten all the leftover pie. I want some, too, you know."

"Don't grow warts worrying about it," Jason said sarcastically. "There's plenty."

Jill's gaze swiveled from her brother to her mother. The level of severity didn't diminish one bit. Dianne met her daughter's eye and mouthed the words along with her.

"Do you have a date yet?"

Jason answered for Dianne. "No, she doesn't. And she's got five days to come up with a decent guy and all she says is that she's working on it."

"Mom..." Jill's brown eyes filled with concern.

"Children, please."

"Everyone in town's going," Jill claimed, as if Dianne wasn't already aware of that. "You've *got* to be there, you've just got to. I told all my friends you're going."

More pressure! That was the last thing Dianne needed. Nevertheless, she smiled serenely at her two children and assured them they didn't have a thing to worry about.

An hour or so later, while she was making dinner, she could hear Jason and Jill's voices in the living room. They were huddled together in front of the television, their heads close together. Plotting, it looked like, charting her barren love life. Doubtless deciding who their mother should take to the dinner. Probably the guy with the toupee.

"Is something wrong?" Dianne asked, standing in the doorway. It was unusual for them to watch television this time of day, but more unusual for them to be so chummy. The fact that they'd turned on the TV to drown out their conversation hadn't escaped her.

They broke guiltily apart.

"Wrong?" Jason asked, recovering first. "I was just talking to Jill, is all. Do you need me to do something?"

That offer alone was enough evidence to convict them both. "Jill, would you set the table for me?" she asked, her gaze lingering on her two children for another moment before she returned to the kitchen.

Jason and Jill were up to something. Dianne could only guess what. No doubt the plot they were concocting included their grandmother.

Sure enough, while Jill was setting the silverware on the kitchen table, Jason used the phone, stretching the cord as far as it would go and mumbling into the mouthpiece so there was no chance Dianne could overhear his conversation.

Dianne's suspicions were confirmed when her mother arrived shortly after dinner. And within minutes, Jason and Jill had deserted the kitchen, saying they had to get to their homework. Also highly suspicious behavior.

"Do you want some tea, Mom?" Dianne felt obliged to ask, dreading the coming conversation. It didn't take Sherlock Holmes to deduce that her children had called their grandmother hoping she'd find a last-minute date for Dianne.

"Don't go to any trouble."

This was her mother's standard reply. "It's no trouble," Dianne said.

"Then make the tea."

Because of her evening aerobics class—W.A.R. it was called, for Women After Results—Dianne had changed and was prepared to make a hasty exit.

While the water was heating, she took a white ceramic teapot from the cupboard. "Before you ask, and I know you will," she said with strained patience, "I haven't got a date for the Valentine's dinner yet."

Her mother nodded slowly as if Dianne had just announced something of profound importance. Martha was from the old school, and she took her time getting around to whatever was on her mind, usually preceding it with a long list of questions that hinted at the subject.

Dianne loved her mother, but there wasn't anyone on this earth who could drive her crazier.

"You've still got your figure," Martha said, her expression serious. "That helps." She stroked her chin a couple of times and nodded. "You've got your father's brown eyes, may he rest in peace, and your hair is nice and thick. You can thank your grandfather for that. He had hair so thick—"

"Ma, did I mention I have an aerobics class tonight?"

Her mother's posture stiffened. "I don't want to bother you."

"It's just that I might have to leave before you say what you're obviously planning to say, and I didn't want to miss the reason for your unexpected visit."

Her mother relaxed, but just a little. "Don't worry. I'll say what must be said and then you can leave. Your mother's words are not as important as your exercise class."

An argument bubbled up like fizz from a can of soda, but Dianne successfully managed to swallow it. Showing any sign of weakness in front of her mother was a major tactical error. Dianne made the tea, then carried the pot over to the table and sat across from Martha.

"Your skin's still as creamy as—"

"Mom," Dianne said, "there's no need to tell me all this. I know my coloring is good. I also know I've still got my figure and that my hair is thick and that you approve of my keeping it long. You don't need to sell me on myself."

"Ah," Martha told her softly, "that's where you're wrong."

Dianne couldn't help it—she rolled her eyes. When Dianne was fifteen her mother would have slapped her hand, but now that she was thirty-three, Martha used more subtle tactics.

Guilt.

"I don't have many years left."

"Mom—"

"No, listen. I'm an old woman now and I have the right to say what I want, especially since the good Lord may choose to call me home at any minute."

Stirring a teaspoon of sugar into her tea offered Dianne a moment to compose herself. Bracing her elbows on the table, she raised the cup to her lips. "Just say it."

Her mother nodded, apparently appeased. "You've lost confidence in yourself."

"That's not true."

Martha's smile was meager at best. "Jack left you, and now you think there must be something wrong with you. But, Dianne, what you don't understand is that he would've gone if you were as beautiful as Marilyn Monroe. Jack's leaving had nothing to do with you and everything to do with Jack."

This conversation was taking a turn Dianne wanted to avoid. Jack was a subject she preferred not to discuss. As far as she could see, there wasn't any reason to peel back the scars and examine the wound at this late date. Jack was gone. She'd accepted it, dealt with it, and gone on with her life. The fact that her mother was even mentioning her ex-husband had taken Dianne by surprise.

"My goodness," Dianne said, checking her watch. "Look at the time—"

"Before you go," her mother said quickly, grabbing her wrist, "I met a nice young man this afternoon in the butcher's shop. Marie Zimmerman told me about him and I went to talk to him myself."

"Mom—"

"Hush and listen. He's divorced, but from what he said it was all his wife's fault. He makes blood sausage and insisted I try some. It was so good it practically melted in my mouth. I never tasted sausage so good. A man who makes sausage like that would be an asset to any family."

Oh, sweet heaven. Her mother already had her married to the guy!

"I told him all about you and he generously offered to take you out."

"Mother, *please*. I've already said I won't go out on any more blind dates."

"Jerome's a nice man. He's—"

"I don't mean to be rude, but I really have to leave now, or I'll be late." Hurriedly, Dianne stood, collected her coat and called out to her children that she'd be back in an hour.

The kids didn't say a word.

It wasn't until she was in her car that Dianne realized they'd been expecting her to announce that she finally had a date.

Two

"Damn," Dianne muttered, scrambling through her purse for the tenth time. She knew it wasn't going to do the least bit of good, but she felt compelled to continue the search.

"Double damn," she said as she set the bulky leather handbag on the hood of her car. Raindrops spattered all around her.

Expelling her breath, she stalked back into the Port Blossom Community Center and stood in front of the desk. "I seem to have locked my keys in my car," she told the receptionist. "Along with my cell."

"Oh, dear. Is there someone you can get in touch with?"

"I'm a member of the auto club so I can call them for help. I also want to call home and say I'll be late. So if you'll let me use the phone?"

"Oh, sure." The young woman smiled pleasantly, and lifted the phone onto the counter. "We close in fifteen minutes, you know."

A half hour later, Dianne was leaning impatiently against her car in the community center parking lot when a red tow truck pulled in. It circled the area, then eased into the space next to hers.

The driver, whom Dianne couldn't see in the dark, rolled down his window and stuck out his elbow. "Are you the lady who phoned about locking her keys in the car?"

"No. I'm standing out in the rain wearing a leotard for the fun of it," she muttered.

He chuckled, turned off the engine and hopped out of the driver's seat. "Sounds like this has been one of those days."

She nodded, suddenly feeling a stab of guilt at her churlishness. He seemed so friendly.

"Why don't you climb in my truck where it's nice and warm while I take care of this?" He opened the passenger-side door and gestured for her to enter.

She smiled weakly, and as she climbed in, said, "I didn't mean to snap at you just now."

He flashed her a grin. "No problem." She found herself taking a second look at him. He was wearing gray-striped coveralls and the front was covered with grease stains. His name, Steve, was embroidered in red across the top of his vest pocket. His hair, which was neatly styled, appeared to have been recently cut. His eyes were a warm shade of brown and—she searched for the right word—gentle, she decided.

After ensuring that she was comfortable in his truck, Steve walked around to the driver's side of her compact car and used his flashlight to determine the type of lock.

Dianne lowered the window. "I don't usually do things like this. I've never locked the keys in my car before—I don't know why I did tonight. Stupid."

He returned to the tow truck and opened the passenger door. "No one can be smart all the time," he said cheerfully. "Don't be so hard on yourself." He moved the seat forward a little and reached for a toolbox in the space behind her.

"I've had a lot on my mind lately," she said.

Straightening, he looked at her and nodded sympathetically. He had a nice face too, she noted, easy on the eyes. In fact, he was downright attractive. The coveralls didn't detract from his appeal, but actually suggested a certain ruggedness. He was thoughtful and friendly just when Dianne was beginning to think there wasn't anyone in the world who was. But then, standing in the dark and the rain might make anyone feel friendless, even though Port Blossom was a rural community with a warm, small-town atmosphere.

Steve went back to her car and began to fiddle with the lock. Unable to sit still, Dianne opened the truck door and climbed out. "It's the dinner that's got me so upset."

"The dinner?" Steve glanced up from his work.

"The Valentine's dinner the community center's sponsoring this Saturday night. My children are forcing me to go. I don't know for sure, but I think they've got money riding on it, because they're making it sound like a matter of national importance."

"I see. Why doesn't your husband take you?"

"I'm divorced," she said bluntly. "I suppose no one expects it to happen to them. I assumed after twelve years my marriage was solid, but it wasn't. Jack's remarried now, living in Boston." Dianne had no idea why she was rambling on like this, but once she'd opened her mouth, she couldn't seem to stop. She didn't usually relate the intimate details of her life to a perfect stranger.

"Aren't you cold?"

"I'm fine, thanks." That wasn't entirely true—she was a little chilled—but she was more worried about not having a date for the stupid Valentine's dinner than freezing to death. Briefly she wondered if Jason, Jill and her mother would accept pneumonia as a reasonable excuse for not attending.

"You're sure? You look like you're shivering."

She rubbed her palms together and ignored his question. "That's when my mother suggested Jerome."

"Jerome?"

"She seems to think I need help getting my feet wet."

Steve glanced up at her again, clearly puzzled.

"In the dating world," Dianne explained. "But I've had it with the dates she's arranged."

"Disasters?"

"Encounters of the worst kind. On one of them, the guy set his napkin on fire."

Steve laughed outright at that.

"Hey, it wasn't funny, trust me. I was mortified. He panicked and started waving it around in the air until the maitre d' arrived with a fire extinguisher and chaos broke loose."

Dianne found herself smiling at the memory of the unhappy episode. "Now that I look back on it, it was rather amusing."

Steve's gaze held hers. "I take it there were other disasters?"

"None I'd care to repeat."

"So your mother's up to her tricks again?"

Dianne nodded. "Only this time my kids are involved. Mom stumbled across this butcher who specializes in…well, never mind, that's not important. What is important is if I don't come up with a date in the next day or two, I'm going to be stuck going to this stupid dinner with Jerome."

"It shouldn't be so bad," he said. Dianne could hear the grin in his voice.

"How generous of you to say so." She crossed her arms over her chest. She'd orbited her vehicle twice before she spoke again.

"My kids are even instructing me on the kind of man they want me to date."

"Oh?"

Dianne wasn't sure he'd heard her. Her lock snapped free and he opened the door and retrieved her keys, which were in the ignition. He handed them to her, and with a thank-you, Dianne made a move to climb into her car.

"Jason and Jill—they're my kids—want me to go out with a tall, dark, handsome—" She stopped abruptly, thrusting out her arm as if to keep her balance.

Steve looked at her oddly. "Are you all right?"

Dianne brought her fingertips to her temple and nodded. "I think so..." She inhaled sharply and motioned toward the streetlight. "Would you mind stepping over there for a minute?"

"Me?" He pointed to himself as though he wasn't sure she meant him.

"Please."

He shrugged and did as she requested.

The idea was fast gaining momentum in her mind. He was certainly tall—at least six foot three, which was a nice complement to her own slender five ten. And he was dark—his hair appeared to be a rich shade of mahogany. As for the handsome part, she'd noticed that right off.

"Is something wrong?" he probed.

"No," Dianne said, grinning shyly—although what she was about to propose was anything but shy. "By the way, how old are you? Thirty? Thirty-one?"

"Thirty-five."

"That's good. Perfect." A couple of years older than she was. Yes, the kids would approve of that.

"Good? Perfect?" He seemed to be questioning her sanity.

"Married?" she asked.

"Nope. I never got around to it, but I came close once." His eyes narrowed suspiciously.

"That's even better. I don't suppose you've got a jealous girlfriend—or a mad lover hanging around looking for an excuse to murder someone?"

"Not lately."

Dianne sighed with relief. "Great."

"Your car door's open," he said, gesturing toward it. He seemed eager to be on his way. "All I need to do is write down your auto club number."

"Yes, I know." She stood there, arms folded, studying him in the light. He was even better-looking than she'd first thought. "Do you own a decent suit?"

He chuckled as if the question amused him. "Yes."

"I mean something really nice, not the one you wore to your high-school graduation."

"It's a really nice suit."

Dianne didn't mean to be insulting, but she had to have all her bases covered. "That's good," she said. "How would you like to earn an extra hundred bucks Saturday night?"

"I beg your pardon?"

"I'm offering you a hundred dollars to escort me to the Valentine's dinner here at the center."

Steve stared at her as though he suspected she'd escaped from a mental institution.

"Listen, I know this is a bit unusual," Dianne rushed on, "but you're perfect. Well, not perfect, but you're exactly the kind of man the kids expect me to date, and frankly I haven't got time to do a whole lot of recruiting. Mr. Right hasn't showed up, if you know what I mean."

"I think I do."

"I need a date for one night. You fit the bill and you could probably use the extra cash. I realize it's not much, but a hundred dollars sounds fair to me. The dinner starts at seven and should be over by nine. I suspect fifty dollars an hour is more than you're earning now."

"Ah..."

"I know what you're thinking, but I promise you I'm not crazy. I've got a gold credit card, and they don't issue those to just anyone."

"What about a library card?"

"That, too, but I do have a book overdue. I was planning to take it back tomorrow." She started searching through her purse to prove she had both cards before she saw that he was teasing her.

"Ms. ..."

"Dianne Williams," she said stepping forward to offer him her hand. His long, strong fingers wrapped around hers and he smiled, studying her for perhaps the first time. His eyes softened as he shook her hand. The gesture, though small, reassured Dianne that he was the man she wanted to take her to this silly dinner. Once more she found herself rushing to explain.

"I'm sure this all sounds crazy. I don't blame you for thinking I'm a nutcase. But I'm not, really I'm not. I attend church every Sunday, do volunteer work at the grade school, and help coach a girls' soccer team in the fall."

"Why'd you pick me?"

"Well, that's a bit complicated, but you have nice eyes, and when you suggested I sit in your truck and get out of the rain—actually it was only drizzling—" she paused and inhaled a deep breath "—I realized you were a generous person, and you just might consider something this…"

"…weird," he finished for her.

Dianne nodded, then looked him directly in the eye. Her defenses were down, and there was nothing left to do but admit the truth.

"I'm desperate. No one but a desperate woman would make this kind of offer."

"Saturday night, you say?"

The way her luck was running, he'd suddenly remember he had urgent plans for the evening. Something important like dusting his bowling trophies.

"From seven to nine. No later, I promise. If you don't think a hundred is enough…"

"A hundred's more than generous."

She sagged with relief. "Does this mean you'll do it?"

Steve shook his head slowly, as though to suggest he ought to have it examined for even contemplating her proposal.

"All right," he said after a moment. "I never could resist a damsel in distress."

Three

"Hello, everyone!" Dianne sang out as she breezed in the front door. She paused just inside the living room and watched as her mother and her two children stared openly. A sense of quiet astonishment pervaded the room. "Is something wrong?"

"What happened to you?" Jason cried. "You look awful!"

"You look like Little Orphan Annie, dear," her mother said, her hand working a crochet hook so fast the yarn zipped through her fingers.

"I phoned to tell you I'd be late," Dianne reminded them.

"But you didn't say anything about nearly drowning. What happened?"

"I locked my keys in the car—I already explained that."

Jill walked over to her mother, took her hand and led her to the hallway mirror. The image that greeted Dianne was only a little short of shocking. Her long thick hair hung in limp sodden curls over her shoulders. Her mascara, supposedly no-run, had dissolved into black tracks down her cheeks. She was drenched to the skin and looked like a prize the cat had dragged onto the porch.

"Oh, dear," she whispered. Her stomach muscles tightened as she recalled the odd glances Steve had given her, and his comment that it must be "one of those days." No wonder!

"Why don't you go upstairs and take a nice hot shower?" her mother said. "You'll feel worlds better."

Humbled, for more reasons than she cared to admit, Dianne agreed.

As was generally the rule, her mother was right. By the time Dianne reappeared a half hour later, dressed in her terry-cloth robe and fuzzy pink slippers, she felt considerably better.

Making herself a cup of tea, she reviewed the events of the evening. Even if Steve had agreed to attend the Valentine's dinner out of pity, it didn't matter. What did matter was the fact that she had a date. As soon as she told her family, they'd stop hounding her.

"By the way," she said as she carried her tea into the living room, "I have a date for Saturday night."

The room went still. Even the television sound seemed to fade into nothingness. Her two children and her mother did a slow turn, their faces revealing their surprise.

"Don't look so shocked," Dianne said with a light, casual laugh. "I told you before that I was working on it. No one seemed to believe I was capable of finding a date on my own. Well, that isn't the case."

"Who?" Martha demanded, her eyes disbelieving.

"Oh, ye of little faith," Dianne said, feeling only a small twinge of guilt. "His name is Steve Creighton."

"When did you meet him?"

"Ah..." Dianne realized she wasn't prepared for an inquisition. "A few weeks ago. We happened to bump into each other tonight, and he asked if I had a date for the dinner. Naturally I told him I didn't and he suggested we go together."

"Steve Creighton." Her mother repeated the name slowly, rolling the syllables over her tongue, as if trying to remember where she'd last heard it. Then she shook her head and resumed crocheting.

"You never said anything about this guy before." Jason's gaze was slightly accusing. He sat on the carpet, knees tucked under his chin.

"Of course I didn't. If I had, all three of you would be bugging me about him, just the way you are now."

Martha gave her ball of yarn a hard jerk. "How'd you two meet?"

Dianne wasn't ready for this line of questioning. She'd assumed letting her family know she had the necessary escort would've been enough to appease them. Silly of her.

They wanted details. Lots of details, and the only thing Dianne could do was make them up as she went along. She couldn't very well admit she'd only met Steve that night and was so desperate for a date that she'd offered to pay him to escort her to the dinner.

"We met, ah, a few weeks ago in the grocery store," she explained haltingly, averting her gaze. She prayed that would satisfy their curiosity. But when she paused to sip her tea, the three faces were riveted on her.

"Go on," her mother urged.

"I...I was standing in the frozen-food section and...

Steve was there, too, and…he smiled at me and introduced himself."

"What did he say after that?" Jill wanted to know, eager for the particulars. Martha shared her granddaughter's interest. She set her yarn and crochet hook aside, focusing all her attention on Dianne.

"After he introduced himself, he said surely those low-cal dinners couldn't be for me—that I looked perfect just the way I was." The words fell stiffly from her lips. She had to be desperate to divulge her own fantasy to her family like this.

All right, she *was* desperate.

Jill's shoulders rose with an expressive sigh. "How romantic!"

Jason, however, was frowning. "The guy sounds like a flake to me. A real man doesn't walk up to a woman and say something stupid like that."

"Steve's very nice."

"Maybe, but he doesn't sound like he's got all his oars in the water."

"I think he sounds sweet," Jill countered, immediately defending her mother by championing Steve. "If Mom likes him, then he's good enough for me."

"There are a lot of fruitcakes out there." Apparently her mother felt obliged to tell her that.

It was all Dianne could do not to remind her dear, sweet mother that she'd arranged several dates for her with men who fell easily into that category.

"I think we should meet him," Jason said, his eyes darkening with concern. "He might turn out to be a serial murderer or something."

"Jason—" Dianne forced another light laugh "—you're

being silly. Besides, you're going to meet him Saturday night."

"By then it'll be too late."

"Jason's got a point, dear," Martha said. "I don't think it would do any harm to introduce your young man to the family before Saturday night."

"I... He's probably busy... He's working all sorts of weird hours and..."

"What does he do?"

"Ah..." She couldn't think fast enough to come up with a lie and had to admit the truth. "He drives a truck."

Her words were followed by a tense silence as her children and mother exchanged meaningful looks. "I've heard stories about truck drivers," Martha said, pinching her lips tightly together. "None I'd care to repeat in front of the children, mind you, but...stories."

"Mother, you're being—"

"Jason's absolutely right. I insist we meet this Steve. Truck drivers and cowboys simply aren't to be trusted."

Dianne rolled her eyes.

Her mother forgave her by saying, "I don't expect you to know this, Dianne, since you married so young."

"You married Dad when you were eighteen—younger than I was when I got married," Dianne said, not really wanting to argue, but finding herself trapped.

"Yes, but I've lived longer." She waved her crochet hook at Dianne. "A mother knows these things."

"Grandma's right," Jason said, sounding very adult. "We need to meet this Steve before you go out with him."

Dianne threw her hands in the air in frustration. "Hey, I thought you kids were the ones so eager for me to be at this dinner!"

"Yes, but we still have standards," Jill said, now siding with the others.

"I'll see what I can do," Dianne mumbled.

"Invite him over for dinner on Thursday night," her mother said. "I'll make my beef Stroganoff and bring over a fresh apple pie."

"Ah...he might be busy."

"Then tell him Wednesday night," Jason advised in a voice that was hauntingly familiar. It was the same tone Dianne used when she meant business.

With nothing left to do but agree, Dianne said, "Okay. I'll try for Thursday." Oh, Lord, she thought, what had she got herself into?

She waited until the following afternoon to contact Steve. He'd given her his business card, which she'd tucked into the edging at the bottom of the bulletin board in her kitchen. She wasn't pleased about having to call him. She'd need to offer him more money if he agreed to this dinner. She couldn't very well expect him to come out of the generosity of his heart.

"Port Blossom Towing," a crisp female voice answered.

"Ah...this is Dianne Williams. I'd like to leave a message for Steve Creighton."

"Steve's here." Her words were followed by a click and a ringing sound.

"Steve," he answered distractedly.

"Hello." Dianne found herself at a loss for words. She'd hoped to just leave a message and ask him to return the call at his convenience. Having him there, on the other end of the line, when she wasn't expecting it left her at a disadvantage.

"Is this Dianne?"

"Yes. How'd you know?"

He chuckled softly, and the sound was pleasant and warm. "It's probably best if I don't answer that. Are you checking up to make sure I don't back out of Saturday night? Don't worry, I won't. In fact, I stopped off at the community center this morning and picked up tickets for the dinner."

"Oh, you didn't have to do that, but thanks. I'll reimburse you later."

"Just add it to my tab," he said lightly.

Dianne cringed, then took a breath and said, "Actually, I called to talk to you about my children."

"Your children?"

"Yes," she said. "Jason and Jill, and my mother, too, seem to think it would be a good idea if they met you. I assured them they would on Saturday night, but apparently that isn't good enough."

"I see."

"According to Jason, by then it'll be too late, and you might turn out to be a serial murderer or something. And my mother found the fact that you drive a truck worrisome."

"Do you want me to change jobs, too? I might have a bit of a problem managing all that before Saturday night."

"Of course not. Now, about Thursday—that's when they want you to come for dinner. My mother's offered to fix her Stroganoff and bake a pie. She uses Granny Smith apples," Dianne added, as though that bit of information would convince him to accept.

"Thursday night?"

"I'll give you an additional twenty dollars."

"Twenty dollars?" He sounded insulted, so Dianne raised her offer.

"All right, twenty-five, but that's as high as I can go. I'm living on a budget, you know." This fiasco was quickly running into a big chunk of cash. The dinner tickets were thirty each, and she'd need to reimburse Steve for those. Plus, she owed him a hundred for escorting her to the silly affair, and now an additional twenty-five if he came to dinner with her family.

"For twenty-five you've got yourself a deal," he said at last. "Anything else?"

Dianne closed her eyes. This was the worst part. "Yes," she said, swallowing tightly. The lump in her throat had grown to painful proportions. "There's one other thing. I...I want you to know I don't normally look that bad."

"Hey, I told you before—don't be so hard on yourself. You'd had a rough day."

"It's just that I don't want you to think I'm going to embarrass you at this Valentine's dinner. There may be people there you know, and after I made such a big deal over whether you had a suit and everything, well, I thought you might be more comfortable knowing..." She paused, closed her eyes and then blurted, "I've decided to switch brands of mascara."

His hesitation was only slight. "Thank you for sharing that. I'm sure I'll sleep better now."

Dianne decided to ignore his comment since she'd practically invited it. She didn't understand why she should find herself so tongue-tied with this man, but then again, perhaps she did. She'd made a complete idiot of herself. Paying a man to escort her to a dinner wasn't exactly the type of thing she wanted to list on a résumé.

"Oh, and before I forget," Dianne said, determined to put this unpleasantness behind her, "my mother and the kids asked me several questions about…us. How we met and the like. It might be a good idea if we went over my answers so our stories match."

"You want to meet for coffee later?"

"Ah…when?"

"Say seven, at the Pancake Haven. Don't worry, I'll buy."

Dianne had to bite back her sarcastic response. Instead she murmured, "Okay, but I won't have a lot of time."

"I promise not to keep you any longer than necessary."

Four

"All right," Steve said dubiously, once the waitress had poured them each a cup of coffee. "How'd we meet?"

Dianne told him, lowering her voice when she came to the part about the low-cal frozen dinners. She found it rather humiliating to have to repeat her private fantasy a second time, especially to Steve.

He looked incredulous when she'd finished. "You've got to be kidding."

Dianne took offense at his tone. This was *her* romantic invention he was ridiculing, and she hadn't even mentioned the part about the Rimsky-Korsakov symphony or the chiming bells.

"I didn't have time to think of anything better," Dianne explained irritably. "Jason hit me with the question first thing and I wasn't prepared."

"What did Jason say when you told him that story?"

"He said you sounded like a flake."

"I don't blame him."

Dianne's shoulders sagged with defeat.

"Don't worry about it," Steve assured her, still frowning. "I'll clear everything up when I meet him Thursday night." He said it in a way that suggested the task would be difficult.

"Good—only don't make me look like any more of a fool than I already do."

"I'll try my best," he said with the same dubious inflection he'd used when they'd first sat down.

Dianne sympathized. This entire affair was quickly going from bad to worse, and there was no one to fault but her. Who would've dreamed finding a date for the Valentine's dinner would cause so many problems?

As they sipped their coffee, Dianne studied the man sitting across from her. She was somewhat surprised to discover that Steve Creighton looked even better the second time around. He was dressed in slacks and an Irish cable-knit sweater the color of winter wheat. His smile was a ready one and his eyes, now that she had a chance to see them in the light, were a deep, rich shade of brown like his hair. The impression he'd given her of a considerate, generous man persisted. He must be. No one else would have agreed to this scheme, at least not without a more substantial inducement.

"I'm afraid I might've painted my kids a picture of you that's not quite accurate," Dianne admitted. Both her children had been filled with questions about Steve when they'd returned from school that afternoon. Jason had remained skeptical, but Jill, always a romantic— Dianne couldn't imagine where she'd inherited that!— had bombarded her for details.

"I'll do my best to live up to my image," Steve was quick to assure her.

Placing her elbows on the table, Dianne brushed a thick swatch of hair away from her face and tucked it behind her ear. "Listen, I'm sorry I ever got you involved in this."

"No backing out now—I've laid out cold hard cash for the dinner tickets."

Which was a not-so-subtle reminder that she owed him for those. She dug through her bag and brought out her checkbook. "I'll write you a check for the tickets right now."

"I'm not worried." He dismissed her offer with a wave of his hand.

Nevertheless, Dianne insisted. If she paid him in increments, she wouldn't have to think about how much this fiasco would end up costing her. She had the distinct feeling that by the time the Valentine's dinner was over, she would've spent as much as if she'd taken a Hawaiian vacation. Or gone to Seattle for the weekend, anyway.

After adding her signature, with a flair, to the bottom of the check, she kept her eyes lowered and said, "If I upped the ante ten dollars do you think you could manage to look…besotted?"

"Besotted?" Steve repeated the word as though he'd never heard it before.

"You know, smitten."

"Smitten?"

Again he made it sound as though she were speaking a foreign language. "Attracted," she tried for the third time, loud enough to catch the waitress's attention. The woman appeared and splashed more coffee into their nearly full cups.

"I'm not purposely being dense," he said. "I'm just not sure what you mean."

"Try to look as though you find me attractive," she

said, leaning halfway across the table and speaking in a heated whisper.

"I see. So that's what 'besotted' means." He took another sip of his coffee, and Dianne had the feeling he did so in an effort to hide a smile.

"You aren't supposed to find that amusing." She took a gulp of her own drink and nearly scalded her mouth. Under different circumstances she would've grimaced with pain, or at least reached for the water glass. She did none of those things. A woman has her pride.

"Let me see if I understand you correctly," Steve said matter-of-factly. "For an extra ten bucks you want me to look 'smitten.'"

"Yes," Dianne answered with as much dignity as she could muster, which at the moment wasn't a lot.

"I'll do it, of course," Steve said, grinning and making her feel all the more foolish, "only I'm not sure I know how." He straightened, squared his shoulders and momentarily closed his eyes.

"Steve?" Dianne whispered, glancing around, hoping no one was watching them. He seemed to be attempting some form of Eastern meditation. She half expected him to start chanting. "What are you doing?"

"Thinking about how to look smitten."

"Are you making fun of me?"

"Not at all. If you're willing to offer me an extra ten bucks, it must be important to you. I want to do it right."

Dianne thought she'd better tell him. "This isn't for me," she said. "It's for my ten-year-old daughter, who happens to have a romantic nature. Jill was so impressed with the story of how we supposedly met, that I…I was kind of hoping you'd be willing to…you know." Now that she was forced to spell it out, Dianne wasn't certain of anything. But she knew one thing—suggesting he look smitten with her had been a mistake.

"I'll try."

"I'd appreciate it," she said.

"How's this?" Steve cocked his head at a slight angle, then slowly lowered his eyelids until they were half closed. His mouth curved upward in an off-center smile while his shoulders heaved in what Dianne suspected was meant to be a deep sigh of longing. As though in afterthought, he pressed his open hands over his heart while making soft panting sounds.

"Are you doing an imitation of a Saint Bernard?" Dianne snapped, still not sure whether he was laughing at her. "You look like a...a dog. Maybe Jason's right and you really are a flake."

"I was trying to look besotted," Steve said. "I thought that was what you wanted." As if it would improve the image, he cocked his head the other way and repeated the performance.

"You're making fun of me, and I don't appreciate it one bit." Dianne tossed her napkin on the table and stood. "Thursday night, six o'clock, and please don't be late." With that she slipped her purse strap over her shoulder and stalked out of the restaurant.

Steve followed her to her car. "All right, I apologize. I got carried away in there."

Dianne nodded. She'd gone a little overboard herself, but not nearly as much as Steve. Although she claimed she wanted him to give the impression of being attracted to her for Jill's sake, that wasn't entirely true. Steve was handsome and kind, and to have him looking at her with his heart in his eyes was a fantasy that was strictly her own.

Admitting that, even to herself, was a shock. The walls around her battered heart had been reinforced by three years of loneliness. For reasons she couldn't really explain, this tow-truck driver made her feel vulnerable.

"I'm willing to try again if you want," he said. "Only..."

"Yes?" Her car was parked in the rear lot where the lighting wasn't nearly as good. Steve's face was hidden in the shadows, and she couldn't tell if he was being sincere or not.

"The problem," he replied slowly, "comes from the fact that we haven't kissed. I don't mean to be forward, you understand. You want me to wear a certain look, but it's a little difficult to manufacture without having had any, er, physical closeness."

"I see." Dianne's heart was pounding hard enough to damage her rib cage.

"Are you willing to let me kiss you?"

It was a last resort and she didn't have much choice. But she didn't have anything to lose, either. "If you insist."

With a deep breath, she tilted her head to the right, shut her eyes and puckered up. After waiting what seemed an inordinate amount of time, she opened her eyes. "Is something wrong?"

"I can't do it."

Embarrassed in the extreme, Dianne set her hands on her hips. "What do you mean?"

"You look like you're about to be sacrificed to appease the gods."

"I beg your pardon!" Dianne couldn't believe she was hearing him correctly. Talk about humiliation— she was only doing what he'd suggested.

"I can't kiss a woman who acts like she's about to undergo the most revolting experience of her life."

"You're saying I'm…oh…oh!" Too furious to speak, Dianne gripped Steve by the elbow and jerked him over to where his tow truck was parked, a couple of spaces down from her own car. Hopping onto the running board, she glared down at him. Her higher vantage point made her feel less vulnerable. Her eyes flashed with anger; his were filled with mild curiosity.

"Dianne, what are you doing now?"

"I'll have you know I was quite a kisser in my time."

"I don't doubt it."

"You just did. Now listen and listen well, because I'm only going to say this once." Waving her index finger under his nose, she paused and lowered her hand abruptly. He was right, she hadn't been all that thrilled to fall into this little experiment. A kiss was an innocent-enough exchange, she supposed, but kissing Steve put her on the defensive. And that troubled her.

"Say it."

Self-conscious now, she shifted her gaze and stepped off the running board, feeling ridiculous.

"What was so important that you were waving your finger under my nose?" Steve pressed.

Since she'd made such a fuss, she didn't have any alternative but to finish what she'd begun. "When I was in high school…the boys used to like to kiss me."

"They still would," Steve said softly, "if you'd give them a little encouragement."

She looked up at him and had to blink back unexpected tears. A woman doesn't have her husband walk out on her and not find herself awash in pain and self-doubt. Once she'd been confident; now she was dubious and insecure.

"Here," Steve said, holding her by the shoulders. "Let's try this." Then he gently, sweetly slanted his mouth over hers. Dianne was about to protest when their lips met and the option to refuse was taken from her.

Mindlessly she responded. Her arms slid around his middle and her hands splayed across the hard muscles of his back. And suddenly, emotions that had been simmering just below the surface rose like a tempest within her, and her heart went on a rampage.

Steve buried his hands in her hair, his fingers twisting and tangling in its thickness, bunching it at the back of her head. His mouth was soft, yet possessive. She gave a small, shocked moan when his tongue breached the barrier of her lips, but she adjusted quickly to the deepening quality of his kiss.

Reluctantly, Steve eased his mouth from hers. For a long moment, Dianne didn't open her eyes. When she finally did, she found Steve staring down at her.

He blinked.

She blinked.

Then, in the space of a heartbeat, he lowered his mouth back to hers.

Unable to stop, Dianne sighed deeply and leaned into his strength. Her legs felt like mush and her head was spinning with confusion. Her hands crept up and closed around the folds of his collar.

This kiss was long and thorough. It was the sweetest kiss Dianne had ever known—and the most passionate.

When he lifted his mouth from hers, he smiled tenderly. "I don't believe I'll have any problem looking besotted," he whispered.

Five

"Steve's here!" Jason called, releasing the living-room curtain. "He just pulled into the driveway."

Jill's high-pitched voice echoed her brother's. "He brought his truck. It's red and—"

"—wicked," Jason said, paying Steve's choice of vehicles the highest form of teenage compliment.

"What did I tell you," Dianne's mother said, as she briskly stirred the Stroganoff sauce. "He's driving a truck that's red and wicked." Her voice rose hysterically. "The man's probably a spawn of the devil!"

"Mother, 'wicked' means 'wonderful' to Jason."

"I've never heard anything so absurd in my life."

The doorbell chimed just then. Unfastening the apron from around her waist and tossing it aside, Dianne straightened and walked into the wide entryway. Jason, Jill and her mother followed closely, crowding her.

"Mom, please," Dianne pleaded, "give me some room here. Jason. Jill. Back up a little, would you?"

All three moved several paces back, allowing Di-

anne some space. But the moment her hand went for
the doorknob, they crowded forward again.

"Children, Ma, please!" she whispered frantically.
The three were so close to her she could barely breathe.

Reluctantly Jason and Jill shuffled into the living
room and slumped onto the sofa near the television set.
Martha, however, refused to budge.

The bell chimed a second time, and after glaring at
her mother and receiving no response, Dianne opened
the door. On the other side of the screen door stood
Steve, a huge bouquet of red roses in one hand and a
large stuffed bear tucked under his other arm.

Dianne stared as she calculated the cost of long-
stemmed roses, and a stuffed animal. She couldn't even
afford carnations. And if he felt it necessary to bring
along a stuffed bear, why hadn't he chosen a smaller,
less costly one?

"May I come in?" he asked after a lengthy pause.

Her mother elbowed Dianne in the ribs and smiled
serenely as she unlatched the lock on the screen door.

"You must be Steve. How lovely to meet you," Martha said as graciously as if she'd always thought the
world of truck drivers.

Holding the outer door for him, Dianne managed
to produce a weak smile as Steve entered her home.
Jason and Jill had come back into the hallway to stand
next to their grandmother, eyeing Dianne's newfound
date with open curiosity. For all her son's concern that
Steve might turn out to be an ax-murderer, one look at
the bright-red tow truck and he'd been won over.

"Steve, I'd like you to meet my family," Dianne said,
gesturing toward the three.

"So, you're Jason," Steve said, holding out his hand.

The two exchanged a hearty handshake. "I'm pleased to meet you. Your mother speaks highly of you."

Jason beamed.

Turning his attention to Jill, Steve held out the over-size teddy bear. "This is for you," he said, giving her the stuffed animal. "I wanted something extra-special for Dianne's daughter, but this was all I could think of. I hope you aren't disappointed."

"I *love* teddy bears!" Jill cried, hugging it tight. "Did Mom tell you that?"

"Nope," Steve said, centering his high-voltage smile on the ten-year-old. "I just guessed."

"Oh, thank you, thank you." Cuddling the bear, Jill raced up the stairs, giddy with delight. "I'm going to put him on my bed right now."

Steve's gaze followed her daughter, and then his eyes briefly linked with Dianne's. In that split second, she let him know she wasn't entirely pleased. He frowned slightly, but recovered before presenting the roses to Dianne's mother.

"For me?" Martha brought her fingertips to her mouth as though shocked by the gesture. "Oh, you shouldn't have! Oh, my heavens, I can't remember the last time a man gave me roses." Reaching for the corner of her apron, she discreetly dabbed her eyes. "This is such a treat."

"Mother, don't you want to put those in water?" Dianne said pointedly.

"Oh, dear, I suppose I should. It was a thoughtful gesture, Steve. Very thoughtful."

"Jason, go help your grandmother."

Her son looked as though he intended to object, but

changed his mind and obediently followed Martha into the kitchen.

As soon as they were alone, Dianne turned on Steve. "Don't you think you're laying it on a little thick?" she whispered. She was so furious she was having trouble speaking clearly. "I can't afford all this!"

"Don't worry about it."

"I am worried. In fact I'm experiencing a good deal of distress. At the rate you're spending my money, I'm going to have to go on an installment plan."

"Hush, now, before you attract everyone's attention."

Dianne scowled at him. "I—"

Steve placed his fingers over her lips. "I've learned a very effective way of keeping you quiet—don't force me to use it. Kissing you so soon after my arrival might create the wrong impression."

"You wouldn't dare!"

The way his mouth slanted upward in a slow smile made her afraid he would. "I was only doing my best to act besotted," he said.

"You didn't have to spend this much money doing it. Opening my door, holding out my chair—that's all I wanted. First you roll your eyes like you're going into a coma and pant like a Saint Bernard, then you spend a fortune."

"Dinner's ready," Martha shouted from the kitchen.

With one last angry glare, Dianne led him into the big kitchen. Steve moved behind Dianne's chair and pulled it out for her. "Are you happy now?" he whispered close to her ear as she sat down.

She nodded, thinking it was too little, too late, but she didn't have much of an argument since she'd specifically asked for this.

Soon the five were seated around the wooden table. Dianne's mother said the blessing, and while she did, Dianne offered up a fervent prayer of her own. She wanted Steve to make a good impression—but not too good.

After the buttered noodles and the Stroganoff had been passed around, along with a lettuce-and-cucumber salad and homemade rolls, Jason embarked on the topic that had apparently been troubling him from the first.

"Mom said you met at the grocery store."

Steve nodded. "She was blocking the aisle and I had to ask her to move her cart so I could get to the Hearty Eater Pot Pies."

Jason straightened in his chair, looking more than a little satisfied. "I thought it might be something like that."

"I beg your pardon?" Steve asked, playing innocent.

Her son cleared his throat, glanced carefully around before answering, then lowered his voice. "You should hear Mom's version of how you two met."

"More noodles?" Dianne said, shoving the bowl toward her son.

Jill looked confused. "But didn't you smile at Mom and say she's perfect just the way she is?"

Steve took a moment to compose his thoughts while he buttered his third dinner roll. Dianne recognized that he was doing a balancing act between her two children. If he said he'd commented on the low-cal frozen dinners and her figure, then he risked offending Jason, who seemed to think no man in his right mind would say something like that. On the other hand, if he claimed otherwise, he might wound Jill's romantic little heart.

"I'd be interested in knowing that myself," Martha

added, looking pleased that Steve had taken a second helping of her Stroganoff. "Dianne's terribly close-mouthed about these things. She didn't even mention you until the other night."

"To be honest," Steve said, sitting back in his chair, "I don't exactly recall what I said to Dianne. I remember being irritated with her for hogging the aisle, but when I asked her to move, she apologized and immediately pushed her cart out of the way."

Jason nodded, appeased.

"But when I got a good look at her, I couldn't help thinking she was the most beautiful woman I'd seen in a long while."

Jill sighed, mollified.

"I don't recall any of that," Dianne said, reaching for another roll. She tore it apart with a vengeance and smeared butter on both halves before she realized she had an untouched roll balanced on the edge of her plate.

"I was thinking that after dinner I'd take Jason out for a ride in the truck," Steve said when a few minutes had passed.

"You'd do that?" Jason nearly leaped from his chair in his eagerness.

"I was planning to all along," Steve explained. "I thought you'd be more interested in seeing how all the gears worked than in any gift I could bring you."

"I am." Jason was so excited he could barely sit still.

"When Jason and I come back, I'll take you out for a spin, Dianne."

She shook her head. "I'm not interested, thanks."

Three pairs of accusing eyes flashed in her direction. It was as if she'd committed an act of treason.

"I'm sure my daughter didn't mean that," Martha

said, smiling sweetly at Steve. "She's been very tired lately and not quite herself."

Bewildered, Dianne stared at her mother.

"Can we go now?" Jason asked, already standing.

"If your mother says it's okay," Steve said, with a glance at Dianne. She nodded, and Steve finished the last of his roll and stood.

"I'll have apple pie ready for you when you get back," Martha promised, quickly ushering the two out the front door.

As soon as her mother returned to the kitchen, Dianne asked, "What was all that about?"

"What?" her mother demanded, feigning ignorance.

"That I've been very tired and not myself lately?"

"Oh, that," Martha said, clearing the table. "Steve wants to spend a few minutes alone with you. It's only natural. So I had to make some excuse for you."

"Yes, but—"

"Your behavior, my dear, was just short of rude. When a gentleman makes it clear he wants to spend some uninterrupted time in your company, you should welcome the opportunity."

"Mother, I seem to recall your saying Steve was a spawn of the devil, remember?"

"Now that I've met him, I've had a change of heart."

"What about Jerome, the butcher? I thought you were convinced he was the one for me."

"I like Steve better. I can tell he's a good man, and you'd be a fool to let him slip through your fingers by pretending to be indifferent."

"I am indifferent."

With a look of patent disbelief, Martha Janes shook her head. "I saw the way your eyes lit up when Steve walked into the house. You can fool some folks, but you can't pull the wool over your own mother's eyes. You're falling in love with this young man, and frankly, I'm pleased. I like him."

Dianne frowned. If her eyes had lit up when Steve arrived, it was because she was busy trying to figure out a way to repay him for the roses and the teddy bear. What she felt for him wasn't anything romantic. Or was it?

Dear Lord, she couldn't actually be falling for this guy, could she?

The question haunted Dianne as she loaded the dishwasher.

"Steve's real cute," Jill announced. Her daughter would find Attila the Hun cute, too, if he brought her a teddy bear, but Dianne resisted the impulse to say so.

"He looks a little bit like Hugh Jackman, don't you think?" Jill continued.

"I can't say I've noticed." A small lie. Dianne had noticed a lot more about Steve than she was willing to admit. Although she'd issued a fair number of complaints, he really was being a good sport about this. Of course, she was paying him, but he'd gone above and beyond the call of duty. Taking Jason out for a spin in the tow truck was one example, although why anyone would be thrilled to drive around in that contraption was something Dianne didn't understand.

"I do believe Steve Creighton will make you a decent husband," her mother stated thoughtfully as she removed the warm apple pie from the oven. "In fact, I was just thinking how nice it would be to have a summer wedding. It's so much easier to ask relatives to travel when the weather's good. June or July would be perfect."

"Mother, please! Steve and I barely know each other."

"On the contrary," Steve said, sauntering into the kitchen. He stepped behind Dianne's mother and sniffed appreciatively at the aroma wafting from her apple pie. "I happen to be partial to summer weddings myself."

Six

"Don't you think you're overdoing it a bit?" Dianne demanded as Steve eased the big tow truck out of her driveway. She was belted into the seat next to him, feeling trapped—not to mention betrayed by her own family. They had insisted Steve take her out for a spin so the two of them could have some time alone. Steve didn't want to be alone with her, but her family didn't know that.

"Maybe I did come on a little strong," Steve agreed, dazzling her with his smile.

It was better for her equilibrium if she didn't glance his way, Dianne decided. Her eyes would innocently meet his and he'd give her one of those heart-stopping, lopsided smiles, and something inside her would melt. If this continued much longer, she'd be nothing more than a puddle by the end of the evening.

"The flowers and the stuffed animal I can understand," she said stiffly, willing to grant him that much. "You wanted to make a good impression, and that's fine, but the comment about being partial to summer weddings was going too far. It's just the kind of thing my mother was hoping to hear from you."

"You're right."

The fact that he was being so agreeable should have forewarned Dianne that something was amiss. She'd sensed it from the first moment she'd climbed into the truck. He'd closed the door and almost immediately something pulled wire-taut within her. The sensation was peculiar, even wistful—a melancholy pining she'd never felt before.

She squared her shoulders and stared straight ahead, determined not to fall under his spell the way her children and her mother so obviously had.

"As it is, I suspect Mom's been faithfully lighting votive candles every afternoon, asking God to send me a husband. She thinks God needs her help—that's why she goes around arranging dates for me."

"You're right, of course. I should never have made that comment about summer weddings," Steve said, "but I assumed that's just the sort of thing a *besotted* man would say."

Dianne sighed, realizing once again that she didn't have much of an argument. But he was doing everything in his power to make her regret that silly request.

"Hey, where are you taking me?" she asked when he turned off her street onto a main thoroughfare.

Steve turned his smile on her full force and twitched his thick eyebrows a couple of times for effect. "For a short drive. It wouldn't look good if we were to return five minutes after we left the house. Your family—"

"—will be waiting at the front door. They expect me back any minute."

"No, they don't."

"And why don't they?" she asked, growing uneasy. This wasn't supposed to be anything more than a ride around the block, and she'd had to be coerced into even that.

"Because I told your mother we'd be gone for an hour."

"An hour?" Dianne cried, as though he'd just announced he was kidnapping her. "But you can't do that! I mean, what about your time? Surely it's valuable."

"I assumed you'd want to pay me a few extra dollars—after all, I'm doing this to create the right impression. It's what—"

"I know, I know," she interrupted. "You're just acting smitten." The truth of the matter was that Dianne was making a fuss over something that was actually causing her heart to pound hard and fast. The whole idea of being alone with Steve appealed to her too much. *That* was the reason she fought it so hard. Without even trying, he'd managed to cast a spell on her family, and although she hated to admit it, he'd cast one on her, too. Steve Creighton was laughter and magic. Instinctively she knew he wasn't another Jack. Not the type of man who would walk away from his family.

Dianne frowned as the thought crossed her mind. It would be much easier to deal with the hand life had dealt her if she wasn't forced to associate with men as seemingly wonderful as Steve. It was easier to view all men as insensitive and inconsiderate.

Dianne didn't like that Steve was proving to be otherwise. He was apparently determined to crack the hard shell around her heart, no matter how hard she tried to reinforce it.

"Another thing," she said stiffly, crossing her arms

with resolve, but refusing to glance in his direction. "You've got to stop being so free with my money."

"I never expected you to reimburse me for those gifts," he explained quietly.

"I insist on it."

"My, my, aren't we prickly. I bought the flowers and the toy for Jill of my own accord. I don't expect you to pick up the tab," he said again.

Dianne didn't know if she should argue with him or not. Although his tone was soft, a thread of steel ran through his words, just enough to let her know nothing she said was going to change his mind.

"That's not all," she said, deciding to drop that argument for a more urgent one. She probably did sound a bit shrewish, but if he wasn't going to be practical about this, *she'd* have to be.

"You mean there's more?" he cried, pretending to be distressed.

"Steve, please," she said, shocked at how feeble she sounded. She scarcely recognized the voice as her own. "You've got to stop being so…so wonderful," she finally said.

He came to a stop at a red light and turned to her, draping his arm over the back of the seat. "I don't think I heard you right. Would you mind repeating that?"

"You can't continue to be so—" she paused, searching for another word "—charming."

"Charming," he echoed. "Charming?"

"To my children and my mother," she elaborated. "The gifts were one thing. Giving Jason a ride in the tow truck was fine, too, but agreeing with my mother about summer weddings and then playing basketball with Jason—none of that was necessary."

"Personally, I would've thought your mother measuring my chest and arm length so she could knit me a sweater would bother you the most."

"That, too!"

"Could you explain why this is such a problem?"

"Isn't it obvious? If you keep doing that sort of thing, they'll expect me to continue dating you after the Valentine's dinner, and, frankly, I can't afford it."

He chuckled at that as if she was making some kind of joke. Only it wasn't funny. "I happen to live on a budget—"

"I don't think we should concern ourselves with that," he broke in.

"Well, I *am* concerned." She expelled her breath sharply. "One date! That's all I can afford and that's all I'm interested in. If you continue to be so...so..."

"Wonderful?" he supplied.

"Charming," she corrected, "then I'll have a whole lot to answer for when I don't see you again after Saturday."

"So you want me to limit the charm?"

"Please."

"I'll do my best," he said, and his eyes sparked with laughter, which they seemed to do a good deal of the time. If she hadn't been so flustered, she might have been pleased that he found her so amusing.

"Thank you." She glanced pointedly at her watch. "Shouldn't we head back to the house?"

"No."

"No? I realize you told my mother we'd be gone an hour, but that really is too long and—"

"I'm taking you to Jackson Point."

Dianne's heart reacted instantly, zooming into her

throat and then righting itself. Jackson Point overlooked a narrow water passage between the Kitsap Peninsula and Vashon Island. The view, either at night or during the day, was spectacular, but those who came to appreciate it at night were generally more interested in each other than the glittering lights of the island and Seattle farther beyond.

"I'll take the fact that you're not arguing with me as a positive sign," he said.

"I think we should go back to the house," she stated with as much resolve as she could muster. Unfortunately it didn't come out sounding very firm. The last time she'd been to Jackson Point had been a lifetime ago. She'd been a high-school junior and madly in love for the first time. The last time.

"We'll go back in a little while."

"Steve," she cried, fighting the urge to cry, "why are you doing this?"

"Isn't it obvious? I want to kiss you again."

Dianne pushed her hair away from her face with both hands. "I don't think that's such a good idea." Her voice wavered, just like her teenage son's.

Before she could come up with an argument, Steve pulled off the highway and down the narrow road that led to the popular lookout. She hadn't wanted to think about that kiss they'd shared. It had been a mistake. Dianne knew she'd disappointed Steve—not because of the kiss itself, but her reaction to it. He seemed to be waiting for her to admit how deeply it had affected her, but she hadn't given him the satisfaction.

Now, she told herself, he wanted revenge.

Her heart was still hammering when Steve stopped the truck and turned off the engine. The lights across the water sparkled in welcome. The closest lights were from Vashon Island, a sparsely populated place accessible only by ferry. The more distant ones came from West Seattle.

"It's really beautiful," she whispered. Some of the tension eased from her shoulders and she felt herself begin to relax.

"Yes," Steve agreed. He moved closer and placed his arm around her shoulder.

Dianne closed her eyes, knowing she didn't have the power to resist him. He'd been so wonderful with her children and her mother—more than wonderful. Now it seemed to be her turn, and try as she might to avoid it, she found herself a willing victim to his special brand of magic.

"You *are* going to let me kiss you, aren't you?" he whispered close to her ear.

She nodded.

His hands were in her hair as he directed his mouth to hers. The kiss was slow, as though he was afraid of frightening her. His mouth was warm and moist over her own, gentle and persuasive. Dianne could feel her bones start to dissolve and knew that if she was going to walk away from this experience unscathed, she needed to think fast. Unfortunately, her mind was already overloaded.

When at last they drew apart, he dragged in a deep breath. Dianne sank back against the seat and noted that his eyes were still closed. Taking this moment to gather her composure, she scooted as far away from him as she could, pressing the small of her back against the door handle.

"You're very good at this," she said, striving to sound unaffected, and knowing she hadn't succeeded.

He opened his eyes and frowned. "I'll assume that's a compliment."

"Yes. I think you should." Steve was the kind of man who'd attract attention from women no matter where he went. He wouldn't be interested in a divorcée and a ready-made family, and there was no use trying to convince herself otherwise. The only reason he'd agreed to take her to the Valentine's dinner was because she'd offered to pay him. This was strictly a business arrangement.

His finger lightly grazed the side of her face. His eyes were tender as he studied her, but he said nothing.

"It would probably be a good idea if we talked about Saturday night," she said, doing her best to keep her gaze trained away from him. "There's a lot to discuss and...there isn't much time left."

"All right." His wayward grin told her she hadn't fooled him. He knew exactly what she was up to.

"Since the dinner starts at seven, I suggest you arrive at my house at quarter to."

"Fine."

"We don't need to go to the trouble or the expense of a corsage."

"What are you wearing?"

Dianne hadn't given the matter a second's thought. "Since it's a Valentine's dinner, something red, I suppose. I have a red-and-white-striped dress that will do." It was a couple of years old, but this dinner wasn't exactly the fashion event of the year, and she didn't have the money for a new outfit, anyway.

She looked at her watch, although she couldn't possibly read it in the darkness.

"Is that a hint you want to get back to the house?"

"Yes," she said.

Her honesty seemed to amuse him. "That's what I thought." Without argument, he started the engine and put the truck in Reverse.

The minute they turned onto her street, Jason and Jill came vaulting out the front door. Dianne guessed they'd both been staring out the upstairs window, eagerly awaiting her return.

She was wrong. It was Steve they were eager to see.

"Hey, what took you so long?" Jason demanded as Steve climbed out of the truck.

"Grandma's got the apple pie all dished up. Are you ready?" Jill hugged Steve's arm, gazing anxiously up at him.

Dianne watched the unfolding scene with dismay. Steve walked into her house with one arm around Jason and Jill clinging to the other.

It was as if she were invisible. Neither of her children had said a single word to her!

To his credit, Jason paused at the front door. "Mom, you coming?"

"Just bringing up the rear," she muttered.

Jill shook her head, her shoulders lifting, then falling, in a deep sigh. "You'll have to forgive my mother," she told Steve confidingly. "She can be a real slowpoke sometimes."

Seven

"Oh, Mom," Jill said softly. "You look so beautiful."

Dianne examined her reflection in the full-length mirror. At the last moment, she'd been gripped by another bout of insanity. She'd gone out and purchased a new dress.

She couldn't afford it. She couldn't rationalize that expense on top of everything else, but the instant she'd seen the flowered pink creation in the shop window, she'd decided to try it on. That was her first mistake. Correction: that was just one mistake in a long list of recent mistakes where Steve Creighton was concerned.

The dress was probably the most flattering thing she'd ever owned. The price tag had practically caused her to clutch her chest and stagger backward. She hadn't purchased it impulsively. No, she was too smart for that. The fact that she was nearly penniless and it was only the middle of the month didn't help matters. She'd sat down in the coffee shop next door and juggled figures for ten or fifteen minutes before crumpling up the paper and deciding to buy the dress, anyway. It was her birthday, Mother's Day and Christmas gifts to herself all rolled into one.

"I brought my pearls," Martha announced as she bolted breathlessly into Dianne's bedroom. She was late, which wasn't like Martha, but Dianne hadn't been worried. She knew her mother would be there before she had to leave for the dinner.

Martha stopped abruptly, folding her hands prayerfully and nodding with approval. "Oh, Dianne. You look…"

"Beautiful," Jill finished for her grandmother.

"Beautiful," Martha echoed. "I thought you were going to wear the red dress."

"I just happened to be at the mall and stumbled across this." She didn't mention that she'd made the trip into Tacoma for the express purpose of looking for something new to wear.

"Steve's here," Jason yelled from the bottom of the stairs.

"Here are my pearls," Martha said, reverently handing them to her daughter. The pearls were a family heirloom and worn only on the most special occasions.

"Mom, I don't know…"

"Your first official date with Steve," she said as though that event was on a level with God giving Moses the Ten Commandments. Without further ado, Martha draped the necklace around her daughter's neck. "I insist. Your father insists."

"Mom?" Dianne asked, turning around to search her mother's face. "Have you been talking to Dad again?" Dianne's father had been gone for more than ten years.

However, for several years following his death, Martha claimed they carried on regular conversations.

"Not exactly, but I know your father would have insisted, had he been here. Now off with you. It's rude to keep a date waiting."

Preparing to leave her bedroom, Dianne closed her eyes. She was nervous. Which was silly, she told herself. This wasn't a *real* date, since she was paying Steve for the honor of escorting her. She'd reminded herself of that the entire time she was dressing. The only reason they were even attending this Valentine's dinner was because she'd asked him. Not only asked, but offered to pay for everything.

Jill rushed out of the bedroom door and down the stairs. "She's coming and she looks beautiful."

"Your mother always looks beautiful," Dianne heard Steve say matter-of-factly as she descended the steps. Her eyes were on him, standing in the entryway dressed in a dark gray suit, looking tall and debonair.

He glanced up and his gaze found hers. She was gratified to see that his eyes widened briefly.

"I was wrong, she's extra-beautiful tonight," he whispered, but if he was speaking to her children, he wasn't looking at them. In fact, his eyes were riveted on her, which only served to make Dianne more uneasy.

They stood staring at each other like star-crossed lovers until Jill tugged at Steve's arm. "Aren't you going to give my mom the corsage?"

"Oh, yes, here," he said. Apparently he'd forgotten he was holding an octagon-shaped plastic box.

Dianne frowned. They'd agreed earlier that he wasn't going to do this. She was already over her budget, and flowers were a low-priority item, as far as Dianne was concerned.

"It's for the wrist," he explained, opening the box for her. "I thought you said the dress was red, so I'm afraid this might not go with it very well." The corsage was fashioned of three white rosebuds between a froth of red-and-white silk ribbons. Although her dress was several shades of pink, there was a smattering of red in the center of the flowers that matched the color in the ribbon perfectly. It was as if Steve had seen the dress and chosen the flowers to complement it. "It's…"

"Beautiful," Jill supplied once more, smugly pleased with herself.

"Are you ready?" Steve asked.

Jason stepped forward with her wool coat as though he couldn't wait to be rid of her. Steve took the coat from her son's hands and helped Dianne into it, while her son and daughter stood back looking as proud as if they'd arranged the entire affair themselves.

Before she left the house, Dianne gave her children their instructions and kissed them each on the cheek. Jason wasn't much in favor of letting his mother kiss him, but he tolerated it.

Martha continued to stand at the top of the stairs, dabbing her eyes with a tissue and looking down as if the four of them together were the most romantic sight she'd ever witnessed. Dianne sincerely prayed that Steve wouldn't notice.

"I won't be late," Dianne said as Steve opened the front door.

"Don't worry about it," Jason said pointedly. "There's no need to rush home."

"Have a wonderful time," Jill called after them.

The first thing Dianne realized once they were out the door was that Steve's tow truck was missing from her driveway. She looked around, half expecting to find the red monstrosity parked on the street.

With his hand cupping her elbow, he led her instead to a luxury car. "What's this?" she asked, thinking he might have rented it. If he had, she wanted it understood this minute that she had no intention of paying the fee.

"My car."

"Your car?" she asked. He opened the door for her and Dianne slid onto the supple white leather. Tow-truck operators obviously made better money than she'd assumed. If she'd known that, she would've offered him seventy-five dollars for this evening instead of a hundred.

Steve walked around the front of the sedan and got into the driver's seat. They chatted on the short ride to the community center, with Dianne making small talk in an effort to cover her nervousness.

The parking lot was nearly full, but Steve found a spot on the side lot next to the sprawling brick building.

"You want to go in?" he asked.

She nodded. Over the years, Dianne had attended a dozen of these affairs. There was no reason to feel nervous. Her friends and neighbors would be there. Naturally there'd be questions about her and Steve, but this time she was prepared.

Steve came around the car, opened her door and helped her out. She saw that he was frowning.

"Is something wrong?" she asked anxiously.

"You look pale."

She was about to reply that it was probably nerves when he said, "Not to worry, I have a cure for that." Before she'd guessed his intention, he leaned forward and brushed his mouth over hers.

He was right. The instant his lips touched hers, hot color exploded in her cheeks. She felt herself swaying toward him, and Steve caught her gently by the shoulders.

"That was a mistake," he whispered once they'd moved apart. "Now the only thing I'm hungry for is you. Forget the dinner."

"I...think we should go inside now," she said, glancing around the parking lot, praying no one had witnessed the kiss.

Light and laughter spilled out from the wide double doors of the Port Blossom Community Center. The soft strains of a romantic ballad beckoned them in.

Steve took her coat and hung it on the rack in the entry. She waited for him, feeling more jittery than ever. When he'd finished, Steve slipped his arm about her waist and led her into the main room.

"Steve Creighton!" They had scarcely stepped into the room when Steve was greeted by a robust man with a salt-and-pepper beard. Glancing curiously at Dianne, the stranger slapped Steve on the back and said, "It's about time you attended one of our functions."

Steve introduced Dianne to the man, whose name was Sam Horton. The name was vaguely familiar to her, but she couldn't quite place it.

Apparently reading her mind, Steve said, "Sam's the president of the Chamber of Commerce."

"Ah, yes," Dianne said, impressed to meet one of the community's more distinguished members.

"My wife, Renée," Sam said, absently glancing around, "is somewhere in this mass of humanity." Then he turned back to Steve. "Have you two found a table yet? We'd consider it a pleasure to have you join us."

"Dianne?" Steve looked at her.

"That would be very nice, thank you." Wait until her mother heard this. She and Steve dining with the Chamber of Commerce president! Dianne couldn't help smiling. No doubt her mother would attribute this piece of good luck to the pearls. Sam left to find his wife, in order to introduce her to Dianne.

"Dianne Williams! It's so good to see you." The voice belonged to Beth Martin, who had crossed the room, dragging her husband, Ralph, along with her. Dianne knew Beth from the PTA. They'd worked together on the spring carnival the year before. Actually, Dianne had done most of the work while Beth had done the delegating. The experience had been enough to convince Dianne not to volunteer for this year's event.

Dianne introduced Steve to Beth and Ralph. Dianne felt a small sense of triumph as she noted the way Beth eyed Steve. This man was worth every single penny of the money he was costing her!

The two couples chatted for a few moments, then Steve excused himself. Dianne watched him as he walked through the room, observing how the eyes of several women followed him. He did make a compelling sight, especially in his well-cut suit.

"How long have you known Steve Creighton?" Beth asked the instant Steve was out of earshot. She moved closer to Dianne, as though she was about to hear some well-seasoned gossip.

"A few weeks now." It was clear that Beth was hoping Dianne would elaborate, but Dianne had no intention of doing so.

"Dianne." Shirley Simpson, another PTA friend, moved to her side. "Is that Steve Creighton you're with?"

"Yes." She'd had no idea Steve was so well known.

"I swear he's the cutest man in town. One look at him and my toes start to curl."

When she'd approached Steve with this proposal, Dianne hadn't a clue she would become the envy of her friends. She really *had* got a bargain.

"Are you sitting with anyone yet?" Shirley asked. Beth bristled as though offended she hadn't thought to ask first.

"Ah, yes. Sam Horton's already invited us, but thanks."

"Sam Horton," Beth repeated and she and Shirley shared a significant look. "My, my, you are traveling in elevated circles these days. Well, more power to you. And good luck with Steve Creighton. I've been saying for ages that it's time someone bagged him. I hope it's you."

"Thanks," Dianne said, feeling more than a little confused by this unexpected turn of events. Everyone knew Steve, right down to her PTA friends. It didn't make a lot of sense.

Steve returned a moment later, carrying two slender flutes of champagne. "I'd like you to meet some friends of mine," he said, leading her across the room to where several couples were standing. The circle immediately opened to include them. Dianne recognized the mayor and a couple of others.

Dianne threw Steve a puzzled look. He certainly was a social animal, but the people he knew... Still, why should she be surprised? A tow-truck operator would have plenty of opportunity to meet community leaders. And Steve was such a likable man, who obviously made friends easily.

A four-piece band began playing forties' swing, and after the introductions, Dianne found her toe tapping to the music.

"Next year we should make this a dinner-dance," Steve suggested, smiling down on Dianne. He casually put his hand on her shoulder as if he'd been doing that for months.

"Great idea," Port Blossom's mayor said, nodding. "You might bring it up at the March committee meeting."

Dianne frowned, not certain she understood. It was several minutes before she had a chance to ask Steve about the comment.

"I'm on the board of directors for the community center," he explained briefly.

"You are?" Dianne took another sip of her champagne. Some of the details were beginning to get muddled in her mind, and she wasn't sure if it had anything to do with the champagne.

"Does that surprise you?"

"Yes. I thought you had to be, you know, a business owner to be on the board of directors."

Now it was Steve's turn to frown. "I am."

"You are?" Dianne asked. Her hand tightened around the long stem of her glass. "What business?"

"Port Blossom Towing."

That did it. Dianne drank what remained of her

champagne in a single gulp. "You mean to say you *own* the company?"

"Yes. Don't tell me you didn't know."

She glared up at him, her eyes narrowed and distrusting. "I didn't."

Eight

Steve Creighton had made a fool of her.

Dianne was so infuriated she couldn't wait to be alone with him so she could give him a piece of her mind. Loudly.

"What's that got to do with anything?" Steve asked.

Dianne continued to glare at him, unable to form any words yet. It wasn't just that he owned the towing company or even that he was a member of the board of directors for the community center. It was the fact that he'd deceived her.

"You should've told me you owned the company!" she hissed.

"I gave you my business card," he said, shrugging.

"You gave me your business card," she mimicked in a furious whisper. "The least you could've done was mention it. I feel like an idiot."

Steve was wearing a perplexed frown, as if he found her response completely unreasonable. "To be honest, I assumed you knew. I wasn't purposely keeping it from you."

That wasn't the only thing disturbing her, but the

second concern was even more troubling than the first. "While I'm on the subject, what are you? Some sort of...love god?"

"What?"

"From the moment we arrived all the women I know, and even some I don't, have been crowding around me asking all sorts of leading questions. One friend claims you make her toes curl and another...never mind."

Steve looked exceptionally pleased. "I make her toes curl?"

How like a man to fall for flattery! "That's not the point."

"Then what is?"

"Everyone thinks you and I are an item."

"So? I thought that's what you wanted."

Dianne felt like screaming. "Kindly look at this from my point of view. I'm in one hell of a mess because of you!" He frowned as she went on. "What am I supposed to tell everyone, including my mother and children, once tonight is over?" Why, oh why hadn't she thought of this sooner?

"About what?"

"About you and me," she said slowly, using short words so he'd understand. "I didn't even *want* to attend this dinner. I've lied to my own family and, worse, I'm actually paying a man to escort me. This is probably the lowest point of my life, and all you can do is stand there with a silly grin."

Steve chuckled and his mouth twitched. "This silly grin you find so offensive is my besotted look. I've been practicing it in front of a mirror all week."

Dianne covered her face with her hands. "Now... now I discover that I'm even more of a fool than I realized. You're this upstanding businessman and, worse, a…a playboy."

"I'm not a playboy," he corrected. "And that's a pretty dated term, anyway."

"Maybe—but that's the reputation you seem to have. There isn't a woman at this dinner who doesn't envy me."

All she'd wanted was someone presentable to escort her to this dinner so she could satisfy her children. She lived a quiet, uncomplicated life, and suddenly she was the most gossip-worthy member of tonight's affair.

Sam Horton stepped to the microphone in front of the hall and announced that dinner was about to be served, so would everyone please go to their tables.

"Don't look so discontented," Steve whispered in her ear. He was standing behind her, and his hands rested gently on her shoulders. "The woman who's supposed to be the envy of every other one here shouldn't be frowning. Try smiling."

"I don't think I can," she muttered, fearing she might break down and cry. Being casually held by Steve wasn't helping. She found his touch reassuring and comforting when she didn't want either, at least not from him. She was confused enough. Her head was telling her one thing and her heart another.

"Trust me, Dianne, you're blowing this out of proportion. I didn't mean to deceive you. Let's just enjoy the evening."

"I feel like such a fool," she muttered again. Several people walked past them on their way to the tables, pausing to smile and nod. Dianne did her best to respond appropriately.

"You're not a fool." He slipped his arm around her

waist and led her toward the table where Sam and his
wife, as well as two other couples Dianne didn't know,
were waiting.

Dianne smiled at the others while Steve held out her
chair. A gentleman to the very end, she observed wryly.
He opened doors and held out chairs for her, and the
whole time she was making an idiot of herself in front
of the entire community.

As soon as everyone was seated, he introduced Dianne to the two remaining couples—Larry and Louise Lester, who owned a local restaurant, and Dale and
Maryanne Atwater. Dale was head of the town's most
prominent accounting firm.

The salads were delivered by young men in crisp
white jackets. The Lesters and the Atwaters were discussing the weather and other bland subjects. Caught
in her own churning thoughts, Dianne ate her salad
and tuned them out. When she was least expecting it,
she heard her name. She glanced up to find six pairs of
eyes studying her. She had no idea why.

She lowered the fork to her salad plate and glanced
at Steve, praying he'd know what was going on.

"The two of you make such a handsome couple,"
Renée Horton said. Her words were casual, but her expression wasn't. Everything about her said she was in-
tensely curious about Steve and Dianne.

"Thank you," Steve answered, then turned to Dianne
and gave her what she'd referred to earlier as a silly grin
and what he'd said was his besotted look.

"How did you two meet?" Maryanne Atwater asked
nonchalantly.

"Ah…" Dianne's mind spun, lost in a haze of half-
truths and misconceptions. She didn't know if she dared

repeat the story about meeting in the local grocery, but she couldn't think fast enough to come up with anything else. She thought she was prepared, but the moment she was in the spotlight, all her self-confidence deserted her.

"We both happened to be in the grocery store at the same time," Steve explained smoothly. The story had been repeated so often it was beginning to sound like the truth.

"I was blocking Steve's way in the frozen-food section," she said, picking up his version of the story. She felt embarrassed seeing the three other couples listening so intently to their fabrication.

"I asked Dianne to kindly move her cart, and she stopped to apologize for being so thoughtless. Before I knew it, we'd struck up a conversation."

"I was there!" Louise Lester threw her hands wildly in the air, her blue eyes shining. "That was the two of you? I saw the whole thing!" She dabbed the corners of her mouth with her napkin and checked to be sure she had everyone's attention before continuing. "I swear it was the most romantic thing I've ever seen."

"It certainly was," Steve added, smiling over at Dianne, who restrained herself from kicking him in the shin, although it was exactly what he deserved.

"Steve's cart inadvertently bumped into Dianne's," Louise went on, grinning broadly at Steve.

"Inadvertently, Steve?" Sam Horton teased, chuckling loudly enough to attract attention. Crazy though it was, it seemed that everyone in the entire community center had stopped eating in order to hear Louise tell her story.

"At any rate," Louise said, "the two of them stopped to chat, and I swear it was like watching a romantic

comedy. Naturally Dianne apologized—she hadn't realized she was blocking the aisle. Then Steve started
sorting through the stuff in her cart, teasing her. We all
know how Steve enjoys kidding around."

The others shook their heads, their affection for their
friend obvious.

"She was buying all these diet dinners," Steve said,
ignoring Dianne's glare. "I told her she couldn't possibly be buying them for herself."

The three women at the table sighed audibly. It was
all Dianne could do not to slide off her chair and disappear under the table.

"That's not the best part," Louise said, beaming with
pride at the attention she was garnering. A dreamy look
stole over her features. "They must've stood and talked
for ages. I'd finished my shopping and just happened
to stroll past them several minutes later, and they were
still there. It was when I was standing in the checkout
line that I noticed them coming down the aisle side by
side, each pushing a grocery cart. It was so cute, I half
expected someone to start playing a violin."

"How sweet," Renée Horton whispered.

"I thought so myself and I mentioned it to Larry once
I got home. Remember, honey?"

Larry nodded obligingly. "Louise must've told me
that story two or three times that night," her husband
reported.

"I just didn't know it was you, Steve. Imagine, out
of all the people to run into at the grocery store, I happened to stumble upon you and Dianne the first time
you met. Life is so ironic, isn't it?"

"Oh, yes, life is very ironic," Dianne said. Steve sent

her a subtle smile, and she couldn't hold back an answering grin.

"It was one of the most beautiful things I've ever seen," Louise finished.

"Can you believe that Louise Lester?" Steve said later. They were sitting in his luxury sedan waiting for their turn to pull out of the crowded parking lot.

"No," Dianne said simply. She'd managed to make it through the rest of the dinner, but it had demanded every ounce of poise and self-control she possessed. From the moment they'd walked in the front door until the time Steve helped her put on her coat at the end of the evening, they'd been the center of attention. And the main topic of conversation.

Like a bumblebee visiting a flower garden, Louise Lester had breezed from one dinner table to the next, spreading the story of how Dianne and Steve had met and how she'd been there to witness every detail.

"I've never been so…" Dianne couldn't think of a word that quite described how she'd felt. "This may have been the worst evening of my life." She slumped against the back of the seat and covered her eyes.

"I thought you had a good time."

"How could I?" she cried, dropping her hand long enough to glare at him. "The first thing I get hit with is that you're some rich playboy."

"Come on, Dianne. Just because I happen to own a business doesn't mean I'm rolling in money."

"Port Blossom Towing is one of the fastest-growing enterprises in Kitsap County," she said, repeating what Sam Horton had been happy to tell her. "What I don't understand is why my mother hasn't heard of you. She's been on the lookout for eligible men for months. It's a miracle she didn't—" Dianne stopped abruptly.

"What?"

"My mother was looking all right, but she was realistic enough to stay in my own social realm. You're a major-league player. The only men my mother knows are in the minors—butchers, teachers, everyday sort of guys."

Now that she thought about it, however, her mother had seemed to recognize Steve's name when Dianne first mentioned it. She probably *had* heard of him, but couldn't remember where.

"Major-league player? That's a ridiculous analogy."

"It isn't. And to think I approached you, offering you money to take me to this dinner." Humiliation washed over her again, then gradually receded. "I have one question—why didn't you already have a date?" The dinner had been only five days away, so surely the most eligible bachelor in town, a man who could have his choice of women, would've had a date!

He shrugged. "I'm not seeing anyone."

"I bet you got a good laugh when I offered to pay you." Not to mention the fact that she'd made such a fuss over his owning a proper suit.

"As a matter of fact, I was flattered."

"No doubt."

"Are you still upset?"

"You could say that, yes." *Upset* was putting it mildly.

Since Dianne's house was only a couple of miles from the community center, she reached for her purse and checkbook. She waited until he pulled into the driveway before writing a check and handing it to him.

"What's this?" Steve asked.

"What I owe you. Since I didn't know the exact cost of Jill's stuffed animal, I made an educated guess. The cost of the roses varies from shop to shop, so I took an average price."

"I don't think you should pay me until the evening's over," he said, opening his car door.

As far as Dianne was concerned, it had been over the minute she'd learned who he was. When he came around to her side of the car and opened her door, she said, "Just what are you planning now?" He led her by the hand to the front of the garage, which was illuminated by a floodlight. They stood facing each other, his hands on her shoulders.

She frowned, gazing up at him. "I fully intend to give you your money's worth," he replied.

"I beg your pardon?"

"Jason, Jill and your mother."

"What about them?"

"They're peering out the front window waiting for me to kiss you, and I'm not going to disappoint them."

"Oh, no, you don't," she objected. But the moment his eyes held hers, all her anger drained away. Then, slowly, as though he recognized the change in her, he lowered his head. Dianne knew he was going to kiss her, and in the same instant she knew she wouldn't do anything to stop him...

Nine

"You have the check?" Dianne asked once her head was clear enough for her to think again. It was a struggle to pull herself free from the magic Steve wove so easily around her.

Steve pulled the check she'd written from his suit pocket. Then, without ceremony, he tore it in two. "I never intended to accept a penny."

"You have to! We agreed—"

"I want to see you again," he said, clasping her shoulders firmly and looking intently at her.

Dianne was struck dumb. If he'd announced he was an alien, visiting from the planet Mars, he couldn't have surprised her more. Not knowing what to say, she eyed him speculatively. "You're kidding, aren't you?"

A smile flitted across his lips as though he'd anticipated her reaction. The left side of his mouth rose slightly higher in that lazy, off-center grin of his. "I've never been more serious in my life."

Now that the shock had worn off, it took Dianne all of one second to decide. "Naturally, I'm flattered—but no."

"No?" Steve was clearly taken aback, and he needed a second or two to compose himself. "Why not?"

"After tonight you need to ask?"

"Apparently so," he said, stepping away from her a little. He paused and shoved his fingers through his hair with enough force to make Dianne flinch. "I can't believe you," he muttered. "The first time we kissed I realized we had something special. I thought you felt it, too."

Dianne couldn't deny it, but she wasn't about to admit it, either. She lowered her gaze, refusing to meet the hungry intensity of his eyes.

When she didn't respond, Steve continued, "I have no intention of letting you out of my life. In case you haven't figured it out yet—and obviously you haven't—I'm crazy about you, Dianne."

Unexpected tears clouded her vision as she gazed up at him. She rubbed her hands against her eyes and sniffled. This wasn't supposed to be happening. She wanted the break to be clean and final. No discussion. No tears.

Steve was handsome and ambitious, intelligent and charming. If anyone deserved an SYT, it was this oh-so-eligible bachelor. She'd been married, and her life was complicated by two children and a manipulative mother.

"Say something," he demanded. "Don't just stand there looking at me with tears in your eyes."

"Th-these aren't tears. They're..." Dianne couldn't finish as fresh tears scalded her eyes.

"Tomorrow afternoon," he said, his voice gentle. "I'll stop by the house, and you and the kids and I can all go to a movie. You can bring your mother, too, if you want."

Dianne managed to swallow a sob. "That's the lowest, meanest thing you've ever suggested."

He frowned. "Taking you and the kids to a movie?"

"Y-yes. You're using my own children against me and that's—"

"Low and mean," he finished, scowling more fiercely. "All right, if you don't want to involve Jason and Jill, then just the two of us will go."

"I already said no."

"Why?"

Her shoulders trembled slightly as she smeared the moisture across her cheek. "I'm divorced." She said it as if it had been a well-kept secret and no one but her mother and children were aware of it.

"So?" He was still scowling.

"I have children."

"I know that, too. You're not making a lot of sense, Dianne."

"It's not that—exactly. You can date any woman you want."

"I want to date *you*."

"No!" She was trembling from the inside out. She tried to compose herself, but it was hopeless with Steve standing so close, looking as though he was going to reach for her and kiss her again.

When she was reasonably sure she wouldn't crumble under the force of her fascination with him, she looked him in the eye. "I'm flattered, really I am, but it wouldn't work."

"You don't know that."

"But I do, I do. We're not even in the same league, you and I, and this whole thing has got completely out of hand." She stood a little straighter, as though the extra inch in height would help. "The deal was I pay you to escort me to the Valentine's dinner—but then

I had to go and complicate matters by suggesting you look smitten with me and you did such a good job of it that you've convinced yourself you're attracted to me and you aren't. You couldn't be."

"Because you're divorced and have two children," he repeated incredulously.

"You're forgetting my manipulative mother."

Steve clenched his fists at his sides. "I haven't forgotten her. In fact, I'm grateful to her."

Dianne narrowed her eyes. "Now I *know* you can't be serious."

"Your mother's a real kick, and your kids are great, and in case you're completely blind, I think you're pretty wonderful yourself."

Dianne fumbled with the pearls at her neck, twisting the strand between her fingers. The man who stood before her was every woman's dream, but she didn't know what was right anymore. She knew only one thing. After the way he'd humiliated her this evening, after the way he'd let her actually pay him to take her to the Valentine's dinner, make a total fool of herself, there was no chance she could see him again.

"I don't think so," she said stiffly. "Goodbye, Steve."

"You really mean it, don't you?"

She was already halfway to the front door. "Yes."

"All right. Fine," he said, slicing the air with his hands. "If this is the way you want it, then fine, just fine." With that he stormed off to his car.

Dianne knew her family would give her all kinds of flack. The minute she walked in the door, Jason and Jill barraged her with questions about the dinner. Dianne was as vague as possible and walked upstairs to her room, pleading exhaustion. There must have been something in her eyes that convinced her mother and children to leave her alone, because no one disturbed her again that night.

She awoke early the next morning, feeling more than a little out of sorts. Jason was already up, eating a huge bowl of cornflakes at the kitchen table.

"Well," he said, when Dianne walked into the kitchen, "when are you going to see Steve again?"

"Uh, I don't know." She put on a pot of coffee, doing her best to shove every thought of her dinner companion from her mind. And not succeeding.

"He wants to go out on another date with you, doesn't he?"

"Uh, I'm not sure."

"You're not sure?" Jason asked. "How come? I saw you two get mushy last night. I like Steve. He's fun."

"Yes, I know," she said, standing in front of the machine while the coffee dripped into the glass pot. Her back was to her son. "Let's give it some time. See how things work out," she mumbled.

To Dianne's relief, he seemed to accept that and didn't question her further. That, however, wasn't the case with her mother.

"So talk to me," Martha insisted later that day, working her crochet hook as she sat in the living room with Dianne. "You've been very quiet."

"No, I haven't." Dianne didn't know why she denied it. Her mother was right, she had been introspective.

"The phone isn't ringing. The phone should be ringing."

"Why's that?"

"Steve. He met your mother, he met your children, he took you out to dinner…"

"You make it sound like we should be discussing wedding plans." Dianne had intended to be flippant, but the look her mother gave her said she shouldn't joke about something so sacred.

"When are you seeing him again?" Her mother tugged on her ball of yarn when Dianne didn't immediately answer, as if that might bring forth a response.

"We're both going to be busy for the next few days."

"Busy? You're going to let busy interfere with love?"

Dianne ignored the question. It was easier that way. Her mother plied her with questions on and off for the rest of the day, but after repeated attempts to get something more out of her daughter and not succeeding, Martha reluctantly let the matter drop.

Three days after the Valentine's dinner, Dianne was shopping after work at a grocery store on the other side of town—she avoided going anywhere near the one around which she and Steve had fabricated their story—when she ran into Beth Martin.

"Dianne," Beth called, racing down the aisle after her. Darn, Dianne thought. The last person she wanted to chitchat with was Beth, who would, no doubt, be filled with questions about her and Steve.

She was.

"I've been meaning to phone you all week," Beth said, her smile so sweet Dianne felt as if she'd fallen into a vat of honey.

"Hello, Beth." She made a pretense of scanning the grocery shelf until she realized she was standing in front of the disposable-diaper section. She jerked away as though she'd been burned.

Beth's gaze followed Dianne's. "You know, you're not too old to have more children," she said. "What are you? Thirty-three, thirty-four?"

"Around that."

"If Steve wanted children, you could—"

"I have no intention of marrying Steve Creighton," Dianne answered testily. "We're nothing more than friends."

Beth arched her eyebrows. "My dear girl, that's not what I've heard. All of Port Blossom is buzzing with talk about the two of you. Steve's been such an elusive bachelor. He dates a lot of women, or so I've heard, but from what everyone's saying, and I do mean *everyone*, you've got him hooked. Why, the way he was looking at you on Saturday night was enough to bring tears to my eyes. I don't know what you did to that man, but he's yours for the asking."

"I'm sure you're mistaken." Dianne couldn't very well announce that she'd paid Steve to look besotted. He'd done such a good job of it, he'd convinced himself and everyone else that he was head over heels in love with her.

Beth grinned. "I don't think so."

As quickly as she could, Dianne made her excuses, paid for her groceries and hurried home. Home, she soon discovered, wasn't exactly a haven. Jason and Jill were waiting for her, and it wasn't because they were eager to carry in the grocery sacks.

"It's been three days," Jill said. "Shouldn't you have heard from Steve by now?"

"If he doesn't phone you, then you should call him,"

Jason insisted. "Girls do that sort of thing all the time now, no matter what Grandma says."

"I…" Dianne looked for an escape. Of course there wasn't one.

"Here's his card," Jason said, taking it from the corner of the bulletin board. "Call him."

Dianne stared at the raised red lettering. Port Blossom Towing, it said, with the phone number in large numbers below. In the corner, in smaller, less-pronounced lettering, was Steve's name, followed by one simple word: *owner*.

Dianne's heart plummeted and she closed her eyes. He'd really meant it when he said he had never intentionally misled her. He assumed she knew, and with good reason. The business card he'd given her spelled it out. Only she hadn't noticed…

"Mom." Jason's voice fragmented her introspection.

She opened her eyes to see her son and daughter staring up at her, their eyes, so like her own, intent and worried.

"What are you going to do?" Jill wanted to know.

"W.A.R."

"Aerobics?" Jason said. "What for?"

"I need it," Dianne answered. And she did. She'd learned long ago that when something was weighing on her, heavy-duty exercise helped considerably. It cleared her mind. She didn't enjoy it, exactly; pain rarely thrilled her. But the aerobics classes at the community center had seen her through more than one emotional trauma. If she hurried, she could be there for the last session of the afternoon.

"Kids, put those groceries away for me, will you?" she said, heading for the stairs, yanking the sweater over her head as she raced. The buttons on her blouse were too time-consuming, so she peeled that over her head the moment she entered the bedroom, closing the door with her foot.

In five minutes flat, she'd changed into her leotard, kissed the kids and was out the door. She had a small attack of guilt when she pulled out of the driveway and glanced back to see both her children standing on the porch looking dejected.

The warm-up exercises had already begun when Dianne joined the class. For the next hour she leaped, kicked, bent and stretched, doing her best to keep up with everyone else. By the end of the session, she was exhausted—and no closer to deciding whether or not to phone Steve.

With a towel draped around her neck, she walked out to her car. Her cardiovascular system might've been fine, but nothing else about her was. She searched through her purse for her keys and then checked her coat pocket.

Nothing.

Dread filled her. Framing the sides of her face with her hands, she peered inside the car. There, innocently poking out of the ignition, were her keys.

Ten

"Jason," Dianne said, closing her eyes in thanks that it was her son who'd answered the phone and not Jill. Her daughter would have plied her with questions and more advice than "Dear Abby."

"Hi, Mom. I thought you were at aerobics."

"I am, and I may be here a whole lot longer if you can't help me out." Without a pause, she continued, "I need you to go upstairs, look in my underwear drawer and bring me the extra set of car keys."

"They're in your underwear drawer?"

"Yes." It was the desperate plan of a desperate woman. She didn't dare contact the auto club this time for fear they'd send Port Blossom Towing to the rescue in the form of one Steve Creighton.

"You don't expect me to paw through your, uh, stuff, do you?"

"Jason, listen to me, I've locked my keys in the car, and I don't have any other choice."

"You locked your keys in the car? *Again?* What's with you lately, Mom?"

"Do we need to go through this now?" she demanded.

Jason wasn't saying anything she hadn't already said to herself a hundred times over the past few minutes. She was so agitated it was a struggle not to break down and weep.

"I'll have Jill get the keys for me," Jason agreed, with a sigh that told her it demanded a good deal of effort, not to mention fortitude, for him to comply with this request.

"Great. Thanks." Dianne breathed out in relief. "Okay. Now, the next thing you need to do is get your bicycle out of the garage and ride it down to the community center."

"You mean you want me to *bring* you the keys?"

"Yes."

"But it's raining!"

"It's only drizzling." True, but as a general rule Dianne didn't like her son riding his bike in the winter.

"But it's getting dark," Jason protested next.

That did concern Dianne. "Okay, you're right. Call Grandma and ask her to come over and get the keys from you and then have her bring them to me."

"You want me to call Grandma?"

"Jason, are you hard of hearing? Yes, I want you to call Grandma, and if you can't reach her, call me back here at the community center." Needless to say, her cell phone was locked in the car. *Again.* "I'll be waiting." She read off the number for him. "And listen, if my car keys aren't in my underwear drawer, have Grandma bring me a wire clothes hanger, okay?"

He hesitated. "All right," he said after another burdened sigh. "Are you sure you're all right, Mom?"

"Of course I'm sure." But she was going to remember his attitude the next time he needed her to go on a Boy Scout campout with him.

Jason seemed to take hours to do as she'd asked. Since the front desk was now busy with the after-work crowd, Dianne didn't want to trouble the staff for the phone a second time to find out what was keeping her son.

Forty minutes after Dianne's aerobic class was over, she was still pacing the foyer of the community center, stopping every now and then to glance outside. Suddenly she saw a big red tow truck turn into the parking lot.

She didn't need to be psychic to know that the man driving the truck was Steve.

Mumbling a curse under her breath, Dianne walked out into the parking lot to confront him.

Steve was standing alongside her car when she approached. She noticed that he wasn't wearing the gray-striped coveralls he'd worn the first time they'd met. Now he was dressed in slacks and a sweater, as though he'd come from the office.

"What are you doing here?" The best defense was a good offense, or so her high-school basketball coach had advised her about a hundred years ago.

"Jason called me," he said, without looking at her.

"The traitor," Dianne muttered.

"He said something about refusing to search through your underwear and his grandmother couldn't be reached. And that all this has to do with you going off to war."

Although Steve was speaking in an even voice, it was clear he found the situation comical.

"W.A.R. is my aerobics class," Dianne explained stiffly. "It means Women After Results."

"I'm glad to hear it." He walked around to the passenger side of the tow truck and brought out the instrument he'd used to open her door the first time. "So," he said, leaning against the side of her compact, "how have you been?"

"Fine."

"You don't look so good, but then I suppose that's because you're a divorced woman with two children and a manipulative mother."

Naturally he'd taunt her with that. "How kind of you to say so," she returned with an equal dose of sarcasm.

"How's Jerome?"

"Jerome?"

"The butcher your mother wanted to set you up with," he answered gruffly. "I figured by now the two of you would've gone out." His words had a biting edge.

"I'm not seeing Jerome." The thought of having to eat blood sausage was enough to turn her stomach.

"I'm surprised," he said. "I would've figured you'd leap at the opportunity to date someone other than me."

"If I wasn't interested in him before, what makes you think I'd go out with him now? And why aren't you opening my door? That's what you're here for, isn't it?"

He ignored her question. "Frankly, Dianne, we can't go on meeting like this."

"Funny, very funny." She crossed her arms defiantly.

"Actually I came here to talk some sense into you," he said after a moment.

"According to my mother, you won't have any chance of succeeding. I'm hopeless."

"I don't believe that. Otherwise I wouldn't be here." He walked over to her and gently placed his hands on her shoulders. "Maybe, Dianne, you've been fine these past few days, but frankly I've been a wreck."

"You have?" As Dianne looked at him she thought she'd drown in his eyes. And when he smiled, it was all she could do not to cry.

"I've never met a more stubborn woman in my life."

She blushed. "I'm awful, I know."

His gaze became more intent as he asked, "How about if we go someplace and talk?"

"I...think that would be all right." At the moment there was little she could refuse him. Until he'd arrived, she'd had no idea what to do about the situation between them. Now the answer was becoming clear...

"You might want to call Jason and Jill and tell them."

"Oh, right, I should." How could she have forgotten her own children?

Steve was grinning from ear to ear. "Don't worry, I already took care of that. While I was at it, I phoned your mother, too. She's on her way to your house now. She'll make the kids' dinner." He paused, then said, "I figured if I was fortunate enough, I might be able to talk you into having dinner with me. I understand Walker's has an excellent seafood salad."

If he was fortunate enough, he might be able to talk her into having dinner with him? Dianne felt like weeping. Steve Creighton was the sweetest, kindest, handsomest man she'd ever met, and *he* was looking at *her* as if he was the one who should be counting his blessings.

Steve promptly opened her car door. "I'm going to buy you a magnetic key attachment for keeping a spare key under your bumper so this doesn't happen again."

"You are?"

"Yes, otherwise I'll worry about you."

No one had ever worried about her, except her immediate family. Whatever situation arose, she handled. Broken water pipes, lost checks, a leaky roof—nothing had ever defeated her. Not even Jack had been able to break her spirit, but one kind smile from Steve Creighton and she was a jumble of emotions. She blinked back tears and made a mess of thanking him, rushing her words so that they tumbled over each other.

"Dianne?"

She stopped and bit her lower lip. "Yes?"

"Either we go to the restaurant now and talk, or I'm going to kiss you right here in this parking lot."

Despite everything, she managed to smile. "It wouldn't be the first time."

"No, but I doubt I'd be content with one kiss."

She lowered her lashes, thinking she probably wouldn't be, either. "I'll meet you at Walker's."

He followed her across town, which took less than five minutes, and pulled into the empty parking space next to hers. Once inside the restaurant, they were seated immediately by a window overlooking Sinclair Inlet.

Dianne had just picked up her menu when Steve said, "I'd like to tell you a story."

"Okay," she said, puzzled. She put the menu aside. Deciding what to eat took second place to listening to Steve.

"It's about a woman who first attracted the attention of a particular man at the community center about two months ago."

Dianne took a sip of water, her eyes meeting his above the glass, her heart thumping loudly in her ears. "Yes…"

"This lady was oblivious to certain facts."

"Such as?" Dianne prompted.

"First of all, she didn't seem to have a clue how attractive she was or how much this guy admired her. He did everything but stand on his head to get her attention, but nothing worked."

"What exactly did he try?"

"Working out at the same hours she did, pumping iron—and looking exceptionally good in his T-shirt and shorts."

"Why didn't this man say something to…this woman?"

Steve chuckled. "Well, you see, he was accustomed to women giving him plenty of attention. So this particular woman dented his pride by ignoring him, then she made him downright angry. Finally it occurred to him that she wasn't *purposely* ignoring him—she simply wasn't aware of him."

"It seems to me this man is rather arrogant."

"I couldn't agree with you more."

"You couldn't?" Dianne was surprised.

"That was when he decided there were plenty of fish in the sea and he didn't need a pretty divorcée with two children—he'd asked around about her, so he knew a few details like that."

Dianne smoothed the pink linen napkin across her lap. "What happened next?"

"He was sitting in his office one evening. The day had been busy and one of his men had phoned in sick, so he'd been out on the road all afternoon. He was ready to go home and take a hot shower, but just about then the phone rang. One of the night crew answered it and it was the auto club. Apparently some lady had locked her keys in her car at the community center and needed someone to come rescue her."

"So you, I mean this man, volunteered?"

"That he did, never dreaming she'd practically throw herself in his arms. And not because he'd unlocked her car, either, but because she was desperate for someone to take her to the Valentine's dinner."

"That part about her falling in your arms is a slight exaggeration," Dianne felt obliged to tell him.

"Maybe so, but it was the first time a woman had ever offered to pay him to take her out. Which was the most ironic part of this entire tale. For weeks he'd been trying to gain this woman's attention, practically killing himself to impress her with the amount of weight he was lifting. It seemed every woman in town was impressed except the one who mattered."

"Did you ever stop to think that was the very reason he found her so attractive? If she ignored him, then he must have considered her a challenge."

"Yes, he thought about that a lot. But after he met her and kissed her, he realized that his instincts had been right from the first. He was going to fall in love with this woman."

"He was?" Dianne's voice was little more than a hoarse whisper.

"That's the second part of the story."

"The second part?" Dianne was growing confused.

"The happily-ever-after part."

Dianne used her napkin to wipe away the tears, which had suddenly welled up in her eyes again. "He can't possibly know that."

Steve smiled then, that wonderful carefree, vagabond smile of his, the smile that never failed to lift her heart.

"Wrong. He's known it for a long time. All he needs to do now is convince her."

Sniffing, Dianne said, "I have the strangest sensation that this woman has trouble recognizing a prince when she sees one. For a good part of her life, she was satisfied with keeping a frog happy."

"And now?"

"And now she's…now *I'm* ready to discover what happily-ever-after is all about."

* * * * *